A TRECHEROUS FIRE!

Logan raged into the inferno, swinging his arms and bellowing protective spells over his family. In the horrific heat of the fire, he fell back once, twice, then got his footing just as the roof crashed down in burning splinters and flaming thatch.

In the darkest part of the smoke, Logan beheld his daughter Aylith, blinded and coughing, straining to remove herself from her overturned loom and the wall that had collapsed trapping her.

I can get to my little Aylith, at least! he thought, never noticing that he could barely draw his own breath.

The girl cried out to him, and Logan threw himself forward, his hands finding firm purchase on each side of her head, his fingers burning with their own fire, the green fire that could make spring appear, the fire that could heal a wounded land.

"My sweet child, hear me! I am dying; someone has to take the Memories. Aylith! Do you hear me?"

Look for
MAGIC: The Gathering

Arena
Whispering Woods
Shattered Chains
Final Sacrifice
The Cursed Land
The Prodigal Sorcerer*

From HarperPrism

* coming soon

MAGIC
The Gathering™

THE CURSED LAND

Teri McLaren

HarperPrism
An Imprint of HarperPaperbacks

This is a work of fiction. The characters, incidents, and dialogues are products of the author's imagination and are not to be construed as real. Any resemblance to actual events or persons, living or dead, is entirely coincidental.

HarperPaperbacks   *A Division of* HarperCollins*Publishers*
10 East 53rd Street, New York, N.Y. 10022

Cover illustration by John Bolton

First printing: August 1995

Printed in the United States of America

HarperPrism is an imprint of HarperPaperbacks.
HarperPaperbacks, HarperPrism, and colophon are trademarks of HarperCollins*Publishers*

❖ 10 9 8 7 6 5 4 3 2 1

For my father, H. C. Patterson, who long ago, gave me the gift of story telling, and my mother, Virginia Patterson, who always seems to be lost in a book.

My heartfelt thanks to Patrick McGilligan and Margaret Weis, who gave me support and a push when I needed it most.

To Debbie Vaughn and to The Raptor Rehab Center of Kentucky, Inc., for bringing me face to face with barn owls.

To Ernie and Jim, Traci, Jim DeLong, Lisa, Anne Carter, Mort and David, Carole, John and Annette, Bob and Stephanie Joyce, Brad and Dawn, Richard, Keith, Leslie, Terri, and all the dozens of others whose candle of friendship has lit a very long, dark night.

Also to Shawna McCarthy, my most excellent agent, and Jill Grinberg, also of Scovil, Chichak, Galen; to the Wizards: Janna, Kathy, and Dave, and especially to Carla Vaananen, who read the manuscript tirelessly, and always offered her best, no matter what the season.

The Parting

HAEN FELT THE BLUE FIREBALL SINGE HIS brow and then shake the earth as it split a rock face many yards behind him, but still he did not give ground. In fact, he could not. He was nowhere near the ground. He pressed his back closer into the Clan Tree's massive main trunk, wrapped his hands more firmly upon a gently swaying branch overhead, and tried not to think just how far up in the soaring oak he had climbed in his desperate effort to protect it. The Clan Tree was not just his home: it was the center of all Cridhe, the force that held together the clan's entire world. He would just have to hope his old friend would not have the heart to send that cold magic through him.

"Nohr, you cannot divide the magic from the Tree," Haen shouted down to his attacker below. "The two belong together; they are not one or the other, they live in unity. The Tree goes deep into the earth. Its roots uphold the heart of the island. It guards the ways of every living thing and holds them in their balance.

Even the seasons change at the same time of year
because of the Tree. Its power cannot be uncoiled from
the living wood without great loss and destruction to
our world. I have Seen it. Do not do this thing!"
begged Haen, his brown, gnarled hands seeming to
meld with the rough bark of the oak. "Yes, Nohr, Haen
speaks truth. You are but one and the clan is many.
We like the Tree—it's always been here, it's beautiful,
and the notions Haen gets from it are always right,
even if he can't exactly explain why or how. Let the old
Tree live, so I can finish besting Haen at the games. So
what if the man's always been a bit barmy, Nohr? He
likes livin' up there. It's midsummer eve—let us make
merry instead of contending. Put down the trader's
firesword. You have never used a weapon and you
don't know what you're doing," called Raphos the
blacksmith testily, his patience nearly worn out by the
long argument. He itched to simply strike the weasel-
faced weatherworker down and have done with him.

Tonight was Festival—all the clan had turned out for
it. But all nine of the elders and most of the village of
eight hundred had now pressed as closely to Nohr as
they dared, provoking the little man's pride and making a quick end to the dispute impossible. Raphos
flexed his huge hands in anticipation of a chance to settle the quarrel in his own blunt way and get back to his
ale, while Nohr glanced around, impressed with his
new command of the crowd's attention.

"I will not," he said quietly, finally locating Raphos
in the swirl of worried, festooned faces. "What will you
do, ironmonger, exile me? I will go farther when I have
loosed the power bound up in this Tree than you and
the nine graybeards could ever send me. That is exactly
the point. Now come down, show me where exactly the
heartline runs, Haen, or you will See your death," said
Nohr, his voice low and preternaturally cold.

Up in the Tree, Haen shook his head slowly. This argument had begun in the tavern hours ago. Haen knew it would end only when Nohr either wore out the drink, or dropped the sword, an unlikely chance.

Haen was the Keeper of the Tree—chosen by the Tree itself and sworn by the elders to keep the wood from fire, ax, disease, and from any other threat.

From drunken weatherworkers with magical swords.

Nohr smiled lazily and slid his eyes to his left, and a big, well-muscled foreign man, his wide shoulders draped in gaudy silk from the little Southern Isle, shrugged and nodded. Nohr raised the sword, its pattern of intertwined snakes glinting in the late sunlight, and another thin streak of crackling blue shot forth. Stinging like a viper, the tiny bolt of frozen light bit through Haen's left shoulder, and a gush of bright blood quickly colored his tunic, then froze into a gelid ooze. Haen crumpled forward a little, trying desperately to hold onto both the Tree and his thoughts. At least Nohr had not hit the Tree.

"Nohr . . . there is enough power for you without killing this Tree. You have the weathersense. You alone, out of all our clan, can determine when the rains come and if there will be storms. We rely on you. Why would you think yourself without esteem? This is not just a tree among the forest. It is our sacred oak, as old as Cridhe. Stop and think. You will unmake our people; our entire history will be lost. Every story of life is written in the rings of the Clan Tree. Destroy that, and there will come a great confusion, such as we have never seen before. And where there is confusion, and envy, there is every evil work. You know that from the elders' teachings, from the book of patterns the Maker has given us. Nohr—the very heavens will fall out of balance; the stars will shake loose from their places in the sky."

Haen looked into the festival crowd and saw Capin, Nohr's second son, standing with Haen's clear-eyed daughter Liana, his best friend. The boy dropped his head. Even at fifteen, Capin apprehended the danger his father had been blinded to.

Blinded by Malvos, that tall, powerfully built, tattooed trader, come lately, he said, to deal in metal, but never very far from either the Tree or Nohr. And the only metal he seemed to possess had been the magical sword. Which Haen noticed he never touched barehanded.

Haen took a rasping breath and continued. "The Tree upholds us, Nohr. Its power binds and keeps our life. You will tear our world from its place in the sky. Things will not fit any longer. Look for other power if you must. Touch not the Tree."

Haen closed his eyes for a moment, his hands still meshed with the bark of the oak, and then remembered something. At the base of the Tree stood an old stone, its ornately carved letters wrought by the Maker's own hand. On one side, facing the clan, where everyone could see, there was the Blessing: "Keep me and I will keep you." On the side that faced the Tree, now invisible for the nearness of the massive trunk, another piece of writing.

The Curse.

It was worth a try. Haen wet his lips and put the pain of his ruined shoulder far away from his mind.

"There's the Curse, Nohr." He recited it, suddenly Seeing it facing a much smaller, younger Tree, the image sharp and clear as if it had just been carved into the smooth, polished rock: "'He who harms me harms all the world. My wound shall be his wound, and the darkness of his wound shall not be taken from him, and shall mark his line unto its last generation.'"

Haen hung his shaggy blond head in exhaustion, his

hands aching with the effort to stay upright. Down below, as the sacred words fell upon his ears, Nohr seemed to hesitate. He dropped the point of the heavy sword and hunched his shoulders as he stared at the stone before the old Tree's trunk.

Haen waited, the burn upon his forehead smarting terribly and his shoulder consumed with fire. How had it come to this? What had happened to his friend? Nohr had been his companion since childhood, but it seemed the traitor who contended with him now was someone he did not know at all. And whence came this terrible anger?

It had to be Malvos.

He was the only explanation. For weeks, the two of them had kept secret counsel, with Nohr neglecting his wind charts and his dew cups to the point that the shepherds were trying to take their own weather readings. Now Nohr had drunkenly traded for this mysterious sword, which could cleave rock and throw frozen flames, and who knew what else. And what was their bargain? Malvos wanted the Clan Tree's power, and Haen knew that taking it would destroy its very life. And for some reason, Malvos needed someone else to perform the actual harvest.

Upon arriving at the clanhold, the trader had first approached Haen with his wheedling flattery. Haen had abruptly turned him down. Then Malvos had found Nohr to be an easier target—the weather-worker's jealousy of Haen's place in the clan was infamous, his self-confidence thoroughly eaten away by the worm of envy. The weathersense drove Nohr out to the edges of the clan's pastures and fields every day, and he seldom received the worshipful thanks for his lonely vigils and readings that Haen got for his more visible care of the Tree. Malvos had made much of Nohr's plight, loudly, publicly, especially in the tavern, ever in feigned sympathy. Then he had generously applied mead to Nohr's favorite injustices at the midsummer eve celebration, which always began with a song from Haen under the Tree. It had been an easy jump to get Nohr out here, ready to do whatever Malvos had put in his mind these last weeks.

It was all too obvious. Haen pushed down the horror of his friend's treachery as he clutched at the branch, the life of the Tree and the clan itself in the balance of Nohr's furious consideration.

He sighed, imagining his shoulder healed, called forth the Tree's power, and let his fingers drink in its energy. Verdant light passed over his hands, and he felt the strong rush of warmth that always came with the Tree's gift. The wound on his shoulder began to thaw and close, matching his mental image, the Tree taking the poison away as the tense minutes passed. He tried to settle his mind about Nohr, to rid himself of all strife and anger, and then gently called down again to the puzzling weatherworker.

"Nohr, please . . . "

"No!" Nohr bellowed up, his eyes hard and his mouth curled into a tight gall of bitterness. "You! You can See the heart of the Tree, can you? You can See into the earth itself. You know how the birds make flight, and when the swimmer will come home to the river from the sea, and you know what to do for the calving sickness, and you always know what is best for everyone. The Tree tells you its secrets and you get all the glory. You get the respect that is mine; I have to do my work without the help of your magic, using only my knowledge and instruments. I do not have your Sight, the Tree's communion, its shelter. I go about blindly, standing in your long shadow, scraping after you, working without thanks or notice to find the favor of the winds and rains."

He waved the sword at the group of villagers surrounding him. When they swayed backward, Raphos, finding his opening, rushed Nohr from behind. Immediately, Nohr whirled and caught him with the point of the weapon and the sword spoke again, blue fire enthralling Raphos with searing cold energy until he fell at Nohr's feet, a ring of glistening rime slowly spreading onto the grass around his body.

Raphos's red-haired wife rushed to her fallen husband, but nobody else dared move, their eyes rapt upon the sword and the besotted madman who wielded it. Malvos the trader smirked and folded his tattooed forearms over his chest.

Nohr continued, seeming not to notice that he had just felled one of his clansmen. "Now, thanks to Malvos here, who has opened my eyes, I have seen something. I know your secret, Haen, your Sight—the thing you take from the Tree to work your magic, to look into nature's secrets and make the healings. It's called mana. Malvos has told me how you use it. And Malvos has told me something that you have never Seen. There are people who can use that mana for far greater things than you ever dreamed of. They're called Walkers, Haen, and they can leap worlds . . . and I will be one of them, Malvos says, when I harvest the Tree. No more of your shadow. I'll have my own sun. I'll have thousands of them!" he concluded, his hand tightening on the hilt of the sword.

Haen winced at the icy obsession in Nohr's voice. "The Tree gives of her power to whom she chooses, Nohr. She chose me when we were but children. You know that. And your gift is no less valuable. Malvos is using you, though I don't yet know why. Can you not see that? Why does he need you to do this thing? Why does he not put his sword to the Tree's mana, as you say, himself? Can you not see that?"

The trader rolled his eyes and shook his head benevo-
lently, dismissing Haen's words as if he spoke of fairy
tales. Still, he said nothing and let Nohr reply on his own.

"I see that you would keep the mana all for yourself,
Haen. So you will always be special, be the chosen one.
I see it more clearly every day. We have been closer
than brothers for all our lives. We have learned our life
patterns together. But I have noticed something.
Always you are favored, and I am not. First by the
Tree, then by the elders. Then by Lumi." Nohr
motioned to Haen's wife, who peeked out from behind
the Tree's trunk. "But finally I grasp that the reason is
because you have cheated me all these years, so now I
choose a different pattern. My own pattern. No more
working for the clan. I will have what I want, right or
wrong. And what care I for a people who have never
respected me? What care I for such friends as you, for
that matter. And as for any curse, let it fall where it
will; I see it not, so I believe it not!" Nohr shouted, his
black eyes gleaming with lust and old pain.

"My taste for this game has soured," he continued.
"You had best take what I so graciously offer you out
of sheer kindness, for I am a kind man—you know I
am," he slurred as he took a pull on the jar in his left
hand, failing to notice the searing look Raphos's wife
shot him. "I offer you your life. But if you continue to
stand in my way without showing me the heartline, the
line of mana, it will please me greatly to destroy both
you and your precious Sight, Haen."

The words drove hard into Haen, wounding as deeply
as the sword's strike. Sensing his pain, the great oak
vibrated comfort and Haen's fingertips melded with its
green influence, a soothing assurance overtaking the
effect of Nohr's threat. Far below the rock-strewn
ground, the tree's deepest roots shuddered and a stream
of bright power flowed into its leaves. They began to

glow softly in the twilight, against the hazy gray autumn sky and the dusky blue mountains to the north.

"Nohr, I beg you to look. The Tree speaks also: do not harvest this mana. There must be other sources. I am sure you can leave this place, as you say, very soon without it. Please . . . the Curse is real, Nohr. It's woven into the Tree with the same thread as the Blessing," he finished desperately.

Nohr looked up into the crown of the mighty oak, a hundred feet farther into the air from Haen's perch, where the newest growth pushed forth, glowing now with golden light. He saw nothing more than always— just an old oak, the towering symbol of Haen's larger favor and acceptance. The Tree never had spoken to Nohr, and it remained silent now. Nohr threw back his head and cackled at Haen's pitiful plea. No, not on Cridhe was there other mana. This, Malvos had said, was the only line. And he should know—he was a professional Finder.

"Come down, Haen, for the final time. Or I will build your coffin from the branches that have been your home."

Haen looked at Raphos's blue-tinged body, his wife sobbing over it, and then back to Nohr's fever-stricken face. The two men locked into a stare, and the villagers instinctively moved away from the Tree, away from Nohr, Malvos merging with them. Haen gazed steadily down, trying to find the friend, the companion he had once known behind those wild, vacant eyes.

Nohr, without blinking, smiled wickedly and shook his dark head in disdain and contempt as he raised his right hand to aim the sword. But before he could fix it to the mana line, or where Malvos had guessed the line would be, another charge of frozen light burst forth and struck the stone at the base of the oak, splitting it in two and the tree lengthwise down to the tips of its roots, shearing the topmost cluster of new growth away.

Haen hurtled into the air, his scream rising with the resounding crack of the living wood, and the branches of the Clan Tree shattered and exploded in a rain of frozen splinters, each one encased in a shroud of ice. The mana line surged upward in a mighty roar and exploded into an arc of green light, jumping from the heart of the broken tree high into the sky, dividing in two. One shaft snapped back into the fallen crown, while the other simultaneously dispersed into the falling fragments of the Tree. Nohr's insane laughter rang out in the litter-filled air, and he danced amid the shower of splinters in delight.

And then the world broke.

A deep rumbling from the depths of the earth shook the ground as it rose to the surface, and a great rift opened up between friend and friend, neighbor and neighbor, between Haen and Nohr, between Capin and Liana. There seemed to be no bottom to the chasm, as if the heart of the island had been ripped out of its breast. The two sides of the split heaved and lurched again, causing Raphos's body to roll slowly into the gap. Three men pulled his screaming wife roughly away in order to prevent her from following him.

Unmoved by the woman's loss, from the back of the small group that had found themselves on Nohr's side of the breach, the tattooed trader shook his head in frustration and frowned silently into his rusty beard.

This would not do. The crazed weatherworker had misaligned the sword. Too much mead, perhaps. The mana line had been disrupted, become useless, its power diffusing into the earthquake and the Tree's remnants. And the sword, Soulslayer, had been torn from Nohr's hand and now lay covered in rubble on Haen's side. How could he get off this miserable onion of a world now? Where would he live until he figured it out? Not a single dwelling, not even a fence, stood upright on this side of the rift.

But isn't that just my luck? How could you leave me here, Tempé? My crime was not so severe—just a little mana from your boundless stores—and my just payment, too, I might add. Why should I apologize?

The planeswalker had stranded him here for skimming a little too much a little too often from one of her lines—Malvos's hunger for the mana had grown with his talent for finding it. But he was positive she had not known about these bumpkins' old tree. Richest line of forest mana he'd ever found, and nearly totally hidden from even his expert senses by some strange warding— perhaps that old curse Haen had used to threaten Nohr. Malvos had seen words work in such ways before. Well, he had nearly pulled it off—nearly made it back to Ilcae, a plane he knew to be frequented by a walker who would trade the whereabouts of Tempé's lines for Malvos's freedom. . . .

But Malvos had time. Much time. His people, the Sangrazul, known far and wide for their peculiar need to consume mana, rivaled even the elven races for longevity. Malvos was young, in the prime of his power, strongly built and formidable, able to withstand the harsh conditions of mana starvation for at least long enough to figure out how to get back to the lines. He was ever a patient man—he would simply wait for another chance, his mind already at work on other possibilities. Soulslayer would come back to him, once he marked it. Tempé probably wouldn't even miss it unless he actually touched it. She had thousands of such toys, although there was supposed to be something special about this one—the pommel stones held their own magic, something to do with cures and blades, nothing that concerned his purposes for the weapon. He would find another like Nohr, who had the talent for magic and a jealous heart that could be made to do his bidding with Soulslayer. How hard could that be?

And then he would sift Tempé for every line she wove. He would make her erase her miserable snakes, those tattooed guardians of his talent she had told him would rise to life and strike him dead should he even think too hard about touching mana, much less do it. No, he would never, never apologize. He was, after all, a Sangrazul.

A sharp whack on his broad back brought the trader out of his high imaginings. Nohr whirled in front of him, jumping up and down insanely.

"I have done it! They could not stop me, and I have done it! Where are we now, Malvos? What plane is this?" Nohr gaped foolishly at Malvos for a few heartbeats, his nose sprinkled with drops of spilled mead, and then stopped and looked around and around, as if he could not believe what he saw.

The same faces in the same place. The grin dropped from Nohr's mouth when he realized the Tree's power had not been harvested, did not leap to his command, had not transported them from Cridhe at all. Instead, upon the center of his chest, a wound had opened where a large, sharp missile of iron, the firesword's tip, had snapped off, ricocheted, and struck him right above the heart.

Malvos's eyes narrowed when he saw the bloody gouge. He looked to Nohr's face, which suddenly blanched as the weatherworker's shaking hand found the metal fragment and plucked it out, never looking at the wound, as if it could not be there if he did not see it. Malvos, though, noticed that it perfectly matched the wound Nohr had given Haen only moments ago. Perhaps this curse . . . he brought himself up sharply. No, the only power in such nonsense was in the fools who believed it. And that could be used by those who didn't.

Nohr let drop his bloody hand and looked dumbfounded at his old friend sprawled in the grass on the
other side of the gaping chasm. Then he snatched up
the new growth from the seared crown of the Tree—
three small twigs upon a slender stalk and an acorn—
and bounded over several large, smoking branches,
heading north toward the mountains. A loud thunderclap boomed overhead and those who had unfortunately found themselves on the other side of the new
chasm ceased their cries and shouts in dawning awareness of their vulnerability, then rushed to follow the
madman. Great black clouds gathered quickly at the
edge of the western horizon, a swift wind pushing
them relentlessly toward Cridhe, toward the unshel-
tered, the innocent and unwilling company that now
followed Nohr toward the mountains, the only safety in
the coming storm.

Capin tore at his tunic as he ran, making a bandage
for his father's wound and begging for him to wait. He
looked back at Liana, who stood stricken and crying on
the other side of the rift. The boy stopped and lifted his
hand to her, promising himself he would come back to
her. Liana slowly nodded at him, as if she read his
mind. Capin turned and ran, his oath silently made and
silently accepted.

Nohr ran madly away, blue robes and tassels flutter-
ing, waving his leafy trophy over his head. Though a
bloodstain darkened the back of his tunic, the mad
weatherworker still appeared to not feel his wound.

Haen lifted his ringing head from the patch of
ground where he had landed and tried to shake the
echo of the Tree's pain from his ears. The shock of the
fall slowed his thoughts and words, and he felt himself
slipping little by little into unconsciousness.

Despite the icy wind and the pain of his wounds, Haen
marveled at the vision the Tree had given to him in its

last moment, its whispers still repeating in his heart. He drifted in and out of a green, waking, dream-song, where all the patterns of life swirled in perfect order through his mind, where the Clan Tree had stored its Memories, the names of every green thing. They glowed and surged, wrapping him in their light, healing him.

By his hand lay a fragment of the Tree's main trunk, its pale rings now visible and glowing with mana. Haen reached for it, touching again the familiar warmth of the wood. He watched in wonder as the future fell into solidity before his inner vision. Faces of those yet to be born gathered up in two lines, the newly formed chasm dividing them becoming a river, Nohr's progeny shadowed in darkness on one side, and Haen's in light on the other, until they merged into the distance, in a brilliant point of power, before an oak just like the Clan Tree. Haen opened his eyes.

"Nohr's line is cursed, but the Tree will grow again," Haen interpreted. "I am still the Keeper. I must keep the names, settle the Memories. But there will come . . . a Mender, who shall restore . . . shall heal. And the lines of Haen and Nohr will merge in a point of light when the Mender comes." Haen dropped his head and slept.

As the ice storm broke overhead, and the new chasm began to fill with sleet, Nohr charged into the thick forest, the trader bringing up the rear of the unhappy group at his own languorous pace.

At Haen's mumbled words, which even Lumi, bending over him, had trouble hearing through the storm, Malvos stopped in his distant tracks, listening. He paused for a moment, smiled to himself, then turned around and made a sign with his hand in the freezing air, marking the magical sword.

Lumi, as did most of the clan, mistook it for a farewell.

Overhead, a small tawny owl circled against the darkening sky, and then flew west, against the raging storm.

CHAPTER
1

Year 520, The Mending

"WHEN? WHEN! I CAN'T WAIT ANY LONGER,
Malvos. It has to be this year. It has to be now. I tell you,
the darkness, the darkness *inside*, beckons to me, and
soon, I know, I will not be able to turn from it. I have to
bring the light this year. I have proclaimed it. I will do it.
I will not be just another cursed man in the line of Nohr.
I have sworn that the Haenish and their evil words will
prevail no longer upon my family. I must secure that
Haenish light spell and work it upon the Clan Tree!"
shouted Nazir, the current Felonarch of Inys Nohr, as
he paced up and down the cold stones of his dusty,
decrepit great hall. A smoky fire of soft coal burned
low in the brazier, but provided almost no warmth.

Nazir clutched at his chest and folded over momentarily, the pain of the old birthmark flaring with his
agitation.

"Give me another draft of the potion, man. I can't
think straight. And have Arn bring RoNal. It's time to

mount the spring raid. I feel the equinox about to dawn," he continued, never slowing his anxious steps.

"Of a certainty, my gracious lord, I will do those very things, yes, I will," said the apothecary Malvos, reaching for a bellpull and waddling to his master's side with another of the tiny stone bottles of the foul liquid that kept Nazir in something of his right mind. Nazir lunged for the bottle and gulped down a dose that had been far too much for him even a week before.

Malvos dropped his gaze and considered. Nazir was very near, yes, very near to the ultimate fate of every single one of Nohr's line, the last stroke of the so-called family curse, the consuming madness from which there was no deliverance. He would fall to it in one of his fits of rage and never regain his reason, nor his magic. Malvos was called the Sifter for good reason. He could read the truth in any spoken word. In years of sifting the Nohrish monarchy, he had seen the same pattern again and again. The men, the women even earlier, reached a certain age and were overtaken by insanity: about thirty years, for the men. Nazir was well into his twenty-ninth year.

And Nazir was Malvos's last best hope. Since Nohr himself, Nazir had the best potential for handling mana; Malvos suspected it came from his mother's people. Unfortunately, it seemed, he also had more sensitivity to the pain of the curse. If Malvos lost this one, where, after these several hundred years, would the apothecary be, but still looking for a man from out of the only two families on miserable Cridhe who could work the mana to help him escape Tempé's prison?

Well, there was Thix. But he had no talent at all, that one. None of the right marks. And the boy cared only for his own entertainment, a personality trait that disgusted Malvos. No, Nazir was the best yet; he had the most skill and the most native gift for magic. But as yet, he had no heir. Malvos had to keep this one alive and well until Tempé's sword could be found. Until the light spell held by the Haenish could be brought together with the Clan Tree's acorn, still in Nohrish possession. Then, with Nazir's help, Malvos could go home. Nazir would not withhold it; the pain of his condition without the tonic would be too much, even deadly. And after more than five hundred years of starving for mana on this dark and barren little rock, he had a mighty hunger for the power. Malvos could nearly taste the sweetness of the glowing forest mana running through his hands again. It had been ecstasy, secretly eating from Tempé's lines.

It would be again. For years, Malvos had quelled his mana hunger with the distraction of honeyed cakes and pastries. Soon he would have the real thing again. But Nazir, last in the direct line of the Nohr, must live until the moment Malvos would make him part a new Tree from its energy. This time, they would get it right. He had heard old Haen's prophecy at the Parting. There would be a Mender. It was Nazir. It had to be. He believed it.

Hearing their approach, Malvos stirred his great bulk and moved to open the door for the boy and RoNal.

Moments later, the big blond man strode in preceding Arn, his boots spit-shined and careless on the stones, mail shirt chiming with his measured steps. RoNal had done this before. Too many times. He knew he had to get the Haenish Keeper this time, or Nazir would have him lashed. He supposed himself to be uniquely favored; three chances was more than any other commander had been given. RoNal was more than fifty, old for a Nohrishman, ancient for a Nohrish soldier.

RoNal had never liked Nazir. But that had never mattered. RoNal was a soldier first, last, and always. He would do as he was told and keep his feelings to himself. That was the only honor in this service he could find. He was a skilled fighter with no taste for the fight. He waited, ready to hear his mission.

Nazir, his dark bangs hanging in strings over his white brows, hardly looked at his commander when he spoke. "I want the girl, too. Not just Logan—the Keeper. I have to have some way to make Logan give up the light spell, and he'll never do it unless his daughter is taken, too. I have to have something to hold over his miserable Haenish head. Besides, if she's healthy, I can get sons on her. And I have heard she is tall and strong. You will know her by her white brows, like mine. Don't come back without her, do you hear?"

RoNal never blinked. He saluted Nazir as though the ruler actually saw and cared, and then walked out the way he had come in, cloaked in his own rough dignity.

Making his way through the bailey, RoNal noticed Thix, Nazir's only living kinsman, standing casual guard. He wondered how he would keep Nazir's nephew in line during the raid. The boy was unmanageable in drill, much less in his first venture into Haenish territory. It was a long trip. If Nazir wanted them to leave in haste, that meant the equinox was close, and there would be little margin for error in timing their arrival. They would, as always, have only one chance at the Haenish Keeper—to arrive and attack on the one day when the thornwall gate was open and the man stood alone to work his peculiar magic.

Thix threw off a salute as RoNal passed.

"Good day, sir." He grinned slyly. "Nice weather for a raid, eh?"

RoNal returned the salute crisply. "One duty at a time, soldier. Your pace is off."

Thix laughed and swaggered around the corner.

RoNal didn't like the feel of this at all. Something prickled at his back and made him want to squirm under his mail shirt. He shook his head and looked

into the long distance toward Inys Haen. The barren
moors were lost in mist and darkness.

It's just another raid. We'll get the Keeper this time,
he thought, trying to cheer himself. His back still
itched, as though the lash were already laid into it.

Waiting for further orders, Arn had watched RoNal go,
thinking that now the room felt far more empty. The
boy carefully fixed his eyes upon his ragged shoes.

More than anything in the world, Arn wanted to
grow up and be like RoNal. Arn had been brought to
Inys Nohr a year ago on the spring raid, taken by a
slaver party. Arn had grown up in the second of the
Far clans, the groups of Nohrish refugees and run-
aways that squatted at the edges of Nazir's territory
and the Haenish light. The Far clans had something of
an uneasy peace with Inys Haen, but Far clanners
stayed to themselves. The Haenish watched them
closely from the other side of the Sobus River—what
had once been the great rift of the Parting, now a deep
waterway that stretched across all Cridhe. But Haenish
was Haenish and Nohrish was not, no matter if the Far
clanners despised and rejected their own Felonarch.

So the four loosely connected clans were on their
own when it came to dealing with Nazir, and very, very
vulnerable in their growing urge toward outright, orga-
nized revolt.

Oddly, Arn's life had been saved by his own personal
revolt. Though he'd been repeatedly warned against it,
Arn had developed a habit of playing away from the village by one of the small streams that fed the river. He
wandered farther and farther into Haenish territory all
the time, finally coming to regularly visit a young
woman who fished with her nets at the bend in the
river. They had never exchanged names, and she always

wore a hat that concealed most of her face, but the two had a sort of good-natured tolerance for one another in the camaraderie of the sport.

One day, when Nazir's troops torched their way through his clanhold, Arn was late home from his secret adventures. When he saw the fires, he hid among the rocky cliffs that overhung the second clan until the raiders moved off. Another raiding party, an hour or so behind the first, had found him wandering around the burned-out circle of crude huts looking for a couple of hunters who had also been away from the village. Thinking to garner favor, the Nohrishmen threw him on the back of a scrawny cow and brought him to Nazir. In a small moment of distraction, if not mercy, the Nohrish ruler did not kill him for sport, as the ambitious leader of the raiding party had assumed he would. Instead, Arn had the great favor visited upon him of being the new tower messenger, the boy before him having graduated to the position of Nazir's sparring partner. Only RoNal and old Feryar the Fool had shown the boy a bit of compassion, helping him stay alive in Nazir's hard service.

Arn rubbed his shoulder, and silently hoped his hero RoNal hadn't just been handed a death sentence. The Haenish Keeper had never been taken. Now Nazir wanted his daughter, too.

"Go." Nazir motioned to the boy and Malvos, still not looking up.

Malvos gave Arn the empty apothecary bottle, as well as several others he'd collected from various places in the room, and followed him out, leaving Nazir alone in the hall, his hands clasping his head.

"I will bring the light. It is me. I am the Mender. I can break this Haenish curse. All I need is the light spell, and I can make it so," Nazir whispered to himself. And he almost believed it.

CHAPTER
2

AN HOUR BEFORE A SINGLE GLEAMING RAY of weak sunlight would shine through the pale gray sky to herald the vernal equinox, in the center of a frost-browned verge, on the village's holiest ground, a lone figure, tiredness tracing his rheumy eyes, his cheeks and mouth, stood listening to the last silence of winter.

The gaunt man shivered against the morning chill. It had been the worst winter since the Parting, bringing a kind of cold that mocked at fires and withered the flesh. Great trees had shattered in spontaneous explosions as the sap froze in their hearts, and every bleak morning, more cattle had turned to ice from standing too still in the byre overnight. The frosts had heaved up several of the long, flat, pillow stones in this yard, too. Had even the dead Keepers felt the deeper chill?

Logan hoped the Mender would come soon. Every year since the Parting, a little less grew, a little less ripened, fewer lambs and calves were born, and it had become harder and harder for the Keepers to see the

Memories in their original brightness. Like the way a friend's face changes from the distance of time, the names of things seemed more difficult to See every year. The thread for the pattern was running out, in more ways than one. Fewer and fewer of the clan even believed there would be a Mender.

The Keeper rubbed his arthritic shoulder through a heavy green woolen cloak and cast his eyes over the desolation that the severe season had wrought.

It was time for life to return.

Today was a tender day, a day for ceremony and vigil, the only day when the Memory of spring could be spoken and made manifest. It was also the only day when it could be revoked.

And it all depends on my living through it, thought Logan with a bitter smile. If he could draw breath for just one more day, the spring Memory would settle and take hold in the growing things. They would receive the light, learn their names again, and bear fruit. But Logan was a very old man, even for a Keeper—nearly a hundred winters. Every new spring, he wondered if he could again summon the power and strength to let the waning visions of growth flow out of his heart and into the waiting world. It took so much out of him, but there was no one to replace him yet. No boy with the marks, the signs of the calling, had been born to Logan to receive the Memories and continue the work.

Logan had married only once, late in his life, to a woman from a distant shore-dwelling clan. He and Selka had had only Aylith, now about twenty, though her diminutive frame and owlish blue-green eyes made her look much younger. No son. No heir. Logan had to hang on.

Logan wheezed a long sigh and searched the bleak horizon to his left, where most of the villagers stood hidden, watching while the Keeper invoked the season. The men and women, armed with scythes and poles and a few odd swords, awaited the expected lightning strike of a spring raid from the Nohrlanders, once their kinsmen, now their sworn enemies. Every year, there were two raids: one at harvest, and one at the vernal equinox, when the Keeper was vulnerable and most identifiable.

From the time of Haen, measures had been taken to stop the Nohrish invaders. The First himself had planted and warded against fire and flood a wall of thornwood, now twenty feet high, thickly grown and bristling with eight-inch-long iron-hard spikes. It had one gate, which had to be opened from the inside at just the right angle for the sun's first ray to strike the standing stone. The stone sat to the east of the circle on the holy ground, where Haen had replaced it. Some said the Curse could still be read upon its weathered, split face. Most thought it was just the natural erosion of wind and weather that had scratched the rock.

The village had lost its lookout tower in the last raid, and it had not yet been rebuilt, and a few of the younger men had asked the elders for extra guards at the gate.

They hadn't had any extra guards when Haen was alive, and there would be none now. Four would have to be enough. After all, the Nohr had never breached the hedge.

Logan wondered at the wisdom of that—he knew that Nazir was a different kind of enemy. From his high mountain passes and cold stone battlements, where the sun always wobbled between dark and day, Nazir of the Nohr could sense the awakening of life at Inys Haen more accurately than anyone before him.

Since the death of his father, Nazir, strangely obsessed with light, and less interested in plunder than the previous Felonarchs, had plotted to capture Logan and his Memories. Several times he had come too close. Yes, Nazir was very different from the two previous rulers, or Felonarchs, as they pompously preferred to be called, that Logan had known. He was much more driven, more focused, more dangerous. Nazir's father and grandfather had died horribly, murdered by one another in their blood-borne madness, taking the top of the tower off in a mana-sparked eruption. Crephas had held his throne for years despite his madness, but that final upheaval had left Nazir, at twenty, to oversee a sprawling, sickened, unwieldy kingdom far beyond its ability to either support or heal itself.

The curse had followed Nohr's family from the Parting to the present. This Felonarch, Nazir, in his fervor, in his relative clearness of mind, in his propensity and talent for magic, posed more of a threat to the Haenish clan than any before him. Logan had seen his black eyes in dreams, staring coldly into Logan's, about to rend his mind like old Nohr had rent the clan.

On the vernal equinox, when the Keeper's identity would be certain, and the thornwall of Inys Haen would be open to receive the first ray of sunlight, perhaps another guard should be posted at the gate rather than at the riverbank, where the Nohr were sure to cross on the stern, frozen face of the Sobus River. But that would break the pattern.

"To think we were once the same clan," Logan recalled, half-aloud.

Hundreds of seasons ago, the story went, at the bitter climax of a personal dispute, the Parting occurred. Nazir's ancestor had destroyed the Clan Tree in his rage, taking away with him part of it, having split the beheaded oak in twain to its roots. The enchanted tree had had a magical hold on the rocks at the heart of the world, and the rending of it rocked the island of Cridhe into climactic chaos. The clouds had rolled in that same day, obscuring the sun permanently and plunging the land into deep twilight for its days and deeper darkness for its nights. The death of the Clan Tree had changed everything, down to the kind of creatures that lived on Cridhe, the way crops grew, and how livestock brought forth their young.

The Parting caused the cycle of the seasons to stop completely. And Haen slept, barely breathing, seemingly frozen in time, wounded in Nohr's attack on the Tree. The clan grew worried as days passed, the elders puzzling among themselves when Haen's brows gradually turned white. And still the impossibly thick clouds hovered over all Cridhe, blocking light, and life, from the inhabitants.

Frost spurred the heels of that dark midsummer eve, and stayed. There was no harvest, and soon, little food could be found in the wild. The remnant of the divided clan at Inys Haen all but died out. The elders and Vale, who had taken Nohr's place as weatherworker, could do nothing about the spindly white crops and the starving livestock. Worse, Vale reported that the stars themselves had come unfixed in the sky, just as Haen had predicted. Sometimes the familiar constellations appeared where they should be; sometimes they were replaced by strange new formations of stars, the like of which Vale had never seen.

The clan murmured and pondered the darkness, grew sickly pale while they ate their last mealy potatoes and slaughtered their precious cattle, and passed another two seasons in expectation of them being their last. Someone had placed the only four remaining branches of the sundered Tree near the old Blessing stone, a sad memorial to the mighty oak that had once grown there. They simply could not bear to burn the Clan Tree's wood for warmth.

Then, on the eve of the next vernal equinox, which came, strangely, only three weeks later, Haen woke from the long dream that had come upon him at the Parting.

And there was fire in his hands.

Before his quarrel with Nohr, Haen had spent his life learning the secrets of time and weather, and leaf and animal, and as its Keeper had protected the Tree until the end. Somehow, in the rending, he said, it had gifted him with the song of its power. Gaunt and near death from the long fast, he went to the several remaining branches of the Tree and desperately spoke the light spell he had learned in his trance, whispering it into the tiniest gleam of sunlight that had miraculously penetrated the clouds, afterward calling aloud the names of trees and plants, virtually believing the seasons into existence again.

The branches took root, the Tree grew, the cold receded, the seeds at last awakened, but the world was still broken; the proper invocation had to be done every new vernal equinox, which now came so irregularly that only the Keeper knew exactly when the light would break the clouds for a tiny instant and align with the broken Blessing stone.

Haen's line, and its new order of Keepers, stretched uninterrupted down to Logan, the whole clan rejoicing at the birth of every son with the white gull-wing brows and the fiery fingers.

Winter was always only a tiny breath away.

At the Parting, amid strife and confusion and storm, Nohr and his followers had fled to the mountains, choosing to brood and bellow among the broad ridges and frozen tarns, where tangled disorder and the mutations spawned of lingering darkness, now outgrown and unchecked by natural predators, roamed, making living dangerous and short. There, Nohr's line venerated their ancient grudges and fostered the arts of battle and exploitation, and regularly raided both Inys Haen and those squatter clans out to the east.

The old fortress town of Inys Nohr was built close to an inlet off the Sea of Sorrows. There was some fishing, Logan had heard, and a great many poor folk had to survive on the eels and the other strange, deepwater things left in a lightless sea. Logan knew the Nohr now had mining and a bit of metalwork. The raiders had started wearing armor over the last several years.

But there was no green farming, no corn in the late fall, no grapes for wine, no pasture for livestock. There was no summer in the mountains, even when the Haenish had light. The Nohr were now, by all accounts, a city of sick and poor, thieves and strangers, and a haven for every unsavory sort who feared the light and loved the darkness that covered their deeds. Logan's people were convinced the Nohr lived only for the sweetness of stolen Haenish wine, and the burning of Haenish candles in the drinking halls at storytellings, and the courage of the Haenish conquest to warm the blood and the bed.

Logan, however, believed the Nohr still had the crown of the Clan Tree somewhere in the uppermost chambers of their ancient, stone tower. Sometimes, when he saw Nazir's eyes in his dreams, he saw the Tree, too. Against all odds, the little oak shoot, with its solitary acorn, had survived, languishing in the eternal twilight, its yellowed leaves continually putting forth and then shedding, the heartline of mana unhomed and pulsing irregularly.

They have become savages, and we have become so bound by our patterns that we dare not change anything, not even the way we thread a needle or plow a field. We are living the same way we lived when Haen brought the first spring. There are just the same number of us, and most are afraid to even venture outside our clanhold, much less our way of thinking, for fear the prophecy will not come true. We and the Nohr will have to bring our powers together someday, somehow. No matter the cost. Otherwise, both peoples will perish. But Nazir knows, thought Logan, *that time is running out. He will come for me again.*

The houses of Haen and Nohr had been divided for more than five hundred years. In the furrow of that long time, myth and rumor and exaggeration had taken firm root and grown up between them, pushing them even further apart. All of Cridhe spoke a common tongue, but what Haenish had to say of Nohrlander and Nohrlander of Haenish could best be expressed with a rude gesture and a scowl.

Logan had counted one hundred and fifty-one days of winter this year before his blood stirred, before he spent a sleepless night with the names of birch and elder and lily shaking his every thought with their demand for life.

Still, we cannot simply give in. They would make us slaves. They have hated us for centuries. They will never give up trying to take what can only be given.

Logan shook his head, trying to dispel the strife he had just re-created in his mind. Things had to be especially clear today. It would probably be the last time he did this.

As Logan turned from the blank sky to face the east again, a few of the surviving cattle shifted restlessly and began to low softly, their breath frosting in the air. A dog, far off, probably with the outer guard, began to bark. Logan wondered if somewhere the porridge wasn't already on, a grainy odor teasing the shaggy longhorned cows and his own appetite, too. But there could be no ease from the cold, no refreshment for winter-starved bodies, until Logan the Keeper, sixth from the First, unmade the winter and remembered the spring.

•   •   •

When the ray of red light poured through the lowered thornwall gate and struck the split in the old stone, filling the breach in the Blessing, Logan recalled the Memory, believed it again, and green fire, answering the sunlight, touched his gnarled, upraised hands. He began to walk, not a little painfully, around the wide sun circle laid out on the withered grass in smooth blue stones.

Since the First's awakening, four oak branches, carefully saved arms of the last tree, were spaced equally in the circle, radiating to the edges, while the Keeper's words, Logan's words, hushed and sweet, radiated to the edges of the clanhold.

"Fourth prime: north. I bind and break the hand of winter, the claw of frost, the strength of storm, the blade of ice, the covenant of crystal."

Logan smiled as he heard the crack and grind of ice thawing in the nearby Sobus River. He moved around the circle.

"Third prime: west. I bind the darkness of the long night, the candle's dying, the sun's cloak, the blackness at noonday, the death of color, the sadness of the soul."

Logan's hands reached higher, and the green fire leapt in response. Under his soft leather shoes, tiny spears of grass pushed forth, still white from their sleep in the earth, to mingle with dog violets. The four dried oak limbs turned pliant and flexible, their buds swelling and their newly formed roots burrowing into the ground at the center of the circle. He paced further and stopped at the next station. The mage wheezed for a long moment and then continued.

"Second prime: south. I loose the waters of life, the morning dew, the rain under the sky shield, the tide of beginning, the flood of birth."

A light mist rose at Logan's knees and settled on his green cloak in pearly droplets; a warm wind quickened

and danced over his thinning white hair. He smiled,
fighting the overwhelming fatigue, moved on and
addressed the final passage. That dog had not ceased
its own invocation, either, he thought, somewhat distractedly. He gathered himself and went on.

"First prime: east. I loose light, the laughter of
heaven, the giver of the green, the power of sight, the
maker of day."

Logan's own laughter rang out as the verdant fire at
his fingertips took wing on the words and flew upward
to form a cloud of phosphorescent light that spread
over the entire clanhold in a blazing green glitter. The
oak branches stood up on their roots at the center of
the circle and wound one around the other to form a
thick green trunk, anchored in the warming loam, their
branches and leaves soaring toward the four prime
directions in lush, sweeping cascades. The cloud lingered and fell softly, touching branch and bole, hedge
and hillock, until every blade of grass and every leaf
had caught its magic, named again by the Keeper, and
come forth in its color. They all reached for the rising
sun, which now filled the east with its own light, the
clouds having rolled away from Inys Haen again. When
the sun had circled that day, the spring would be completely remembered, set in its course for its season, and
could not come undone. Logan prayed the day would
pass unchallenged, that he could draw breath until that
evening, that his last act might be to have a son. He
lifted his eyes and scanned the northern horizon, now
verdant with new pasture, and hoped he would see
nothing more than grass.

Nothing is what he saw. But it was a tense, prickly
nothing. The dog had stopped its barking and the
morning stillness settled around Logan again. The
entire clan had encircled the holding, men and women
armed to stand the day's watch. Surely they were safe.

Logan left the holy circle and turned uneasily to make his way around the cow byre and seek out his breakfast, thinking that Aylith, who could barely reach the treadles on her loom, and was far too small to fight—though not by her own estimation—must be the one already cooking. His wife would be at her place by the riverbank, bent on defending the water she so loved. Logan wondered often what would become of his daughter—she had the mage marks, the white gull-wing brows and the firefingers, but she was female, and the elders would never let her inherit his Memories or his position in the clan. After all, no woman had ever held the Memories.

But before Aylith, no woman had ever had the marks. Logan had secretly turned this over in his mind since his daughter was born. He knew he might someday have to make a terrible choice. His daughter was the most headstrong young woman in the village. Aylith constantly argued with the elders' interpretations of the patterns, despite their superior status and great age. She could outfish any of the men except her cousin Jedhian, and worst of all, she openly voiced her disbelief in the coming of the Mender. Aylith had even refused every suitor thus far, though they were not many. Logan thought perhaps Jom, one of the shepherds, cared for her and might someday bring his courage to the question; Aylith could, *if* she set her mind to it, make someone like him a good wife. She was a good weaver, had quite a talent for the cunning design—and she had a startling way with a kettle of oats.

Logan stopped short.

An odd, new odor mingled with the porridge: too much wood burning and the acrid, throat-searing combustion of straw and dried mud . . . and something else; he could not place it.

It was too quiet. He turned to look for the fire and saw the cattle standing stock still, their eyes wide and terrified, their heads craning to look over the byre wall. In a heartbeat, the eerie silence erupted into shouts and screams and the frenzied calling and stamping of the penned cattle.

A young, black-haired Nohrish warrior, knife in his teeth and torch in his hand, ran from hut to hut, setting the wattle-and-daub buildings ablaze at their thatch roofs. He grinned evilly at Logan as he made for another cottage. Logan gulped a huge breath and raced toward the cluster of low buildings, a supernatural speed in his steps, arriving just as his hut and six more near it shuddered into flame. The air around his head filled with the sounds of joined battle outside the thornwall, the spit and crackle of devouring fire, and the smell of sulfur and pitch. The Nohrish soldier's laughter rang in Logan's ears above it all.

Logan raged into the inferno, swinging his arms and bellowing protective spells over his family. In the horrific heat of the fire, he fell back once, twice, then got his footing just as the roof crashed down in burning splinters and flaming thatch.

In the darkest part of the smoke, Logan beheld his daughter Aylith, blinded and coughing, straining to remove herself from her overturned loom and the wall that had collapsed it trapping her, the flame riding the snapped warp of the piece in progress.

I can get to my little Aylith, at least! he thought, never noticing that he could barely draw his own breath.

The girl cried out to him, and Logan threw himself forward, his hands finding firm purchase on each side of her head, his fingers burning with their own fire, the green fire that could make spring appear, the fire that could heal a wounded land.

"My sweet child, hear me! I am dying; someone has to take the Memories. Aylith! Do you hear me?"

Logan felt the smallest pressure of her acknowledgment. He gasped, choking on the smoke, reciting the ancient words.

"Receive the secret of life, the song of the Clan Tree, precious and magical. Keep the Memories, use them only to make the dead live, the sleeper awaken, to protect, to heal, and guard them with your own life until you pass them on. They are your true nature!" he shouted against the roar of the fire with the very last of his air.

The green fire in his hands sprang higher as Logan finished the invocation that had been spoken to every man who had ever kept the Memories. Aylith opened her smoke-stunned eyes wide against the roiling blackness and felt her father's hard, desperate touch raise her up into a dream of daylight, a song of life, where all the names of green life dwelt in quiet, protected order, where planets rotated in time with suns and every arrival and every passing was marked and laid in her keeping. Logan himself stood in the center of the beautiful dream, his face stricken and helpless, and then greatly surprised. His smiling mouth moved with a silent, strange acknowledgment as his gray eyes clouded and closed.

Outside the vision, with an effort from beyond his last strength, and nearly beyond death, Logan flung his daughter out into the coolness of the new spring morning to safety.

Aylith tumbled out onto the tender grass several yards from the fire and rolled a little way down the earthwork, unconscious of either her own salvation or her father's sacrifice. She drifted in the new dream, looking among the bright words and images, rapt at the music of life.

Above and behind her, the fire found Logan's body very quickly, green flames flashing for a brief moment among the orange.

• • •

Some long time later, when the point of an iron dou-
ble-edged sword touched her chest, Aylith awakened
and looked up the wet blood gutter to see the hard-set,
helmet-framed face of the Nohrish commander staring
down at her. She turned her head slightly and saw the
open, startled, dark eyes of a dead Nohrish soldier collapsed over her left arm, his leggings down around his
knees and her charred cloak in his hand. On his middle
finger was a golden ring, wondrously wrought in the
shape of an eagle's head. Aylith shifted his body with a
sharp tug and then returned her dress to a more mod-
est drape. The big soldier cleared his throat and spoke.

"Get up, girl. Don't worry, Thix never had time. I
have a law against rape. Humiliates the worthy enemy.
No respect."

The man pricked at her ribs with the cold, black
blade, and the pressure brought a sharp frown to her
face.

But whether from inability or resolve, Aylith did not
move. The Nohrish commander twitched his long,
blond mustache and continued to stare down his sword,
the other soldier's blood congealing rather quickly on it.

"Get up. I know you understand me. I am RoNal."

She continued to look through him.

Then suddenly he bellowed a great war cry at the
stunned girl, his head flung back and his chest heaving
under the massive leather sark and the tightly knitted
mail shirt. But one blue eye never left Aylith's face.

The girl sat up and gave him her best Haenish battle
scream in answer.

RoNal, more surprised than he had been in years,
laughed, not unkindly, and said, "You are scrawny and
soft, and much smaller than the Felonarch expects, but
you have more courage than any of your people. Some

are dead, but the rest have all run away. See?" He motioned to the empty clanhold with his free hand. "And they ran much farther than Nazir's nephew."

He rolled the young man's body away from her. Aylith looked out over the smoking debris and vacant cattle byre, then past the dead soldier, her glance freezing on the pile of rubble that had been her home. Her father . . .

"Perhaps you are young enough to forget this day," RoNal chattered on. "I have saved you from death today. Perhaps the Maker has wrought for you another pattern, another life."

He trailed off, noticing Aylith staring at the burned cottage. Tears welled in her eyes, but she would not spill them. RoNal went on after a moment, more softly.

"You will come with us and you will no longer be Haenish dirt. You will be my daughter. You will probably marry a great ruler. It is a good day!" He forced a smile, revealing several large yellow teeth, nodding his head hopefully at her.

Aylith gazed up at him in wordless shock, her sight passing behind him to watch a single snowflake flutter toward the frost-stung grass. Gray-black billowing clouds rolled across the clean blue sky, while the pale sun hovered at the edge of the horizon, and then disappeared behind the clouds, into winter again.

CHAPTER
3

JEDHIAN THE HEALER CHECKED HIMSELF over for battle damage, found some, most of it minor, and then bound up a deep slash on his leg that was just beginning to hurt. His scarf would hold, but the leg could be a problem. He planned hastily, thankful he had fared better than his friend Jom, who lay still and cold not three feet away from Jedhian, the edge of a Nohrish battle-ax lost in his neck. Just beyond Jom, and equally dead, the owner of the ax and two of his friends communed in eternal silence, stiffening monuments to Jom's skill with his shepherd's crook.

Jedhian peered through a withered prickleberry bush, just outside the thornwall, and watched as the retreating Nohr gathered everything they could, as quickly as they could, divided it, and packed three war parties off toward the mountains. He saw a large, blond, mustachioed man gather the last group together and chain Aylith's hands and feet, and another tall soldier in the same battle dress as the leader took charge of her as they moved out of the clanhold, through the thornwall gate and toward the Sobus River. His uncle Logan must be dead, because he had not been taken. The old man was so frail to begin with; Jedhian knew he could not have survived this attack.

The gate. He had known there would be trouble with that. Hadn't he told the elders that they needed more men there? And where was everybody now? Dead or hiding, most likely.

Jedhian studied out the situation for awhile. The Nohr had breached the thornwall and likely killed the Keeper. No telling what that could mean. More importantly, Nazir's raiders had his cousin Aylith. The Nohr almost never took prisoners. Why now? Why her?

By Haen's white brow, it's cold! he thought, clutching the flaps of his old cloak together and shivering furiously in the lightly falling snow. He wished ardently for his newly woven bhana. Left behind because of its bright colors, it had probably burned with his hut, he thought miserably. He picked all the shriveling berries from the bush, shoved them into his pocket, took a deep breath, and dug out the ax from Jom's body, wiping its blade on the frost-burned grass, his hands shaking. No surgery he had ever done was more painful.

Some time after the Nohrish raiders drove the cattle out of the gate, he rose quietly to follow, staying under cover and skirting the ruined clanhold.

As he crossed the refrozen Sobus, making his way through the great chunks of ice that looked like scattered teeth, he heard a dog barking behind him. Looking back, he searched the riverbank until he found Nesa, Aylith's sheepkeeper, her body a black-and-tan blur of excitement, a few yards from the point he knew the raiders had crossed.

Jedhian's mouth went dry and he slipped and slid back to the clanhold's side of the riverbank, dreading what he might find.

"What is it, Nesa?" he whispered as he reached the firmer ground. The dog whined and licked his face, but in no wise settled. Instead, Nesa bounded off down the riverbank a little farther, encouraging him to follow. Jedhian saw what she had summoned him for.

In a thin patch of red-stained snow, Selka, Aylith's mother, lay very, very dead, the work of a Nohrish sword and a berserk mind. A trail of tracks, the hooves of the cattle through the new snow, and Aylith's soft boot prints among them, passed not three feet from the body. He read the prints with a practiced hunter's eye. Aylith had turned, and dug in her heels, struggling with the captors. They had lifted her bodily and gone on.

He was in a hurry, but there was nothing to cover the body, and none of the clan in sight. He could not go back into Inys Haen and risk the collected elders seeing him and forbidding him to leave again. There was nothing for it. She would have to be buried.

Jedhian set his back to the task, thinking he could make up the time on the trail. Since they had captured Aylith alive, she would probably stay alive at least until the raiders got to Inys Nohr. They were only a mile or so ahead of him by now.

The ground had frozen quickly at the sudden return of winter, so Jedhian had a harder time with the burial than he had supposed. But after a quick search for Selka's weapon, or a large enough freshwater clamshell, or just anything that would make the digging easier, he came upon a bit of metal just at the river's edge, apparently frost-heaved from deep mud by the looks of the one visible edge. He loosened and worked at the blade, for it became obvious that he had a sword of some type in his hands, until it reluctantly pulled from the icy mud with a dull *thwick*.

Jedhian whistled softly when he had hastily cleaned the remainder of the muck off the old sword. Stylized snakes, of a sort Jedhian could not identify, wound themselves around the hilt and down the blade in a sinuous, graceful pattern. Attached to either side of the pommel were two stones, unequally balanced, each one fastened with a hinge and lock in the middle, but when Jedhian tried to open the stones, the curious metal hardware refused to budge. Perhaps the years this old blade had spent buried in the soggy riverbank had locked the stones permanently.

The sword, for all its beauty, was not much of a weapon anymore. Its blade would not cut leather, thought Jedhian, and the tip was broken. Nonetheless, digging would be easier with it. He spent a couple of hours on the shallow grave, and with every plunge of the broken sword into the unforgiving earth, Jedhian could feel the Nohrish slash on his leg open a little wider. He tried not to think about what they had done to Selka. He tried harder not to think about how much time he was losing. But finally the job was done. Wiping the freezing sweat from his face, Jedhian sent Nesa, reluctant but obedient, back to the village, and set out over the snow-dusted moors, toward Inys Nohr.

CHAPTER
4

ON THE FIFTH DAY OUT FROM THE RUIN OF Inys Haen, RoNal stopped the raiding party and made camp early. The Nohrland foothills rose gray and stark behind the smoky cookfire, the sky holding only the faintest trace of pink light. Still shocked and numb, Aylith wrapped herself more tightly in the red-and-blue bhana they had thrown her, and inhaled the familiar smells of the clanhold, still sharp upon the cloak despite its baptism by smoke and fire. It was Jedhian's cloak, newly received for his birth moon. Her throat ached at the thought of her cousin's laughter and their long walks in the gloaming, the present comfort of his cloak seeming somehow too dear.

If they had this bhana, Jedhian must be dead, too. He would never have given it up. He had helped her find the wildflowers to dye it, also using the roots in his medicines. Their sweet perfume rose in her memory even now. Jom had laughed at him for its patterns and colors, pretending to be blinded when the healer wore it. And Jedhian had laughed, too.

Her cousin. Her best friend.

She blinked back the stinging tears yet again and tried to think only that she was happy at least to have the bhana, something soft to hold on to in the midst of hard changes. Last night, as the freezing mist had settled on her uncovered face, she dreamed of rescue, of Jedhian, of the horrors of the fire, and the final touch of her father's hands on her head, and much more about the strange things he had put into her mind. She awoke several times, her woolen tunic stiff with the cold, while visions of the land before her danced in their green finery, all traces of the winter gone. She heard the seeds buried in the frosted earth calling to her, pleading for another chance to grow. And the song of the Clan Tree rose and fell with her every breath, swelling to deafening crescendos of radiant growth. She had clutched at her head and then swooned back into troubled sleep, pleading all the while with Logan for silence. But the song never ceased, the names repeating themselves over and over in her mind with the same urgency, as though there were one final chance left them to live.

The Nohr are rightly cursed, she thought to herself. *Let them rot in their darkness forever!*

RoNal had chained her hands in front today and left her feet unfettered, thinking that she would have nowhere to run. He was right. Though she had plotted a dozen escapes, the raiding party had taken an arduous route across the barren moors, around the squatter clanholds that had sprouted at the edges of Haenish light. The last one she had seen, two days back, had been razed to the ground some time ago, its rough quarried stones thrown down and the cottages' roofs all caved in. Large plate-shaped fungi had spread across the charred stones, feeding upon the fire's grim leavings.

At least they had left something standing at Inys Haen, Aylith thought. There were many huts the fire had not swallowed, and she had seen only six or seven bodies tossed on the pyres. Surely her people would come for her. Surely. She had curled her lip and hissed at the two brutes in front of her, their coarse accents grating on her ears. With every step away from Inys Haen she was forced to take, her heart hardened further toward the Nohr and especially toward Nazir, their famed ruler.

The traders who brought tin and iron to the clanhold always passed through Nohrland, and the tales they told of this monster made Aylith's hair rise. One of them said he had lost his brother, a pot mender, to Nazir's temper; the man had been found with his throat ripped out. They said Nazir could look in your eyes and make you blind, that Inys Nohr was full of white-eyed folks who had stared too long at the Felonarch. Some said he was better than his murdered father, though. That one had killed off all his own brothers and sisters in order to make sure they would never steal his throne.

And they were taking her to this beast who had as much as with his own hand killed all her family. She fought down the brief flash of her mother's hand in the snow, her fingers blue and still gripping her only weapon, a small pair of sheep shears, which now dangled from the belt of one of the men sitting in front of her, closer to the campfire. Her family and how many others? And for what? So that Nazir might take away her people's last bit of hope? As long as Keepers brought the spring, the Haenish could survive. They could even believe, if they chose to.

What will come of them now that Logan is gone, and they don't know about me? They will scatter like sheep. . . . she thought, knowing the elders kept the clan from despair largely through reminding them constantly of the prophecy.

And the fire—as long as she lived, fire would be different now. No longer the warming, friendly thing it had been before.

The smell of it clogged her nostrils now with the memory of destruction. Her home lay in ashes. Logan's ancient, stricken face still flashed before her eyes at every turn of the trail, at every break of a twig and especially, especially, at every wisp of smoke.

RoNal stirred the fire with his sword, and spat the shell of a grubnut into it with a well-practiced arc.

"You will eat this," he said, his voice gravelly and tired from the day's travel. He carved off a hunk of the boar he'd killed that afternoon, now roasting toward indigestibility before them.

Oh, yes, I will eat, Aylith secretly resolved. *If I am going to Inys Nohr, let them think they have taken a prisoner. But if it still exists, if it is more than an old story, I will take back whatever is left of the Clan Tree. I can't believe in a Mender, but it's enough that Nazir obviously does. Let him try to mend without any power! I will escape somehow and return in time for the next equinox. Maybe the elders can teach me to use the Memories. Whether they like it or not, I'm all they've got, now. There may never be a Mender, but there will always be a Keeper. The Nohr will never have our light!*

She sighed and put out her bound hands for the meat. RoNal jerked back his knife, baiting her. He laughed in great ugly waves at his jest, spewing meat and recently stolen Haenish wine from his mouth, and repeated the offer again and again. On the fourth try, Aylith rose up and deftly snatched the food off his knife, a thin, brittle smile on her face. RoNal drew back, his eyes alight with laughter.

"You will make a fierce warrior, I think," he teased, choking down a wayward morsel. "You have the heart for it, if not the size. And perhaps Nazir will not kill me, after all, for losing your sorcerer again," he added, somewhat more soberly as he finally swallowed the tough, dry meat.

Nazir.

Aylith bit savagely into the burned, foul-tasting pork, thinking all the while who her first kill would be if they ever, indeed, gave her the chance to swing a sword.

The next day, the clouds even darker than usual, and promising snow, Aylith awoke to rough shaking and another portion of the boar for breakfast. It was nearly frozen, the fire having died sometime before midnight. In this wild, barren landscape, the Nohr had left only one man to keep watch every night. She would bide her time. Stay alive. Someone would come. Jedhian would have. They would surely know she was missing by now. She only had to keep believing.

And it would be easy, a small matter if the timing were right, she thought, needles of driving sleet now lacing into her cheeks. If someone came for her before they reached Inys Nohr, there was every chance of taking this slovenly group by surprise. And there were only four of them. Not all those bodies on the pyres were Haenish, she recalled with bitter satisfaction and more than a little wonder, thinking again of the Nohrish soldier RoNal had killed, apparently just before the man—someone had called him Thix—could rape her. From what she had overheard, and as best she could make out from their oddly inflected speech, this party had originally been seven. RoNal was the easiest to understand, and the most talkative. Aylith didn't quite know what to make of the man who, it seemed, had both saved and enslaved her. He was the leader, without apparent challenge, having declared Aylith his new "daughter" when he made a very short speech at Inys Haen to sort the booty.

"Mine," he had said as he pointed to a huge pile of soot-covered objects and six trembling cows strung together near it, and "Yours," when he pointed to two other, thinner, but equally terrified cows and a butter churn. "Mine! Do not touch her," he'd growled as he had put her down rather brusquely by the string of better cows, thereby quelling the lascivious grins on the big dumb faces of the other two men. Despite the dirt and the remains of several recent meals, Aylith could see that they were twins. Aylith wondered which one would get the butter churn.

The other Nohrish warrior in the party and her new sister, too, from his terse introduction, was named Lorris. Aylith had never seen a woman in armor before. Lorris stood as tall as RoNal and had enormous gray eyes, and dark blond hair tightly braided under her bronze, boar-crested helmet. A long scar jagged down her left forearm and hand, and Aylith guessed her to be about the same age as her herself: twenty years. She was much bigger than Aylith, her hands nearly half again Aylith's palm span, her fingers an inch longer. RoNal's other daughter reminded her of a big gray lynx, slanted eyes unblinking and cunning, a solitary huntress.

Lorris had grimaced tacitly at Aylith when they first met, apparently quite annoyed that the wispy girl had been put in her charge for the journey home. Now she stood glaring down at Aylith, large face tilted in impatience and sword in hand.

Aylith rolled over in the bhana and elbowed her way up, wincing at the prickles in her feet as she stood too

quickly. Her thin boots were little protection against
the night's chill. Before she could request water, Lorris
was stalking away.

"Get moving, Haenish," she called back over her
shoulder, a blast of icy wind catching away some of her
words. "You'll freeze otherwise. And then my father will
take your bride price from my pay. And do not even
begin to think of yourself as my family, do you hear?"

Aylith heard only the first and last of what Lorris
said. But Lorris's cutting tone was enough to bring a
flush of heat to her face and make her fingers tingle.
She looked down at her hands and saw green light pulsing at her fingertips, and quickly hid them in the bhana.

Do not concern yourself, she raged silently at Lorris,
her eyes furiously darting around the camp to check if
the magic had been seen. When she held out her hand
again, the flame had quenched.

The day, if it could be called such, lasted only a few
hours, with thick dark clouds blanketing the sky. They
had walked out of the ice storm, but winter's long grimace still stretched across the land from the last season, and no green thing had grown where they now
passed. They were just about to pass the point where
the last bit of Haenish light allowed for it, anyway.
Here and there grew thorny switches of prickleberry
bush, this year's buds formed and waiting, but no
bunch of leaves pushed forth, no sprig of their flower
perfumed the air. At odd moments, Aylith saw the
same landscape in her mind, burgeoning with new
growth and innumerable shades of green, with blossoms she had never encountered before—but suddenly
knew the names of—and then the vision would be gone
again, the heather and fern, blackened from frost and
dried from cold, crunching under foot into powdery

dust, and the livestock trying to eat last year's broom wherever it poked out of the rocks. The Haenish cows, already exhausted from living through the harsh winter, stumbled frequently, and the party made small progress. Though there was little cover—they were now too far from Inys Haen for trees—there seemed every opportunity for her rescue, and Aylith constantly scanned the southern horizon, thinking that even Jom could not miss their wide and incautious trail.

But no one came.

At the end of the day's travel, while Lorris glared at her and RoNal made a fire, the two younger men, still nameless to Aylith and totally indistinguishable from one another, began to care for the animals. Aylith sat down near a low outcrop of white granite, out of Lorris's direct view, tired beyond words, her heart heavy with the realization that no one was coming to rescue her.

Not now, not later. She was alone.

She slumped against the crumbling rock wall, finally letting hot tears well in her eyes and spill onto her dirty cheeks. Still she made no sound. The brutish Nohr had taken away everything she loved, but they would not have the satisfaction of hearing her fear and grief. She gave herself to the pain in great silent sobs, uttering wordless curses upon Nazir with every breath. Finally, the heaviness lifted and the pain subsided. She sat quietly, empty and numb.

Before long, Aylith felt very cold and confused, but only pulled Jedhian's bhana over herself to sleep for awhile. The bhana seemed especially warm and comforting, and she fell immediately into a deep dream.

Suddenly, her body afire with a searing pain, Aylith tumbled forward and tried to tear the bhana away, for every part of her skin it touched felt like a flayed, salted wound.

"Help!" she croaked, fighting the sleep and unable to completely gain her senses. With her violent lurch, the bhana had tightened its deadly embrace and snaked one corner of itself over her head.

"Ah, by Nohr! She is such baggage!" cried Lorris, dropping her handful of scrub and racing to Aylith's struggling form. But when she saw what was happening, her tone changed. "It's a shroud, Father— Fire! Quickly!"

RoNal, already roaring anger at the possible loss of Nazir's pardon, charged over and began waving a burning torch all around the bundled, thrashing girl. RoNal attacked again and again, heartened by Aylith's muffled screams, until the beast quivered and detached from her head, and then curled itself away from Aylith's hands and feet, leaving ugly red welts on them and a gust of fetid acid in the air around her. RoNal twitched the writhing animal away from her body, and Aylith, freed from the creature's grip, but not her hand-bindings, jerked backward and rolled into the rock face, hitting her head and knocking herself out.

RoNal cursed and kicked the shroud into the fire, where it sizzled and popped for a moment, then blackened and shrank into a thin, transparent membrane before it turned to ash, twisting off in the air on a tongue of fire.

"That was a little one. She was fortunate. Look, the blisters are fading even now, and her skin looks to be barely peeled. It didn't get much of a grip, I suppose." RoNal grimaced in utter amazement as he gently turned Aylith's limbs over to check for further injuries. "The headache will be worse. See to her, Lorris. Things are bad enough already. I can't be delivering damaged wares," he said brusquely, barely hiding some genuine concern for the girl. He then walked slowly over to the fire and sat down to his supper, his mind constantly churning over what he would have to tell Nazir about the Keeper. About the raid. About Thix.

Lorris fanned the last of the acid cloud out of her eyes and opened her canteen to clean the nick above Aylith's ear.

"You have defied death again, Haenish. You are the first person I know to survive a wrapped shroud, little one or not, and my father knows it, too."

She passed the cold cloth over Aylith's bruised head, the cut already only a red streak near her hairline. "And how is it your wounds close so quickly?" Lorris said, mostly to herself, since Aylith lay unmoving and limp. "And who is that fine big man who now follows us, hmm?"

Lorris removed the girl's acid-soaked clothing and finished washing the shroud's vitriol off her body.

When Aylith awoke, she felt very strange, as if she had been too long in the sun on a bright day, and she was dressed in one of Lorris's spare fleece tunics, which was far too large, but warmer.

"What happened?" she asked as Lorris handed her a cup of hot wine and the real bhana. The angry red sucker sores on her face and arms had diminished, but her head pounded ferociously. Aylith took the wine but would not touch her own weave-work. She let Lorris drop it at her feet and kept an eye on it for movement. She poked at it now and then with a dry broom twig.

"Well, you knocked yourself senseless. And you lived through a shroud wrapping. That would be all," said Lorris, her eyes bright with sarcasm and a hint of new respect.

"What's a shroud?" asked Aylith, taking another sip of the spicy wine and still studying the bhana. It was the first hot drink she'd had in days. Her mind began to clear. She nudged the bhana with her boot.

"You don't know about shrouds? You can't be serious. Oh, I suppose the wondrous Inys Haen has no vermin."

Aylith held her tongue, thinking, *Yes, we do. They visit at least twice a year.*

"They are very common in the mountains," Lorris continued, "though this is a bit farther down-country than usual for them. They crawl close to travelers and mimic clothing or a blanket, and all the while, they are lulling you to sleep and making you colder with some kind of inaudible song. When you reach for something to warm yourself, they find your hand, or crawl over you, and soon, you are completely enveloped, and sooner, you are dead—they dissolve their prey from the outside in." She pointed to Aylith's clothes, now a heap of mush and thread.

"They can copy after any fabric or leather they sense. And you can't kill them with a blade; it only helps them to multiply. Never cut a shroud, remember that. Or tear one, either, even though it's very easy to do. The pieces can grow and rejoin into something pretty big, like a blanket or even a tent. Try to use fire to try to peel them off if they aren't fully wrapped, although that's difficult. Eat green things—if you can find them—it helps to repel them and slows the poison. The grass-lovers taste bad to them. That's why they leave the cattle alone."

Lorris bent low to Aylith's face. "They were meant to be Nazir's toys—his father and the Sifter made them from the lint of Haenish garments and dark magic up in the tower, my mother says. They thought they were creating an invisible cloak. You really never have seen one before?" Lorris looked at Aylith in clear wonder.

Aylith shook her head. Strands of sandy hair, now very cold from their washing, stuck to her face.

"How would I know? I have lived in the clanhold all my life. I have never been farther outside the holding of

Inys Haen than the western seashore. And I have never wanted to," she said as she looked toward the forbidding countryside. "My father said traveling would be too dangerous and unsavory. I think he was right."

Lorris whistled softly and then half-smiled at Aylith.

"You are doing pretty well, then, for a light-lover. Um . . . what is your name?" she asked hesitantly.

"Aylith of Inys Haen."

"Aylith," said Lorris, her accent thick on the new name, making the "th" sound like a "t." "I have never heard of any person who survived a complete wrapping. And you have almost recovered from it. Does every Haenish have this power? What charms do you wear? Do you eat with the cattle? Or maybe are you a sorcerer, like Nazir?" she offered, her gray eyes lit in laughter at the sheer impossibility.

Aylith rubbed at the fading red rings on her hands and stared over at the fire. Logan's smiling face seemed to glow in the dancing flames.

Aylith looked into the fire a long time before she answered. "I don't know, Lorris. I don't know."

Lorris shrugged and left her alone. Aylith thought long about her vow and the mystical power of the Memories. Somehow, she would learn to use them. There had to be a way. It felt just beyond her reach. When she looked down, the dry broom twig in Aylith's hand had sprouted three tiny new leaves, their tender edges burned with the cold.

CHAPTER
5

ANOTHER NIGHT OF THE TREE'S DREAMS had deprived her of much sleep, but the next day brought the war party to the outskirts of Inys Nohr, and Aylith took a small comfort in the nearness of the journey's end. All morning long, they had climbed steadily, until Aylith thought they must surely be walking upon pure sky, not land at all. She had never been this far up in the air, and found herself gasping for breath and a little dizzy. She had kept up well enough, though, and Lorris, now a little kinder toward her, had called for frequent stops to help Aylith adjust to the altitude.

The Memories still flooded her mind when she lost her concentration, but the landscape had altered alarmingly. All around, where Aylith knew there should be trees, could see them swaying in their golden autumnal splendor or raining their cones in heavy gusts upon the earth, there stood instead thick bunches of overgrown fungi, clusters of rubbery gray clubs and sickly brown platelets. Gigantic blue puffballs sprayed their dark spores into the air, the fine purple particles floating for hours before settling like ash on everything for several hundred yards, staining the light cover of snow a strange, unnatural lavender. When they rounded the bend on a crop of bright orange stinkworts, Aylith nearly lost her meager breakfast. The odor of rotting meat cloyed at her nostrils and set her against food for the remainder of the day. Aylith wondered how the fungi and worts could grow here—but then remembered Logan once dreaming there had been hundreds of years of jungle here before the long winter. The slow rot of a rainforest could produce enough decay to host the giant mushrooms for a very long time. The cold seemed not to bother them at all.

Further up the pass, where a treeline should have marked the mountain face, great landslid boulders, eroded from their higher perches during the vegetation kill after the Parting, gave place to oily bogs and pockets of quicksand. On one of his hunting trips, Jedhian had seen an area he had described like this, called the Slicks, just past the fourth Far clan. Aylith supposed it must be similar, and marveled at how hard it was to see the mire before you were upon it. Not a second later, one of the twins went down to his waist in the fetid murk, completely disappearing before his brother pulled him out. When Aylith passed the same place only seconds later, the black pool had already slicked over, tiny white crystals forming over its dark surface, instantly forgetting the disturbance. She shuddered, wondering how many others had fallen alone and now lay frozen at the bottom of such a pit.

The darkness here seemed much more pervasive as well. The very little light that passed between the head-high clusters of mushrooms and waving, ferntcled fronds of mold diffused into a dirty gray haze, with no apparent source. These outlands of Inys Nohr lay in cold, perpetual twilight and decay.

"Is it always this dark here? It's like winter at home," asked Aylith, when Lorris sat down to adjust her bootlace.

"Dark? I suppose you would think it is. Nazir has proclaimed a new dawning and that we will grow green things in this valley." Lorris chuckled ruefully, waving her hand over the burgeoning crop of boulders. "In fact, he has promised all of Inys Nohr that it will be this very year. But I don't believe him. I have never believed him," she added, her voice hard at the edges.

"I have never seen much more light here than this, even when you call forth the spring at Inys Haen," continued Lorris. Then, as if she considered the differences for the first time, "It's more fun to raid for grain and cattle, anyway. I don't think I would make any kind of green-farmer at all. Takes you too long to get anything. We grow some food here, but none of it's what you are used to eating. But the fishing is interesting."

Aylith didn't like the sound of her tone, but kept quiet.

An hour or so after their last stop, the legendary Tower at Inys Nohr became a visible fact for Aylith. Although she had heard the myths and the stories about this dark fortress, seeing it for the first time, even from a distance, still made her stop in her tracks. In the swirling mist of a mountain pass, Inys Nohr's dark, stone-hewn tower rose like a massive granite tree trunk, its limbs chopped and its crown broken away, as if from an old violence. Aylith gazed in amazement at the enormous black vines that wrapped themselves upward on the tower's tumbled walls, apparently holding the structure together. Patches of orange and yellow lichens mottled the tower's ancient face, and the moat inside the bailey held syrupy-looking, reddened water. Pockets of steam rose now and then above the moat and small, erratic movements broke the water's thick surface. The low wind that wafted outward from it smelled of death. She recalled Lorris's comment about the fishing with a shiver.

"Welcome home," said Lorris.

"My point," panted Nazir as he swept his opponent's feet out from under him. The shorter man dropped hard to the mat and stayed there, preferring defeat to further injury.

"You always fall for that one." Nazir chuckled, clearly enjoying his pun more than his sparring partner.

The other man, sweating, bruised, blackened blood from his torn scalp flaking to his shoulder, lifted himself painfully off the practice mat and limped to the sidelines. Nazir took a cloth and wiped the sweat from his white brows and smiled hugely. His black hair glistened from exertion and he took a deep, satisfied breath, the puckered, raised birthmark above his heart rising and falling in rhythm to his pulse. It had been an excellent morning. He had beaten five of them; well, all right, one had died too soon, and on his own. But it had still been good sport. And the last raiding party would be returning today; he could feel it in his fingertips. This time, after so many years, they were bringing Logan, for he could also feel the charge in the air that bespoke the Haenish sorcerer's power—the energy signature of the Clan Tree.

RoNal had had other orders, too: take care of Thix. Nazir chuckled as he wondered if RoNal had ever grasped what he had really intended. Only Thix remained in the line of Nohr to threaten Nazir's absolute rule. And though Nazir had been crowned extremely young himself, Thix was too immature at

eighteen to take the throne. Thix would be too immature at any age to take the throne. But he had lately
shown himself to be every bit as cunning and mean as
Nazir, and far more ambitious. Sending him into a raid
would help to assure that ambition would never come
to fruit. Nazir could take no chances; the light that
would save his people, save his name, and save his
reign must come by his hand alone. He could never
share that honor.

Nazir had spent his life in study of the historical
chronicles of his family and his people. He alone knew
how the Haenish had mistreated his ancestor Nohr,
how they had laughed at his weathersense and called
him silly for his dreams of traveling to the stars. Nazir
had poured his precious time into turning the fragile
pages of those dusty volumes, his hand the first to
touch them other than the historians', to trace the line
of his fathers. Where was Thix at the same age?
Drinking with the women at the wharf, or cheating at
cards in the barracks. Of all his family, only Nazir had
wept over the raggedly enscribed stories, felt the pain of
the generations of madmen who never got the chance to
see their old age. Who never got the chance to avenge
Nohr's treatment at the hands of the Haenish.

Yes, RoNal would have to kill the young man when
he got out of hand, as Nazir knew he would. Such
beauty in that . . . then Nazir would have a perfect reason for putting RoNal himself to the lash. And the men
in his ranks would have to respect that. RoNal was a
traitor. No doubt about it. He had to be. Nazir just
knew.

The madness was gaining on him. How long before
it completely overtook him? Someone had to come
after him, to continue his soon-to-be-established rule
over the Haenish, keep his policies and establish
Nohrish dominance. Nazir had to have a son. Finding a

suitable woman to help him get an heir was almost as important as finding the Haenish Keeper. And of suitable Nohrish women, there were none. The birthrate for Inys Nohr had dropped remarkably in the past several years, and more than half the children who came safely into the world left it before they became adults.

Inys Nohr was dying; Nazir had known it for years. Slowly, painfully, from a myriad of diseases, from poverty and hopelessness, but most of all, from darkness. A Haenish woman, born and bred in sunlight, nourished with the fruit of long bright days in the summer, was Nazir's only hope. But his restless people could never know. He could never hope to hold their respect and subservience if they knew he intended to take a Haenish woman, even if it was for the assurance of his line, and their hope of daylight. Even if he would never love her.

Nazir traced the strange raised skin of his birthmark and felt the darkness gathering inside him, trying to pull him down into a deep, winding, internal passage, where every other member of his family had ended, sooner or later, since old Nohr had brought down the curse upon his house.

"Logan. Keeper. You and I, old man. You and I. We will finish what our fathers' fathers began. And this time, I will be the one to seize the light. You will give over the secret spell and I will work it upon the Clan Tree's seed. Then I will take your daughter, and your grandchildren will be Nohrish. They will rule from this tower over your miserable Haenish countrymen. Perhaps I will even travel a bit, like old Nohr had wanted to. . . . "

He smiled again and tossed the sweat-soaked rag, torn from a slave's dress, into the center of the practice ring.

As Nazir turned to leave, Arn the page skidded into the room at full run, nearly crashing into his master.

"Sir! They come, sir. The last party in. Sir, they have a girl with them," he panted, pale, transparent cheeks flushed and voice breaking in excitement.

Nazir stopped and deftly caught the boy's scabious arm, wrenching it upward.

"You saw them? A girl, you say? Good. But they bring no old man? Do you lie to me, Arn, and I will break this for you again," said Nazir, ice and fury warring in his voice.

"Sir! I would not, sir. Look out the portal right now, sir, and see if she is not just herself and no old man at all, begging sir's mercy."

The boy's face had gone completely red under Nazir's brief interrogation, but returned to its normal shade of paste when the Felonarch let him go. His shoulder dropped to its normal lopsided position, which was an uncomfortable slouch, a birth injury and a badly mended break marring his posture.

"Yes, I will do that, Arn. Thank you for the suggestion," menaced Nazir, an odd look crossing his chiseled white face as he strode to the carved stone window and leaned over the deep sill.

Indeed, Arn spoke the truth. As the war party passed below, Nazir saw no trace of Logan.

"By Nohr's knuckle bones!" he swore loudly, and bit the inside of his lip as fury won out. Nazir watched what was left of his last raiding party shuffle wearily into the stone-paved courtyard, a few odd cattle and common goods in tow. He pounded the wall when he saw with them only one prisoner: a small, sandy-haired girl, her hands bound before her, wearing overwhelmingly large clothes of Nohrish military make, her neck twisting far to the left and then back as she gawked all around.

Fresh, hot blood throbbed into Nazir's mouth and he spat it out into the milling party below. RoNal looked up suddenly, puzzled, and then saluted. Nazir rolled his eyes.

"Can RoNal never get him! The best soldier in my army cannot capture one old man? I tell you, that man has become too thick with those Albions to serve me," he muttered to himself. "And what useless baggage have they brought me instead?" he snorted, getting a closer look at Aylith. "She is hardly any prize. I had thought Logan's daughter to be of larger frame and sturdier build. She's as twiggy as a willow, and no taller than a good-sized hound. Ugly, too. Look at those bug eyes. Oh. But where is my nephew Thix?" he added absently, a wicked smile begging at the corner of his mouth.

The prize had been lost again. And yet, his fingertips still tingled.

There was something here to be learned, at least. Ignorance was not one of Nazir's faults. He had studied well his family's errors. He would not repeat them. He would be the one. He breathed deeply and calmed himself.

Perhaps the Keeper had somehow changed his shape. Perhaps it was only a trap on Logan's part to make him think the Keeper was dead or had escaped again, and when Nazir saw what he had, he would turn the ragged creature out, and the Keeper would go free, change back to his original shape, and return to Inys Haen.

"Arn, go to and fetch me clothes, my best—no, my blue robe instead," he ordered, suddenly changing his mind on how he would greet his newest subject.

Arn swallowed hard and left, rubbing his most recent bruise, but glad he still had the use of both arms to do the errand. He smiled to himself, though, despite the new pain. He had not told Nazir all of what he had seen. Not about the way the air shimmered around the girl, nor the way he could see a trace of green in her footprints.

Nazir paced for a moment, thinking and stretching, then leaned against the cold stone of the fortress wall, letting the grain of the rock press into his bare back. His hand wandered to the small scar on his chest. The burning, reddening line tingled slightly as he touched it. A new possibility crossed his mind.

Logan is not here, and should he really be dead or escaped, the power yet sings. Can it be? Has Logan given his daughter the secrets? he wondered.

"What have you in mind, most excellent lord?" oozed a voice from the far corner of the room, where the gargantuan Malvos, seated on a tattered bench, shifted under his gaudy silk drapery and bore down on a cream and honey pie.

"Malvos, do you hear even the thoughts in my head now?" said Nazir, slipping his boots on and searching for a shirt. "Sometimes you seem to be part of the air itself, taking in sounds without putting any back. That irritates me. Do make some noise now and then."

"Of course, my gracious lord. Thank you for not having my head removed for its insulting silence," the huge man muffled between bites of the dwindling pastry. "I thought only to leave my lord to his exertions without care toward my inferior self. I have been quite happy here with the several new 'samples' the first party brought back from the fourth Far clan of Caer Glammis. Would my lord enjoy for me to leave him? I was also just thinking about an ingredient for your elixir. Something to take away your increasing melancholy." . . . *and to better keep the mirke from showing,* he thought behind his eyes.

Nazir had not as yet noticed that he had one or two of the blue-gray patches on his scalp. And a little *more* ardré would take care of that. Until Malvos didn't need him anymore. Then he could turn as blue as any of the mirke-faced Albions in the mines, for all Malvos cared.

Nazir grimaced in disgust as Malvos licked his tattooed fingers for the last bits of pie shell, but let him stay for the moment. As always, Malvos was useful, if revolting. Only Malvos could tell if the girl were Logan in disguise, or a new Keeper. But later, privately, where Malvos could not hear, could not even go—Nazir would take over the interrogation.

Nazir had pried it out of Arn that certain rumors circulated among the Haenish and the Far clans concerning the confusion of his and Malvos's identities. Nazir had found that fortuitous on several occasions. Perhaps it would serve him again.

"Malvos . . . stop gorging for a moment, clean yourself up, and prepare. I have need of your talents. We will play the game."

Malvos raised his bushy red brows in surprise and quirked the side of his capacious mouth. His little green eyes, hidden for the most part in folds of flesh, gleamed suddenly with more intelligence than Nazir liked to see. The fat man wiped his decorated hands on a lace napkin and brought his massive body off the bench and ambled over to Nazir, chuckling softly.

"I will do you proud, my lord." He grinned. "'Tis sport I can enjoy."

"Go to the hall in a moment or two. Be seated upon my throne. I will bring in the girl myself. Watch that cavernous mouth of yours. Say little and do less. Only sift her well. We may have Logan himself, or we may have a Haenish spy. Where is that boy with my clothes?" clipped Nazir, already striding out the door, his iron-toed boots ringing sparks on the stone pavement.

Malvos smiled and followed patiently, silently, as usual.

•   •   •

Aylith winced and breathed through her mouth as the
party passed first the tanner's shop and then the can-
dlemaker's. These lay just inside the outer gate. A layer
of soot covered everything in some degree, and she
could hear the ringing of a smith's hammer not too far
away. The forge's brimstone rose heavily on a steam
cloud. At Inys Haen, the open stalls and fresh air in the
glen had taken away the more pungent odors from
those trades. Within the high rock walls of Inys Nohr,
however, no cleansing breeze diffused their potency.
And so many people! She had never seen a crowd as
large as that which filled the bailey, and this was only
the tower area.

The people of Inys Nohr seemed very like those from
Inys Haen, she thought with a start. Except that they
were far poorer, far dirtier, and more of them seemed
to be ill. Some went about with woven leather veils
that came down over their mouths, hiding who knew
what malady, and others had something else wrong
with them—they looked dappled, with large patches of
blue-gray skin mixed with the pale. And some had eyes
that seemed eerily colorless and much larger than
usual. She saw a few who shaded their vision, even in
the near darkness of Inys Nohr. Were the Haenish stories of the white-eyed people true? These last were
chained; heavy slave manacles at their wrists and
braided iron collars at their throats.

"Lorris . . ." she called, bringing the tall soldier
closer. "What is it . . . these people, their skin? The
chains? Are they prisoners?"

"Not prisoners. Albions. Well, Mirkalbions, to be
formal. The mirke part is the blue skin and hair. Only
the ardré keeps it under control—some kind of fungus
they eat. But it causes it, too, from what my mother
told me. They are Nazir's slaves; they work the mines.
They're the only ones he can make go down there. The

mines . . . are deadly. Cave-ins all the time," came the terse reply.

Aylith stared at her, unsatisfied with the answer. "That's all I know," insisted Lorris.

Aylith let it drop, but the hopeless look on those miners' faces lingered in Aylith's mind long after the chain gang had moved on. There were no slaves in Inys Haen. There weren't any mines, either. All of Inys Haen's precious ore came from somewhere else, brought in by traders. Though now she had some idea of how it felt to walk around in chains, Aylith shuddered as she tried to imagine what it was like to dig in the mines, to be underground, inside the earth itself.

Even so, the differences between the inhabitants of this fabled fortress and the clanfolk she had known all her life were fewer than the similarities. Women sat together and worked. Men still did their jobs. Children still played, sometimes too hard. People still spoke to their friends and shunned their enemies in the bailey. Aylith stopped and stared for a moment, a remarkable observation striking her. If it weren't for the dirt, the noise, the sickness—and most of all, the darkness— many of these people could even be . . . Haenish.

"Lorris . . . your mother, tell me about her," said Aylith as they passed a woman carrying a young child.

Lorris gave her a pained look. "Why do you care?"

"I just thought . . . she sounds like someone who knew a lot about things. We never thought any of, uh—we thought that everyone in—"

"That everyone in Inys Nohr was dim and without sense? We hear the same thing about you Haenish. My mother was very special. She was Nazir's favorite nurse. She knew a lot about things in the tower. She was very beautiful, too. Tall, like me. She had hair the color of flame. I loved her . . ." Lorris said, trailing off into a wordless memory.

"My mother came from the western fisherfolk and is . . . was a weaver, and she taught me to be one, too," said Aylith, tears welling again in her eyes.

Lorris gave her a long look. "Maybe we do have something in common, Haenish," she said far more harshly than she intended, tugging on Aylith's chained wrists to move her along.

A street stretched down into the main part of the heap of stone buildings at the bottom of this hill, and then on toward the wharf, teeming with even more inhabitants.

The noise, from the deafening calls of the hawkers in their shabby stalls to the steady trundle and thrum of the mines just outside the wall, brought Aylith to wonder how anyone here ever slept, or prayed, or even spoke to one another without shouting.

Before them, the tower now rose in an imposing display of decrepitude. Aylith saw that its base was hardly more than a pile of boulders tumbled one atop the other, never mortared in, and falling to further ruin without apparent notice or regard. The lichens she had seen earlier altogether amazed her in their enormous scale and, to her great puzzlement, the crumbled peak of the tower, several hundred feet up, gave off a faint glow of green and gold. Staring up at it, she stumbled ungracefully on a heaved paving stone, and thereafter paid more attention to what lay before her than above her.

"This is the back way in, because we have the animals. But we will have to go before Nazir immediately. Such is his custom. And I think today, he will not be pleased with us. We should have brought back two prisoners. And there are other reasons . . ." Lorris sighed as a passing group of tired miners, chained to their wheelcart of coal, banged against her sword. She turned angrily toward the shuffling group, but kept walking.

Aylith looked back at Lorris, set her teeth, and kept moving into the crowded courtyard. The gate swung open before her, its iron spikes grating cruelly across the paving stones. The exhausted company passed through a long portal, dank with mold and crawling with clicking insects, and for once, Aylith was grateful for the darkness; she could see only the dark orange glimmer of torchlight at the entry tunnel's end. Behind her, the sound of the animals' hooves echoed off the granite walls, and the rest of the party grew quiet, their voices suddenly far too loud for comfort in the narrow stone passage.

Aylith wondered what sort of man this Nazir must be. In all her years with Logan, she had remembered him speak of the Nohrish wizard but once, when he had come to power. Logan's eyes had suddenly changed when he had been told of old Crephas's murder and the new name that had been declared ruler of "Nohr and all her principalities." Logan had said then that Nazir was different. He had had a strange vision about the young Nohrish heir, but could never make the words plain, never find enough meaning to the symbols to be able to more than vaguely speak about it with Aylith.

RoNal now gathered himself into military composure to face his commander, but the big soldier looked like a man who had just seen his own death. Lorris did not fail to notice it.

A groom in a worn-out blue cloak met them at the other end of the tunnel, and his stoop-shouldered boy took the cattle aside. The hooded groom looked Aylith straight in the eye, searching her face quickly, expertly, startling her for a moment, and then greeted Lorris, RoNal, and the other two men.

"Arn will return your portion of the goods after Nazir has had his pick," he mumbled. "The Felonarch will see the girl alone. All of you may go to your quarters and

await his orders later," said the servant. "Except you,
RoNal. Report to the block and give up your sword.
You will then answer for the loss of Logan. And the
whereabouts of Thix."

An odd, pained look passed over Lorris's face, but
she only moved aside with the twins. RoNal blanched
under his beard as he looked at the groom, and his eyes
seemed to lose their focus. He turned around, carefully
keeping his glance from meeting Lorris's. He touched
Aylith gently on the shoulder.

"You are brave, girl. Keep your courage," he said
quietly, and trudged heavily off, leaving Aylith standing
with the groom.

"Please come with me," the man said softly, his voice
now clear and compelling and full of music from
beneath the hood. "My master would like to speak with
you. He is concerned about your journey and wishes to
welcome you to Inys Nohr."

Having no choice in the matter, Aylith walked forward through a pair of massive doors, decorated with
eagles emblazoned over sinuous, carved snakes curling
and knotting over themselves intricately, their heads
biting their own tails. At the end of the great hall,
under rafters covered with gray, frothy cobwebs, down
the long, threadbare aisle carpet, sat a gigantic man in
a polished wooden chair, its arms—and his—covered
in designs of the same serpent motif.

"Do make yourself comfortable, my dear. Well, on
your knees, of course," intoned the mountainous man,
rolling his fingertips across the serpents' fangs and
pointing to the bare, gritty spot on the paving where
the shabby carpet ran out before his throne. "I am so
glad you could join us today. Really brighten things up,
don't you?"

He stared lecherously at her ill-fitting clothes. "Yes.
Yes. Care for a tart? Help you fill out that tunic."

He produced some sort of sweetmeat, waved it before Aylith's nose long enough for its honeyed aroma to tantalize her, and then popped it into his mouth. His piggish eyes lolled toward the groom, who had not left Aylith's side. Now the hooded man pressed even closer. She felt the servant's hand tighten ever so slightly on her arm, and when he motioned for her to kneel, she saw his other hand move in some kind of gesture to the enthroned giant.

So this was Nazir. Aylith stared up at the man in utter amazement, for no one at Inys Haen had ever achieved such size. Or such decoration. Surely this Nazir was every bit as terrible as she had heard.

"Be assured," whispered a smooth voice in her ear. "He didn't want to hand you over to the frog on first sight. You'll be given a chance," said the groom. "Just stay calm and let him dither for awhile. He likes to listen to your voice."

Aylith blanked her face and said nothing. She had thought of what she would and would not tell Nazir since they had captured her. The fat man wiped his mouth on his sleeve and continued.

"What is your name, girl?"

"Aylith, daughter of . . . RoNal," she said clearly, and perhaps a little too slowly, finding it difficult to concentrate. She had almost said, "Daughter of Logan."

"Ah, lovely name, yes. But you are not Nohrish, neither are you part of any Far clan. You obviously mean to say you are recently adopted by RoNal. And what does that adoption mean, eh? Surely you understand that is just a quaint custom of his, being our oldest commander, used to keep the other troops from tampering with the, ah, goods."

Aylith looked at him evenly. "I would rather be a daughter than goods, even if the chains are the same."

The man drummed his fingers on the carved serpent heads and again looked over to the groom. The girl was remarkably self-possessed. Malvos had expected a quivering puffball. The hooded man stepped away from Aylith and stood beside the throne.

"Would Your Excellency like to know anything else about our guest? Or what has become of the Haenish Keeper?" he prompted smoothly.

The giant peered down at Aylith, his face a bemused question. She took more time than before and said carefully, the words coming hard, "You know that I am from Inys Haen. I know not where the last Keeper is. I believe him to be dead, sir. He was a very old man and could not have survived the fire. I know that his hut was burned. That is all I have to tell you." She could not keep the note of defiance out of her voice.

The groom slid his gaze over to her and then composed his face. When he met the enormous man's cold glance again, something passed between them, and the giant locked his eyes upon Aylith's and said, "You are telling the truth?"

She nodded, feeling curiously unable to look away from the big man's stare. He nodded in turn, and then the big man spoke again, his voice icy and distant.

"You may take her away, man, and give her back to the twins, and do see if she cannot be more forthcoming than that in a bit, when she's had a chance to think for a moment in a . . . more conducive setting. I like not her attitude. Perhaps she will enjoy a conversation later."

With that, he smirked evilly and held out a porkish hand for the groom to kiss. After the servant reluctantly did so, he hurried Aylith out, his eyes blazing, looking as though he were plotting murder.

CHAPTER
6

JEDHIAN PEERED CAUTIOUSLY THROUGH the chink in the broad stone wall outside Inys Nohr and suppressed another coughing spell, this time not so successfully. He crouched painfully, patiently, in a heap of frozen garbage, his broad face covered with the soot of Inys Nohr and the grime of rough sleeping. The dull, subterranean sounds of mining had served to cover any noise he had made this close to the wall, and to the inevitable guards upon it or inside it. But that noise also hammered at his mind, making it hard for him to think, to plan, to study the problem he had set for himself.

To get in.

It had been a long, hard journey, and all he'd seen of Aylith was her tracks. When he had entered the mountains, he had suffered the painful and disheartening effects of the Nohrish countryside, his nose and ears swelling nearly shut at times, especially when he passed through the mold forests with their boughs of hanging spores and the regular geysers from the

ripened puffballs. But he had managed to stay just far
enough behind so the war party had not heard him
snorking and blubbering as he followed.

But now he was here, alone and creeping around the
outside of the stronghold of his clan's ancient enemy,
and all he could do was try not to sneeze.

They had probably taken Aylith through the gates
and into the tower. A fetid, red-stained moat ringed the
rising hulk nearly all the way around, preventing him
from getting any closer. But there was one bit of solid
ground, with a lone sentry slowly pacing the distance
between a door and a small iron grate. A looping black
vine hung within grasping distance of the ground there.
It was a chance. He took heart.

Jedhian was also comforted that his cousin yet lived.
He was sure of it. Aylith had a presence about her that
Jedhian could sense anywhere, long before he could see
her, most times. She had never been able to hide from
him, to her great frustration in their childhood games.

The tower loomed over him, its pinnacle shattered,
the ruined walls defiantly raking the dark Nohrish sky.
Jedhian sighed, his arms and legs weary from the climb,
and his heart suddenly full of self-doubt. What was he
doing here, with no help whatsoever? He berated himself. How could he hope to bring the both of them out
of this one? Perhaps he should have waited for help . . .
but then, Aylith might not have that kind of time.

He startled a bit as a large white grub surfaced next
to his foot and wriggled blindly in the rotting garbage.
Jedhian was reminded he was on foreign ground. And
the Nohr, by all accounts, were dangerously short-tem-
pered. Especially Nazir. Jedhian had heard that Nazir
was even older than Logan had been, that even though
he never ate, he was a huge toad of a man, and that he
had snakes for fingers. He was rumored to never have
married, for he was so ugly that no woman could bear

the sight of him, even in the near darkness of Inys Nohr. And there were stories that he could fly and turn a person to dust—Jedhian's aunt had known someone gone to dust that way—or wood or water with the power from the old Clan Tree top that he kept in his tower . . . this tower.

Jedhian sank lower in the musty rubbish pile in order to peer up through the crack in the wall at the fortress. The great leafless black vines—Logan had called them "bitteroots"—snaked all through the jumbled rock work, and seemed to squeeze the tower together into tortured uprightness. He wondered what would happen if those vines were ever poisoned or hacked down. They had insinuated their way into the blocks so deeply that he doubted the tower would stand without them. But they were huge, with thick, curling trunks larger than a bullock's middle, and their slick, glassy surface looked hard and flinty, like it could turn any blade with no trouble at all. Not for climbing, either. Well, not unless you could climb anything.

Like me, thought Jedhian, smiling bleakly to himself, and then sneezed horribly, silently, into his shoulder four times.

Nazir rounded the corner at a full run, his mind on the Clan Tree and his anger seething out his fingers in spurts of blue light. When he got to the door of the great hall, he snuffed out his fingers, poking them quickly into his mouth, one at a time, and composed his face with a couple of quick breaths and a promise to himself to see Malvos served to the frog on a silver platter with a turnip garnish. When he strode back into the hall, the enormous man was still seated on the majestic throne, looking as though he were expecting to stay there; indeed, as though he belonged there.

"Remove your flatulent self from my chair this exact moment, Malvos," menaced Nazir as he bounded down the end of the black-and-gold runner that stretched from the door to just short of the throne.

He stopped directly in front of the limp-lidded giant and waited. Only then did Malvos yawn and begin to shift himself languorously out of the chair, taking just a little too long for Nazir, but not long enough to kill for it. Yet.

"I thought that went rather well, do you not agree, Your Worship?" Malvos grinned. "Looks like you have discovered a dirty little Haenish girl. Pleased?"

Nazir took his place in the too warm seat and regarded Malvos from the superior position.

"Did you have to make me kiss your adder-enveloped hand, you great hulking parasite?" he said, not answering, and thinking about just how many men it would take to lift Malvos, totally dressed, and whether or not there was a vessel in the pantry large enough to carry him down to the frog. Then he smiled, his dignity slightly restored by the small fantasy, but the necessity for Malvos's presence still all too apparent by the pain in Nazir's chest.

Never doubting his position with Nazir, Malvos bowed so deeply that he nearly lost his balance, and said, "But of course, Honored One, no one could leave the presence of yourself without such a courtesy. 'Twas necessary for the girl to believe she had seen you and not just your lowly but beloved servant, was it not?"

"Malvos, you use up entirely too many words every time you open that cavern you call a mouth. All right, though. But do not ever do it again."

"Not at all, sir, nor did I enjoy it in the least, nor will I ever," lied the apothecary. "If I could be given the great privilege of your thoughts, divine sir, I should, however, enjoy that. What would you have of this girl?

She told the truth, you know. You have indeed killed Logan. I could not sift any lies in the words at all. And beyond that . . . there is some sort of an impenetrable warding."

"Why, Malvos, you admit your shortcomings?" Nazir crowed in amazement.

"Yes, well, if I cannot reach through, no one can, my discerning master. What is behind that warding will stay behind it. Only she can open that door." *I have seen it before . . . in Haen himself,* he thought secretly. "I never said I could sift for the light spell. Only for lies."

And only for mana. . . . he said to himself. *And she has a talent there. What else, I do not know. Yet. But what if she had as much talent as Nazir?* Malvos never dropped his vacant smile. There were some things even Nazir did not need to know.

"But the greensong still calls to me. And she has the marks; I can see that even through the dirt on her face. She must have the secrets," Nazir murmured, his eyes glazing over.

The girl was really quite beautiful in an odd, Haenish way. The lift of her chin when she spoke. How she was not afraid of Malvos, only curious. Should she not be the Keeper, perhaps she was a worthy possession after all, even though he could not use her against Logan any longer. He would soon see. In an hour or so, when she had had some time in the pit, just long enough to never want to go back there, he would find out exactly what lay in Aylith's heart and mind. He tried to discard the image of her tender face from his thoughts and slouched lower in the chair. Then he pulled himself up with a start, remembering that another duty awaited: RoNal.

"Have old Feryar bring the girl and let her wash. He can surely handle that much of a task." Malvos shook his head in silent disagreement, but Nazir did not see it. "You will need to prepare a potion for me to give her. Something relaxing, something that will make her trust me. I will now spend some moments in conversation with RoNal. He must acquit himself of his error and explain the whereabouts of my nephew. The game continues for yet awhile, Malvos. Do try not to choke on something before I can win it. And stay out of this chair."

"One more thing, if I might, gracious sir. Do you plan yet to keep this Aylith of Inys Haen?" asked Malvos, a little too much interest in his voice.

Nazir moved lazily toward the door and smiled crookedly at the silk-robed apothecary. "There are some things even you do not need to know, Malvos."

CHAPTER
7

AYLITH SAT ON A HARD ROCK LEDGE hunched in the pitch-black cell and shivered. She didn't know how long it had been since the groom had handed her over to the pair of burly twin guards she had traveled from Inys Haen with. They had seemed to take particular relish in blindfolding and shoving her into this cesspool of a dungeon. It was hard to tell just where she was, however, because they had moved her up and down several staircases, and she thought she must be at least one level under the tower. Both the temperature and the wildlife here were subterranean. She could hear the chitter of rats and the drip of foul water somewhere just beyond her ledge. She had worked the blindfold off easily, but there was nothing to see.

Of all the impressions that flooded her mind about this awful place, she had found herself returning again and again to the stoop-shouldered boy who had taken the animals upon their arrival. There could be no doubt—it had to be the same lad from the second Far squatter clan who had fished beside her long ago. He had grown up, and his face had changed, but it had to be him. Perhaps there was a friend here, after all. She considered how she might get out of the pit.

There was a seam of dim light that marked the doorway, where she knew the twins stood silent guard. When the seam became a streak, and then a block, she blinked, fish-eyed at the sudden brightness and in surprise of the visitor who stepped soundlessly into her cell. A very tall, very thin silhouette passed between Aylith and the light, and a voice like wind on a psaltery said, "Hello. I am Feryar. Nazir has sent me for you." He lowered the soft voice even further. "Do not be afraid. I will help if I can. I think I know you."

Aylith then noticed the outline of the face, the long fingers and the pointed ears: an elf. She had seen one once, as she passed through the clanhold toward the westernmost sea. The elf had told stories of a place called Loch Prith—where it was always both day and night and juicy fruits hung from lush branches, never out of season. Of course, the elf had said, Loch Prith was deep underground and had never been seen by humans. Aylith and Jedhian, eight-year-old explorers, had tried to dig their way to the magical place. When the elf had left, the music she'd played on a stringed instrument for the clan had stayed in Aylith's head for days, making every chore seem lighter, every duty more pleasant. Aylith smiled even now at the recollection. Feryar beckoned, and she unfolded herself painfully and stepped down onto the floor, wincing as her boot crushed some many-legged thing she did not want to know anything else about.

When Aylith came closer, Feryar paused for a moment before he held out his hand, the air between them alive with energy. This girl seemed to glow with the green-song. It clung all about her, new and fresh. Her hands, especially, radiated its warmth and joy. He smiled in the dimness, marveling. Finally, the Mender had come. She would restore the Clan Tree, just as the First Keeper had told him, centuries ago, when he and Thrissa were sent by the Gwylfan from the west. How long had it been? Surely the counting of time had escaped him since he had alighted at Inys Nohr, tirelessly serving the successive tyrants of Nohr's line, protecting them against themselves, pretending dull-wittedness and forgetfulness, to watch and wait for this . . . girl! Feryar grinned wider, his golden eyes glowing in the darkness.

When the elf took Aylith's hand, warmth moved up her arm and she felt instantly restored. But what had caused that burst of the greensong when he beckoned her? Aylith stood rooted to the spot until Feryar pulled a little against her hand.

They moved quietly through the heavy iron door, into the corridor, beyond the guards, and into a very dark passage. Aylith felt no fear and went gladly, thinking that anything to come had to be better than her brief stay in Nazir's pit. She had begun to hear the sounds of something very large and wet down there.

They walked upward several levels as the spiraling ramp took them into warmer and relatively cleaner air. Everything about Inys Nohr was dark or sooty, thought Aylith as she brushed against the filthy stairwell, and longed for the wide clean brightness of Inys Haen and the tidiness of her cottage. But that home was burned to the ground, and Inys Haen would now be every bit as dark as here, she recalled. Logan had not lived to settle in the spring, and what would that mean? Another year and more of ice, as in the time of the great Parting? Now the power to change that lay solely with her. And she had no clue as to how to use it.

It sprang into voice from quiet corners of her mind, or receded just when she had begun to follow a familiar

pattern. The names of growing things she had not seen
or touched echoed in her thoughts like a foreign
tongue, almost making sense, but flowing away before
she understood. When would the equinox come again?
Would she be ready to take Logan's place? Would she
even be free?

As they climbed upward and turned another corner,
Aylith shivered with more than the leftover chill of the
dungeon, and a strange stirring mounted in her heart.
As they ascended, the greensong flashed with astonishing clarity for a brief second, and then again, causing
her to stop and cover her ears. Feryar waited patiently,
never asking for explanation. When the song receded,
they moved on.

The elf climbed in such silence that many times,
when she could not see him directly in front of her in
the darkness, she thought him to be a specter, or a
wraith. But then the torchlight would catch his face,
and the illusion would pass. At last the steep stairs
ended, and they came to a widened room of sorts, its
roof patched badly, where tables and scrolls and various maps lay scattered in casual disarray. The room
ended in a small wooden door. There were no latches
upon it; instead, it bore a single keyhole in the middle,
a sort of gold-green light shining through it.

Aylith felt the green stirring within her grow even
stronger, but Feryar motioned her to a steaming tub of
fragrant water standing behind a screen.

"Nazir says that he wants you to be comforted in
your stay here," he said, his voice official and his eyes
veiled. He handed her a dress, this one smaller and
made of softspun blue wool.

"Haenish wool, Haenish indigo," she muttered.
"Nohrish weave," she added distastefully, noting the
coarseness and give of the garment.

Though she doubted Nazir's desire for her well-being,

especially since he did not see fit to release her hands, which were still in chains, Aylith needed no further prompting and stepped behind the screen and gratefully into the foaming bath while Feryar waited by the door.

Within a few moments, dried and dressed, Aylith stood peering around at the room's curious furnishings. Tacked to the walls were wide vellum sheets with charcoal drawings of wings in all sorts of positions, and scale models of animals that she had never seen before topped disheveled wooden reading stands. Hanging just about the height of the elf's head, huge moths, their pale green wings spanning several feet, turned soundlessly on wires, dancing in darkness where they once had sought light. The largest of them, strangely missing its wings, hung alone and off to the side. Dried plants of absurd proportions were stacked against another wall, near the only window.

Feryar silently moved to the outer door and cocked his head, listening. He then motioned her quickly to the small wooden door, and to her amazement, put his hand to the keyhole, his little finger disappearing inside it, and the door swung open.

"The Sifter hates this. He's too big ever to get in, and that in itself has probably kept things rightly aligned." Feryar smiled.

In this tiny, hidden oriole, over to one side, by an even tinier window, stood a large glass case, its contents the source of the odd gold-green light Aylith had seen from the courtyard and through the keyhole. There was just enough room for one person. One *small* person. Feryar nodded, and she drew closer; immediately, the Memories burst into her consciousness in great waves of color and sound, all but bringing her to blindness and deafness. From outside the oriole, Feryar offered his hand to help support her. When her senses cleared, he spoke.

"We don't have long. I will tell you what you must know. This is the crown of the Clan Tree, and it bears the sacred oak's only fruit." He pointed a long finger at a shimmering acorn. "You must take it when the time is right. You will speak the Memories over the seed, and it will grow into a new tree. This tree will be at Inys Haen, where the first tree stood, where the Blessing stone yet stands—do you know it?" he said gently, the spill of pine needles in his voice.

She nodded. The fingers on her outstretched, bound hands suddenly sprouted points of green fire, and the Tree answered with a brief surge of light.

"Oh, girl, do not let Nazir see that! Can you not control your gift? Have you no idea of the danger you are in?" said Feryar, his golden eyes wide with warning.

Aylith only looked at him and shook her head. There seemed to be a great deal about this gift that she did not understand, but Feryar had said he would help. And he seemed to know more than she did about all of this.

"I don't know. My father, my real father—he was the Keeper. He gave me his Memories in the fire, but he didn't have the time to show me what to do with them or how to use them. All he could do was protect them somehow, until, I suppose, I figured them out. They haunt my dreams and their power washes over me sometimes, my fingertips bring the green fire all on their own, and then it's gone. I should have had a brother. The Haenish Memories pass from father to son; it's the way of the pattern, but now . . . It's winter again and somehow, *I'll* have to work the light spell."

Her words poured out in a rush. The old Clan Tree was real. Now she would have to make good her silent vow. "I guess I must get back to Inys Haen with this acorn before the next equinox. And that could be anytime; I don't even know how to know when. I should not be the Keeper."

Feryar took hold of both her hands and looked levelly into her blue-green eyes, his golden ones never blinking.

"No. That is not so. You see your destiny. You know what it is you must do. You will teach yourself how when the time calls for it. It's already inside you. The pattern is set. Do not fear. You are the one." And he smiled, his sad, lean face falling to creases, his perfect teeth flashing white in the dim light. "But you are not just the Keeper. You are the Mender."

Aylith gazed into Feryar's huge amber eyes and found no guile, no trickery.

"The Mender? That's ridiculous. All these years, Feryar—there is no Mender. It's just a pretty story Haenish fathers tell their daughters when the winter stays too long. The elders tell the weary villagers the same thing. It keeps them happy. The Mender means the end. The curse will be lifted by the Mender, if anyone still believes that. The Mender comes only when . . . the lines of Haen and Nohr merge."

She recalled RoNal's comments about marrying an important man and thought of the man on the throne, his hands alive with the serpent tattoos, his teeth dark with the stain of decay.

"No, I am not the Mender. Why are you telling me this, how do you know it, and what does it mean? Why did they choose me as prisoner, anyway?" she puzzled.

Before Feryar could answer anything, his ears caught a sound beyond the door to the room, though Aylith had heard nothing. He rushed her out of the Clan Tree's oriole, just as the outer door flew open and the hooded groom strode in, wiping his mouth, a small stone bottle in his hand. He . . . was much better looking than Aylith had recalled.

"The master says you may go now, Feryar," he chimed sweetly, as though he spoke to a dim child.

Feryar, suddenly looking much duller of wit, took his glance pointedly away from outside the room's window, where a slight vibration and a flash of movement had drawn his attention.

The old elf bowed his head and rolled his eyes toward Aylith, a warning in them, but the answers to all her questions moved out the door in ghostly silence.

CHAPTER
8

JEDHIAN PANTED FOR BREATH AS QUIETLY
as he could at the tower's base, the rough climb over the
wall and the altitude having winded him. Fortunately,
true night had fallen, and a darker one he'd never seen.
He was certain no one had noticed him; in fact, there
was no one at all in the bailey, the stolen animals settled
in their new byre and the residents long ago indoors.
The guard had turned his corner, and Jedhian figured he
had at least two minutes before the soldier would be
back. A few dim candles shone from the windows of the
tiny stone huts, and smoke rose from nearly every chim-
ney. The smell seemed very different from the hearth
fires at home. He guessed they did not burn turf here,
or any wood—that was probably too precious. The fuel
had to be something else. Whatever, this place was
dirty, decrepit, and cold, and Jedhian realized that he'd
need some shelter of his own very shortly.

The bitteroot stalk under his gloved hand felt even
colder than the air. It seemed to be as cold as ice, as slick
and black as obsidian, and every bit as hard. Of course,

his newly sharpened knife had not even dented it, upon a quick and perfunctory test; he had not bothered to try the old sword. So now the chore was to get himself up the vine and into the dark room next to the little overhang where the gold-green light shone forth. His aim was a large, barred window. Aylith was there. He could feel it.

Jedhian took his knife and made a few expert nicks in the palm of each glove. The surface of the soft leather opened easily under the blade into little nubby cuts. He rubbed his hands together to create a bit more roughness, then blew his nose into a big square of motley cloth and began his ascent. He found a tentative grip on the rocks of the tower wall, the confiscated Nohrish hand ax helping to some degree, but straddling the vines required no small effort. By the time Jedhian was warm again, he hung some hundred feet in the air, right outside the lacy wrought-bronze window.

He cautiously peered into the room from his precarious perch and saw an elf making his way to the door. Though Aylith stood in the center of the room facing toward Jedhian, she did not seem to see him. A hooded man motioned her to a seat and then sat down opposite her, taking his cowl down and smoothing back his dark hair as he offered her something to drink. Jedhian tried to catch Aylith's attention, but after her first swallow, she seemed entranced by the stranger, as if she could look nowhere but into his eyes. When Jedhian strained his ear through the freezing grillwork, he could barely make out what they were saying. Something about Logan, about the Memories, and about . . .

No! blasted Jedhian, his voice silent but his mind screaming. *It cannot be. Aylith has the Memories now? That is impossible. But that is what she just said. Perhaps she lied to save herself. . . .*

There must be magic here, though the man hardly looked like a sorcerer. More like a gardener—and a poor one. He had some kind of dried herbs hanging in front of the window, and just now they were nicely obscuring Jedhian's view. Jedhian leaned into the bronze work a little more, both hands resting on the corroding lower railing, and heard Aylith speak.

Ah, don't tell him anything else, please, he thought fervently. *One more inch over and I can get to you. Hold on, dear cousin, hold on.*

Hanging on to that thought and little else, Jedhian brought his left foot closer to the narrow sill and stepped directly onto a crumbling piece of granite, causing a shower of stones to break loose and leaving his foot pumping wildly in dark nothingness.

He instantly slid several feet down the bitteroot, lost the hand ax, and the old sword, and tore his ear on the freezing bronze work. He came to rest on a curl of the vine some two stories lower, a piece of the corroded railing still in his hand. Was everything at Inys Nohr rotten? His ear throbbing and his heart racing, he found a more solid handhold and started up again. But above him, someone opened the window grate, sending more loose rocks on the sill cascading over him and, after a very long time, falling down to crack off the tower's base and thud into the soft ground below.

Jedhian pressed even more closely to the ragged tower wall, adrenaline and cold making him shake uncontrollably. Just then, a silent flurry of dun-colored wings brushed over his face and nearly sent him the rest of the way down the wall. The bird, no more than a foot high, put out three-inch talons, one of them oddly bent, and grabbed onto the cascade of Jedhian's cloak. He started to fall backward, but then realized that for its size, the bird was not heavy, nor was it attacking, and Jedhian regained his balance. The owl then folded its wings, climbed to his shoulder . . .

And spoke to him. Jedhian nearly fainted.

"I apologize for both the delay and the fright. You cannot stay here; do not be afraid. I will help if I can." The owl's words sounded like water rushing, like the music of dry reeds in the wind.

Jedhian cautiously looked over to meet two of the most enormous golden eyes he had ever seen. The owl blinked, and Jedhian took another short breath, then closed his own eyes and opened them again. The bird was still there. Jedhian realized suddenly just how cold he was, and his teeth began to chatter. The bird spoke again.

"We have to get you down. I can't talk much out here. You can't help her from here, either, and Nazir will be coming soon. He heard you. Let go."

Jedhian shook his head and gripped the side of the wall more tightly. Altitude sickness. Had to be, he thought. Or maybe the cold . . . had he lost too much blood?

"Let go. And don't call out. Let me bear your weight; if you struggle, I might veer and drop you into the moat. The fishing is interesting there."

Jedhian looked up, then down, then sighed and loosed his hands, thinking that it had been a long gamble anyway. Perhaps he was not that far from the ground, and it was sort of soft. . . .

The owl dug in its talons, flapped its wings, and silently hoisted Jedhian out from the tower wall, and flew him down to the bailey yard. Though the bird could not have weighed more than a whisper itself, hauling a fifteen-stone man didn't seem to tax its abilities in the least.

Jedhian didn't have time to cry out. He may have been too dumbfounded to do so anyway. But before he could pose any kind of response to the bird, it took off, leaving him where he had started, with one very tall, very well armed, difference.

Standing over him, dressed in full armor, was a soldier, helmet down and sword drawn. Jedhian sneezed, loudly, coarsely, and with resigned satisfaction.

• • •

"What? You want me to go somewhere? Can you not speak? Am I to be slain by silence before you use your blade? Come on man, say out," demanded Jedhian, wiping his nose.

The owl had flown noiselessly to a nearby ledge, but stood swaying back and forth, its golden eyes unblinking and its curious, asymmetrical ears hearing everything from what Jedhian said to the rat chewing on plaster inside the wall. The bird was distinctly disturbed, though, and took off into the night when the tall warrior grunted and slapped Jedhian on the sole of one boot with the flat of the broadsword. With an equally brusque gesture, the sentry demanded Jedhian's knife, the only weapon left him. The healer rose, gave it over, and walked forward, turning his head every so often to be able to see the armored man in back of him.

They marched on until they came to a small, fungus-covered door in the tower base, an entry never to be seen or noticed by the casual eye. But when they got fairly close, Jedhian noticed a peculiar clump of pale, fleshy stalks rising up in front of the secret entrance, their black, ruffled, hood-shaped heads cast in his direction. The tiniest disturbance of air around the plants brought forth a low whistle, its pitch and tenor that of a mourning woman, a keening that Jedhian found impossible to remove from his mind.

Widowweeds. His aunt had told him about these, too. The much larger version, wild in these mountains, she said, would lure you into their bogs with that song and then you would drown in the icy pools of deep, fetid water where their roots fed. These little ones must serve as some kind of sentry for this forgotten room. A person could never sneak up on widowweeds.

When the creaking door swung open, Jedhian glared

back at the inscrutable suit of armor still behind him and stepped inside. When he next touched solid ground, he had fallen several yards down a wide tunnel, madder than six geese in the same sack. Before he could pick himself up, the soldier jumped down behind him, then stood, the boar crest helmet scraping the ceiling. The soldier groped the wall for the cresset, then reached for a rope to swing shut the door from the inside.

Then, to Jedhian's great surprise, the warrior struck fire to the torch with a flint, deftly removed the heavy bronze helmet while still holding steady the broadsword, and let her dark blond hair fall to her shoulders.

Jedhian forgot his anger momentarily and settled for shock instead.

"You are an idiotic, light-dwelling, Haenish fool! You made enough noise out there to get the entire legion out of its dice game and into your face," charged Lorris, her eyes flashing in the rising torchlight.

"You . . . you are a woman," was all Jedhian could manage, not surprisingly, since he'd only just fallen several stories, had a conversation with an owl who saved him from the rest of the drop, and now stood eye to eye with a woman who looked like she could take any man he'd seen at Inys Nohr in a sword fight. Without using a sword.

"Yes, I am. And you are still an idiot. What were you thinking? What were you doing up the tower? Had it been Iggar's watch, you would be dead now."

"You know where I'm from, but you do not kill me. Why? Why am I not dead on your watch?" Jedhian said, his curiosity now overtaking the shock.

Lorris bade him sit and leaned against the wall, still holding her sword at the ready. Then she remained silent for a moment, thinking, sorting the words.

"I have known you followed us since the second day

out from Inys Haen. But you were alone. I watched you, but no one else noticed; I am sure."

She took a deep breath and searched Jedhian's eyes.

"I cannot prove this, but I think Nazir believes my father has chosen against him, and failed to bring the Keeper because he hopes to overthrow Nazir's rule and bring Inys Nohr to the Far clans, where there is more light. Nazir cannot rule there. He cannot even go there; my mother said it has something to do with the Keeper. But his charge concerning RoNal is not true. My father is loyal to his promise of service. Something Nazir cannot understand—that a man could despise his commander and carry out his orders all the same. Thix, Nazir's nephew, broke formation in the raid and set fire to the Keeper's hut. He tried to savage the girl we brought in. RoNal had to kill him. For that, RoNal is to be lashed. I believe that Nazir sent his nephew to his death to keep the throne and used my father to make certain of it. And he used his nephew to dispose of RoNal as a commander who has become too popular and whom he no longer trusts. Of course, he will have to punish my father for the crime that Nazir knew would happen. That way, my father—and never was there a better soldier—will die honorless in the eyes of his men. Nazir will use that to keep them in line and rid himself of the man he suspects leads the rebellion."

"And you? What part in this did you play? You were also part of the raid on my village. Why should you tell me these things?" countered Jedhian.

"I am RoNal's daughter; he is all I have in the world. My mother is long dead of the hack. I followed him to service when I was ten, so that he could protect me and make good his pledge to my mother to rear me himself. Now I must protect him. I do not want to see my father shamed so, and should he live through the lash, he would be crippled for the rest of his life, though that would not be long. The plague would surely take him, like it takes anyone here with a wound—very quickly." She critically eyed Jedhian's bound-up leg and his bleeding ear.

"Either way, he dies a lowly, shameful death, without his name recited in the battle lists and carved into the Wall of Honor. I am thinking we can help one another. You want Aylith back. No doubt you are promised to her," Lorris added boldly, to Jedhian's astonishment, "and I want my father to escape the lash. And there is only one way. Why do I tell you these things? So you will know I really mean what I say. I trust you for one reason; you are Haenish. Everyone here is suspect. I do not know of anyone, aside from the boy my father has helped, who could hear this. And he is just a boy. Time is short; what I am about to say is unthinkable. Help me to kill Nazir."

Jedhian considered for a moment, wondering what this would cost him.

"And if I help you to kill Nazir?" Jedhian replied, thinking this seemed all too simple. The help he needed when he dangled on the tower wall, and now this offer, had appeared from inside Nazir's very ranks. Still, there was something earnest about this strange, beautiful Nohrish woman. And the owl—if there had really been an owl—had flown away.

"Whatever you ask," the tall soldier replied.

"All right. What have I to lose? I will need you to release my cousin and arrange for us to get away from here safely."

"Your . . . cousin?" Lorris smiled, her voice pitched to a whisper.

And that was a good thing, for they both heard the sound of mourning women rise from beyond the rotting wooden door at the same time.

CHAPTER
9

AYLITH FELL HARD TO THE FLOOR AS THE sudden sharp wrenching of metal and the shuffle of rock brought her out of the trance. Nazir rose up swearing, stormed to the window, where the odd noise had come from, threw open the broken grillwork, and squinted outside.

Nothing. But "nothing" had not bent and torn this piece of wrought bronze, no matter how old it had been. Nazir looked back to see Aylith, dizzy, on all fours and coming to rapidly.

Well, RoNal had almost done well, despite his certain treachery. She was not Logan. She was Logan's daughter, and she truly was the Keeper. No, she was far prettier than that old buzzard that had fathered her, and it was obvious now that she was clean and dressed in clothes that fit. Nazir had had a very uncomfortable reaction to that fact. It was both agony and delight to be in her presence. After seeing her enter the city, he had not expected to find the girl pleasing; she was

Haenish, and so small. But the blue of her eyes, the curve of her lips, and the strength of her will were all enticing. Nazir now wondered just who had been entranced, despite Malvos's lulling potion.

He had been so close. Malvos was right, there was some kind of warding in place; the spell was there, he could all but hear it in her thoughts. This would have to be even more delicately executed than he had imagined. She had called the secrets "Memories" . . . and they lay just beneath the surface of the girl's consciousness, not quite settled, and to invade her mind, or in any way make her clutch harder at them, would send them immediately into some psychic chasm. They would become part of her very life, wound into her spirit and infused with her soul forever, and only she could make the transfer, at her own choosing. That, he figured, would be only at the point of her death. But if he could get to them soon, before she realized them fully . . .

He would have to find a way to coerce her into giving them up. He could have taken them easily from Logan on the promise of letting Aylith—and of course, his grandchildren—live in light for the rest of their lives, which would have to be spent at Inys Nohr. Logan could never have refused his only daughter's life and health, not even for his people. That was the way and the weakness of the Haenish. They loved. And they loved their families above all else.

When Aylith shook her head and stared up at him suspiciously, he beamed in what he hoped looked like benevolence and offered his hand to help her.

"My dear, you have just fainted. Are you well? Could it be that you have not eaten in too long? Perhaps the wine was too strong. Come, sit down again and rest, and I'll ring for Feryar to bring you refreshment. You were just telling me about your poor family,

I believe," Nazir said smoothly as he pulled the bell cord in the corner.

Beside it, a large stuffed eagle brooded down at Aylith, its eyes unblinking and its talons curled around a golden ring perch. She gave a little start as she noticed the raptor for the first time, and then settled back into the chair, realizing it was not alive.

Nazir chuckled at her reaction and said, "That's Atalanta. She belonged to one of the rulers. They keep her up here now, out of the way, where I live. All of this stuff once served the last king, but now it's just attic trapping." He paused, and listened, then went on hastily.

"I've rung for Feryar. He's to bring you something to eat. He'll be at the door immediately. Please just rest," his tone undeniably a warning and an order.

Nazir had bolted the door from without and was gone by the time Aylith fainted and fell to the floor again.

The sounds had drawn him to the cellar door, and Malvos now stood amazed that in all his years at Inys Nohr he had overlooked this place. Apparently, there were still some secrets to this old pile of rocks. The termite-infested wooden door creaked softly open onto the darkest pit Malvos had ever seen, and he had seen some dark ones. After all, Tempé had jailed him in dungeons all over the seven planes of Parnash, each one a little less "civilized" than the one before.

But this hole looked like any old root cellar opening, part of the original tower, probably, and not safe to be used now. All of that was convincing evidence for there to be no one there at all—except for the smell of a quenched cresset and the stifled breathing he heard far in the back of the cellar. Two of them: a man and a woman. A romantic rendezvous? No. He smelled

Nohrish armor oil, too. And the unmistakable odor of a light-lover. Malvos smiled evilly into his rusty beard and called to the occupants of the cellar.

"Hello, the house! Will you not come to greet a visitor? I have need of your hospitality. *Now,*" he added threateningly.

Jedhian swallowed hard against the blade pressing upon his throat. Lorris sighed and pulled her prisoner up in front of her.

"If you talk to him, I will slit your throat as you speak," she mouthed into his ragged, bloody ear, her free hand cupped firmly, painfully, around it.

"Light-dweller," she whispered, her voice carefully uninflected, "that is Malvos. Do you understand? Malvos. He can sift spoken words for lies. I will return for you later, if you do as I have said. Otherwise, when he gives you to Nazir and Nazir gives you to the frog, I will not know you. And the frog is very hungry, I hear, since they did not feed your darling cousin to him."

With that, she shoved Jedhian toward the opening and he emerged from the tunnel, smiling weakly up at the biggest man he'd ever seen. The price of the fellow's cloak alone would keep a family for a winter, he figured. Then he saw the man's ham-sized hands, their snaking tattoos seeming to writhe like living serpents when he moved his fingers. *Malvos,* she had said. Not Nazir. Malvos. And all of the wisdom of Haenish aunts drained away like the blood in Jedhian's face.

Malvos surveyed Jedhian critically and chortled.

"You have come for your little friend, is that not so? She is occupied. You will have to wait for her in our guest house," he invited, his green eyes dancing. "And is someone else there?" the big man cooed down the tunnel doorway.

But as soon as he said it, he knew the other person, whoever she was, had departed. Into solid rock? This was a tasty development. . . . The tower had even larger mice than he had known.

"Come with me, light-dweller. I know a place you will find very comfortable. And we will discuss who left you to answer for yourself later."

Malvos bit the last edges off each of the words he spoke in a way that made Jedhian's skin crawl. But at least Jedhian had not been forced to speak. Malvos talked enough for both of them.

Lorris, some several stories higher now, helmet faceguard down and continuing to race through the secret, cramped, passage, caught her mail shirt on a roughly hewn rock, and halted long enough to free it. She could only hope that Malvos would not be able to identify her voice. But that beast could hear as well as a night bird. And where was she going, anyway? She took a deep breath and peered around the corner, into a landing that led to the tower's main staircase. She stepped cautiously onto it, checked her sword, and strode directly into Nazir, just as he clattered down the steps in a dead run.

"Soldier! Come with me," he bellowed, never stopping to see if she followed.

Lorris gulped, fell in behind him, horrified at every step they took, winding downward, to the very place she had just run from. And the very person. Lorris felt her mouth go completely dry and hoped that the handsome outlander, whose name she had not even yet discovered, would have the sense to remain quiet. She herself would have no problem doing so.

When Nazir and Lorris found them, Malvos and Jedhian were heading toward the nearest door into the great hall, Malvos's hand on Jedhian's collar and his little silver-and-bone dirk against the Haenish healer's ribs. Jedhian himself was not a small man, standing as tall as a Nohrish spear and having the shoulder width of an ox yoke, but next to Malvos, he looked like a child. Lorris caught his eye through her visor and warned him with a glare. He did not even smile, nor did he change stride. Were this man under her father's command, he could be trusted, she reasoned. He was self-possessed under great strain of mind and body. She would not be ashamed to fight beside him. If he could fight.

Nazir stopped in front of Malvos and stood waiting. The big man immediately handed Jedhian over to him and said, "Take him to the pit, groom. And meet me in my chambers momentarily."

And with that, he walked away with remarkable speed and a sudden regal bearing. Jedhian was now thoroughly confused, but he said nothing, still thinking about how close Lorris's hand was to her sword.

Nazir passed Jedhian to Lorris, and then looked at him rather too carefully for a servant. Jedhian began to understand. This man standing there, slightly winded, his hood thrown back, probably from the run down from the high room, his white brows so much like Aylith's, like her father's, also—this must be Nazir. But why was the Felonarch pretending to be a groom? Jedhian composed his best gaming face and looked dully back at Nazir, keeping his revelation to himself.

Nazir motioned for Lorris to carry out Malvos's order and moved away into the hall after the apothecary, leaving Lorris and Jedhian before the hall's side door.

Lorris had drawn her sword again but had raised her visor, and when she spoke, her tone seemed relieved. "You did well, light-dweller. We will finish our talk now. I think Malvos did not notice me. This is the name you will call me: Lorris."

She smiled, noting the fine fall of Jedhian's chestnut hair upon his shoulders. *He is taller than I,* she thought pleasantly. No one but her father and Malvos had that kind of height in Inys Nohr. Nazir came close, and looked the least like old weaselly Nohr of any of his other ancestors.

"Move toward that iron gate, light-dweller. That's the pit. No, don't turn around and don't speak to me in front of anyone. They will hold you in the pit until Nazir makes a choice about what to do with you. Make no commotion; that will only attract the frog. Look for me, do you hear? I will come for you," Lorris whispered to Jedhian's back.

He cleared his throat in response, and the gate guards took him roughly into the tower and moved him down the passage to the pit. Lorris lost sight of him as he passed the first turn, but not before he had grinned back over his shoulder at her.

I told him not to turn around, she thought, a small smile lifting her mouth. *And I forgot to ask him his name.*

CHAPTER

10

AYLITH RECOVERED HER SIGHT BEFORE HER
balance. She tried to get up, to find purchase on the
mildewing, silverfish-infested carpet, but the hypnotic,
vine-scrolled patterns kept making her lose her equilibrium. Finally, she closed her eyes and stood up, left
hand braced against the small table that had viciously
bruised her shin when she had fallen.

The groom's conversation had been invasive; she
had felt him walking around in her mind, examining
things, lightly prodding to see her thoughts, the questions he had asked now returning to her memory. His
touch on her hand had felt like fire, like anger itself.

The wind whistled round the outside of the tower
room, but she could still hear the supposed groom's
steps drumming down the stairwell far below. Aylith
looked around, searching for guards, for hidden
entrapments, for alarms. *He must suppose the bolted
door to be enough,* she reasoned as she turned to look
at the massive wooden portal, its shining keyhole
drawing her like a beacon. She looked around the

shadowy room, at the hanging insects and the bizarre constructions and the stuffed bird, and recalled an earlier conversation with Lorris that had filled most of an afternoon's uphill climb.

Nazir's father had certainly been tenacious, if not successful, in his legendary attempts to use living things to spark the tree's remaining power into light for the Nohr. Too late, she thought, he must have seen that those dreadful experiments only drained the tree constantly, until the dry husk of its once glorious crown now stood sadly corrupted with scabious lesions and rot. Or perhaps he never did see it. She shuddered to think of his other victims—those animals and people the erratic force had fused into mutants and changelings. Some went to the frog, but it fed only once a week or so, Lorris had told her. The army had to dispose of most of them, shoveling the expired wretches down into the cold, dank earth just far enough to prevent makana or other vermin from taking the corpses. And strangest of all, Lorris had said, a very few yet alive had been carried through the night sky in absolute silence, always west, in the clutches of a small, tawny bird.

Aylith tried the wooden door to the oriole. Feryar had not had time to lock it again, and it swung open on noiseless hinges. She bent toward the Clan Tree's case and lifted the glass. Now was her chance, perhaps her only chance. She might never be alone with the acorn again.

Aylith moved to the heavy outer door and listened for footsteps. Hearing only the ever-circling wind against the tower's height, she then padded over to the window and looked down into the empty darkness. Nothing.

Suddenly she heard someone sliding the bolt on the door—if she could be ready, she could slip out just when it opened and take her chances on the stairs. Feryar should be coming up soon; perhaps he could hide her for awhile, until she could make her way out of the city.

Her heart pounding and her head still reeling a bit, she moved back to the oriole, put her hand quickly into the Clan Tree's casement, and snapped off the acorn with a sharp, decisive crack and tucked it into her pocket. Though her fingertips flared green briefly, the Tree's pale light was immediately quenched, leaving the oriole in total darkness. She turned and ran smack into Feryar, who was bearing a tray of meats and mushrooms. He put them down gracefully, seeming to need no light to see, steadied her, and then smoothed his silver hair back in an odd preening motion. The great golden eyes bore down on her and blinked, one at a time, as he smiled his silent greeting.

"Oh," she gasped, trying to keep her voice low, "it's you."

"Yes. And you have done well," he whispered, looking over to the empty case, the twig of the Clan Tree drooping and obviously dead. "Come out of there. You must make haste. There is a small room at the tower's base. There is a staircase, carved inside the tower wall, that falls away from the main one; look for the swell in the landing and hide yourself in the wall. There is a small cellar at the end of the stair, unused since the time of Nazir's great-grandfather, when its walls fell in. Don't worry—it's safe now, though everyone has either forgotten about it or thinks it's still ruined. I will try to get the key for your chains. Only hurry, he talks with Malvos now, but will return very soon."

She cocked her head at him and narrowed her eyes, the truth dawning in them even as Feryar spoke.

"I thought you knew." The elf chuckled. "Yes, he is Nazir. The big man is the apothecary, the Sifter. He is of the Sangrazul. He makes medicine and listens for lies. He can hear from afar, and he is very dangerous. So is Nazir. And I believe you are not finished with him. Now run!" He swung the wooden door closed and placed his hand back to the keyhole.

"Feryar, what of you? He will be furious that you let me go," she said as she looked into his gentle, golden eyes. "And why are you helping me?"

"I am long in this service, my dear. In yours, too. The prophecies have ordained my presence here, and I have survived more than Nazir has yet to imagine. And besides, I am Feryar the Fool. Fools can get away with nearly anything. Oh, that reminds me—someone has come for you, from your home." He grinned.

She smiled, squeezed his long, leathery hands in hers, and then fairly flew down the tower staircase, her bound hands out before her to prevent a deadly tumble, her silent feet hitting only every other step or so. When she reached the third floor, Nazir's voice, enraged and petulant, filtered up through the stonework. Aylith looked desperately for a place to hide, finally noticing the promised enlarged landing just below. She rushed into the nearly invisible crack in the wall, and to her great relief, the hidden door extended into an actual tunnel—darker, but far safer than the staircase or landing.

Which is where Nazir now stood, panting, clutching his chest and swallowing something from that stone bottle of his.

Ah, and did he hear me? she chided herself. *But no . . . he is just getting his breath. And up he goes to find that I am flown.*

With that moment of certainty, at least, she relaxed and felt for the acorn, its smooth, oddly warm presence reassuring her of its safekeeping. Amazingly, the green-song had quieted, its rhythms receded to deep in her mind. She could not wait here long, though. The footsteps grew ever more faint above her and soon they would stop. *How far to the little room?* she wondered, and stepped carefully into the darkness, clutching the acorn in her pocket, not risking its light as her guide. *And who has come for me?* she marveled.

Down, down into the tower wall she moved, until the narrow staircase evened out into an earthen-floored cellar of sorts. Above her head, the gray outline of a very small, round portal interrupted the blackness, and she knew she had reached the outside somehow. A thrill ran through her; she was almost out, and so far, no one was following her or had even guessed her whereabouts. She stepped gingerly toward the door, wondering how she would be able to reach it, when her hand brushed something sharp and irregular on the wall.

A high-pitched clicking sound erupted from the creature she had dislodged as it fell to the floor of the cellar. Aylith backed rapidly away from whatever now scrambled at her feet, and caught her balance again by finding the wall. This time, to her great relief, she also found a cresset, still warm—no, glowing at the heart of the coals. . . . Aylith groped it down from its hook and began to blow on it urgently, a crease of red flaming up at her breath. When the cresset took full fire, she had to shield her eyes from its brightness. After another moment, the small room took shape.

There were smooth walls, hollowed out long ago, by the looks of them, and a little milking stool off to the corner. She nervously searched the ground for whatever she had disturbed, but all she saw were human footprints: her own behind her, and before her, the deep ones of a man and the armored ones of . . . Lorris.

She had seen days of those very tracks when they had brought her from Inys Haen, and they were unmistakable now. The telltale left heel where Lorris had lost a hobnail from the sole as they crossed the Sobus. The bent toe on the other boot, a little deeper dug into the soft earth for its misalignment.

And three feet away from the footprints, hiding behind the milking stool, a cat-sized spider, its back covered with bits and pieces of refuse and rags, odd stones and fish hooks stuck on with varying degrees of success. The spider clicked and cowered at the light, protecting the largest and most exotic addition to its camouflage. . . .

Jedhian's knife.

When he saw that Aylith was gone, Nazir's bellow of anger woke the birds in the mews, the cattle in their byres, and the rats in the pantry. Malvos, also in the pantry, and startled even more than the rats, clapped a still hot meat-and-raisin pie to his ear before he remembered that his hand was thus occupied, and fumed both at the waste of the food and the burning discomfort of his impromptu ornament.

"Oh, and what is it now, my gnat-brained prince, my fractious, peevish, overbearing nightslug of a ruler? Got your shirttail caught in the Haenish trollop's corset? You Nohr are a bunch of wailing wonders. I can never get a moment to myself to eat. If it weren't for the damnable fact that you are my only hope out of this manaforsaken lump of a world, I should have poured your precious potion into the moat and given you over to your curse and the raving blue mirke."

Malvos finished digging the remnants of his dinner out of his ear and ambled to the biscuit box, taking a hefty handful of the sweet cakes and stuffing them into his belt pouch. It sounded like a long night ahead. And Feryar the Fool had just taken the last of his favorite morels up to the girl, leaving only some year-old, dried

Haenish turnip tops in the barrel. He did *so* despise the
produce of this world. Pity.

"I'm on my way, my feeble, imbecilic excuse for a
mage; Your Bumpkinship's every pathetic contentment
is all I ever dream of," he muttered between bites of
biscuit and pulls on a jug of new Haenish wine he'd
found a moment earlier.

He sighed and lumbered up one of the staircases that
led to Nazir's room, while an obese, foot-long black rat
made his own lazy way to Malvos's discarded pie.

When Malvos huffed up the last step, he found Nazir
lacing into Feryar with all the energy he could muster,
lost in the all-absorbing rage of Nohr's curse. Nazir's
birthmark would be thoroughly inflamed by now, and
this could take awhile, thought Malvos, deciding to
leave. But then, he reconsidered, there were all those
steps.

He leaned instead against the stone wall outside the
room and munched the last biscuit, enjoying the tirade
and waiting for Nazir to become malleable. Yes, the
girl was gone. *Of course she was, you fool,* he thought,
laughing to himself, *you let her out of your sight.* And
the acorn?

At this, Malvos's eyes popped wide and his hands
began to tremble. His precious hope? Gone? *You fool,
Nazir! How could you have done this?* In instant
answer to his own question, Malvos remembered the
irrational behavior that always preceded Nohrish madness.

Well, the girl could be found. And the acorn would
be with her. She couldn't have gone far, and Nazir
could sense the Memories when she was near. Inys
Nohr was totally isolated and the winter had not lifted.
How could she hope to survive the journey home? No,
she was still somewhere very close, and there was,
after all, a very easy way to flush her out and get her

back. This could be even the better for her running, thought Malvos, calming himself. The young Haenishman now cooling in the pit obviously had come for Aylith. Nazir needed a way to find her and get her to give up the Memories, and Malvos could smell a way to get into Inys Haen.

Now, if the frog just hadn't eaten him yet. . . . Malvos grinned and licked the last of the crumbs from his fingers. Some things were sweeter even than honey-cakes.

CHAPTER

11

JEDHIAN WRAPPED HIS HAND AROUND THE chain that secured him to the dank, weeping, stone wall and hauled himself up it as far as he could. Which was just short of being able to see out the dirty grate above his head. It was morning, or what passed for it here. A thin veil of haze filtered down into the abject darkness of the pit but, so far, had not given relief to anything of interest, anything of hope. Jedhian felt like a fox in a cage trap. But Lorris had promised to come to him, and somehow, he believed she would do what she had said. And she'd seen some hard fighting, he guessed, remembering the lightning streak of a scar that ran down her arm and hand. He wondered if the wound were Haenish——if perhaps he himself had ever faced Lorris in a battle, never knowing that he fought a woman.

A groan startled him out of his reverie, and he searched the darkness for the origin of the sound. To his left it came again, this time much weaker. It did not sound amphibian, to Jedhian's great relief.

"Hello . . . are you hurt? Are you also chained?" he said in his best imitation of Lorris's clipped accent.

"I . . . am not chained. I am laid upon a bench. I have been . . . flogged. Who calls to me?" The voice, a man's, was deep and resonant, commanding, even, despite the obvious agony of its owner.

"I am Jedhian. Of Inys Haen. And who are you, my friend?"

"RoNal, of Inys Nohr."

Jedhian's mouth went suddenly very dry. He croaked out another question, nonetheless. "You have been flogged, you say? By Nazir?"

"And who else, you fool? Only he won't do it himself. Too much gone to anger; kills 'em straight-away every time. He wants me to die slow and shameful. And I guess I will. I feel the plague at work already. My stripes are like to gone white with it by now. I can feel it walking."

Jedhian turned toward the voice; there was just enough weak light now to reveal the man who shared the pit. RoNal lay on his stomach, his head wrapped with rags made from his shirt, his eyes swelled almost completely shut. His back had been laid open with many slashes, the work of a zealous torturer. And though Jedhian could give no color to the bruises on the man's back, they were indeed some of the worst he'd ever seen. RoNal was right; overlaying each long, raised stripe of the whip crept a layer of cottony white fungus. To Jedhian's utter amazement, it was moving, slowly undulating in throbbing waves.

"Oh . . . what have they done to you? How do you yet live? I am a healer, RoNal—if I can get loose here, maybe there's something I can do for you."

Jedhian jerked again at the chains and found that if he let one whole side of the chain be drawn up to the wall, the other lengthened enough to just reach the dying man. One arm, one hand, was better than none.

"Oh, no, Haenish—come not close to me, you'll give yourself the plague as well. There is no cure; I am a dead man, only without the dignity of dying quickly on the field with my sword in my hand. But this is better than the hack—that would take weeks. There is naught left for me but to bear the walk of the beast bravely, without crying out when it takes me. I . . . I'm grateful for your company. Makes it easier. If you get out of here, bear witness to my daughter Lorris that I was her father to the last, and no traitor. I hope she can still be proud of me.

"And tell her that . . . I served truly but blindly. I do not want her to follow me into this death. Please."

Jedhian lifted RoNal's facial bandages enough for the commander to see the man he spoke his last requests to.

"I will, man. I will," Jedhian promised.

Just then, a terrible rending sound shook the cell and a deep basso filled the damp air with a deafening croak. Jedhian's nostrils stung with the acrid breath of the creature they could neither see nor run from.

Do not make any commotion, Lorris had said. . . .

The frog.

A loud splash located the creature in the far right corner of the huge pit, several yards away now, and coming closer with each shuffling hop. Jedhian felt the spray of dirty water on his face and spat the foulness from his mouth, trying to think of what to do, how to distract the monster. But RoNal had another plan.

The dying man sat up painfully and said his last words to Jedhian.

"Do not make another move, no matter what you see or hear. Close your eyes when you don't hear me anymore. Do not open them until you think it's completely dark again or they come for you. The frog eats only once a week; you'll be safe. Get out of here. Tell my daughter I love her. Promise me that you'll take her out of Inys Nohr if you can. She owes no time and has yet to swear allegiance to the Felonarch's service for life. If this is my reward for thirty years of loyalty, I know that Nazir will not stop until he destroys my whole house. . . . "

And with that, RoNal gathered himself and lunged forward from the bench, waving his hands, singing a battle song, and laughing, laughing, until Jedhian heard another big splash and the *thwoop* of the frog's lightning-fast tongue. Then a gulp, and the wrenching of sinew and bone as the creature rearranged RoNal's body, perhaps not yet completely dead, to fit down its gullet.

Several moments later, when Jedhian could no longer bear his own stillness, he opened his eyes to see four great yellow ones blink from the corner where RoNal had disappeared. But the eyes of the frog were not amphibian, nor were they like any reptile's Jedhian had studied. They were distinctly human, and so was the huge, naked body, its flesh pale and just a bit phosphorescent— Jedhian estimated the thing to be twenty feet long in a stretch—and it squatted in the filthy pool amid the regurgitated bones and hair of countless other victims.

The beast sat motionless and content, digesting, a look of total vacancy upon its fungus-encrusted, wide-mouthed face.

Jedhian swallowed hard and said a silent thanks to the enemy soldier whose last act, perhaps his bravest, had secured Jedhian his life and a chance to save Aylith's.

There will be a memorial for you in the wall, RoNal, if I have to carve it with my own hand, he thought.

Aylith jubilantly snatched up the Haenish knife from the spider's shell and tried several different ways to cut the shackles from her hands. But the links were tight, and the knife unwieldy. Finally, she managed to pound

the links apart, the other hand coming more easily in a
moment more.

With a flood of pain, the blood rushed back to her
hands, and her fingers flamed green for a moment at
the release of the pent-up power.

Ah . . . now I can make it, she thought, overjoyed
that her cousin yet lived —and was close by somewhere. She tucked the knife into her belt, kirtled up
the long tunic, and wished for a cloak, remembering
the hard, cold trip from Inys Haen. "Nevertheless, I
will make it," she muttered.

She threw sand into the cresset to extinguish it, and
hoisted herself to the opening as quietly as she could,
employing the little stool. Just as she was about to open
the door, the widowweeds sounded their dolorous warning. Aylith had never heard anything like it and froze
against the cellar wall, under the door, listening. Two
sets of footsteps, one much heavier and more ponderous
than the other, slowly passed in front of the door, and
she could hear the men's voices for a short time.

". . . known that he's to be publicly beheaded tomorrow unless the girl comes forward and gives over the
seed and the light spell."

"Perfect. You are sometimes worth your very expensive keep, Malvos. . . . We will publish it abroad within
the servants' earshot. They're the only true source for
information, anyway. Well, except for Feryar. He doesn't
seem to hear anything I tell him," Nazir muttered.

"Thank you, my sublime, salubrious sovereign."

The steps and the conversation grew fainter. After
another several moments of silence, Aylith let out the
breath she had been holding. So they had Jedhian, she
realized, her confidence falling. And she was, by herself, no help for him. Her fingers made a slight glow on
the door latch, and she let herself slip back down into
the little room.

The cresset well and truly snuffed, she sat in near darkness, thinking about what to do. The acorn found its way to her hand and she idly tumbled it around, its glow becoming ever more faint. The tower room had been lit only by the acorn's glow. Now the last of its green light winked out. She dropped the seed into her pocket and brought her fingers up before her face, trying to force a bit of fire from them. Nothing.

How did you get it to work, Father? she pleaded silently. *Jedhian is about to lose his life, and I must use the power you gave me to help him. Why can't I bring the fire? You never showed me. What good are the Memories when I can't use them? They might as well still belong to you.*

With those bleak thoughts, the darkness seemed to get a little darker. But as she sat and pondered the situation, an image from long ago, from a childhood fishing trip, brought her answer.

When she was twelve, Logan had taken Aylith and Jedhian to the Sobus on a day when the sky looked like the indigo cloth she wove for the village. They had brought nets made of the hiroo plant that grew near the water's edge and dropped them down into the cool depths of the river, hoping to catch dinner. Aylith had set out to best her cousin, throwing her net furiously, hardly letting it open before drawing it up with a sharp jerk every time. While Aylith's net had come up empty time and time again, Jedhian hauled in fish after fish. This only added to her frustration, so she threw down her net on the shore and refused to fish any longer.

"Why can't I do this?" she had stormed. Logan had quietly answered, "Because you are trying too hard. You want to be a good fisher?"

"You know that I do, Father! What a question. I have thought of nothing else all day but how many fish I could catch."

"Then be a good fisher."

"How? I don't know where to start, or what to do."

He looked at her with a tolerant smile.

"Show me the first thing. Just the first right thing."

Aylith frowned at him, but gathered the net in her hands and threw it out over the glassy water in a perfect arc. It dropped with a quiet splash, the old loomstones they used for weights taking it under instantly.

"Now show me the next right thing."

Aylith sighed, drew the line in, and dragged the net ashore. There were a dozen flapping shiners in it, their fins catching the sun's brilliance in wet rainbows.

"What . . ." Aylith began, amazed at the fish in her net.

"You were trying to do it all at once. Every task is many little tasks. Do the first right thing. Then do the next right thing. And you will be a good fisher."

Logan smiled at her, and this time, Aylith smiled back. She picked out her spot and threw the net again and again, just for the joy of seeing it spread out and hover above the clear water, then sharply break the glassy surface.

And she took home more fish than ever before. Even more, she noted now in the dark cellar, a smile coming to her lips, than had Jedhian.

"So this is the first right thing."

She took a deep breath and thought of light, as Logan had told her he did when using his hands to heal. The tips of her fingers glowed briefly. Aylith relaxed, then, and began to see the pattern she sought.

"This will work. I know it," she breathed, her frustration turning to faith.

And light.

With those last thoughts, Aylith's fingers burst again into green flame, this time illuminating the hollow of the little cellar with incandescence and her heart with hope. She put out one finger and drew a line in the air.

It remained. She crossed it with another, and then another, until she had the pattern of Jedhian's cloak floating in front of her, twisted in gleaming light. She tried the edge of the knife against it, poking, slashing, using all her strength to force the weapon through. But the pattern held, turning the weapon without so much as a change in shape. After a few moments, it vanished and she sat in darkness again, a plan forming in her mind. "Use the power only to heal, to protect. . . ." Logan had said.

This would take some thought. And some practice, she resolved. She began to trace the darkness with the glowing tips of her fingers, calming her mind and summoning the fire on sheer faith, walking slowly into that green world in her heart where life slept, where Jedhian's only chance lay. For the next few hours, she plaited power into the air faster and faster, crossing and looping the lines in intricate patterns of strength, weaving a fabric of green light that stayed and glimmered and formed a force around her for longer and longer until she dissolved it, at first, by dropping her concentration, but later only by will.

When Feryar found her, she lay fast asleep against the earthen wall, the air above her head still charged with yards and yards of glowing, ephemeral chain mail.

"Get up, my girl. I will help you to go. You have the Mending to do." He chuckled, batting the weakened remnants of the glowing stuff from before his face.

"Ah! Feryar . . . it's you. Could you see the light from back up the stair? Am I found out?"

Aylith jumped up from her sleep, trying to collect her thoughts. The practice had taken a lot out of her. No wonder it had always tired her father so. She pushed back her tousled hair and looked at Feryar closely for the first time since he had gently shaken her awake. The old elf's face was badly bruised and a thin sliver of a cut ran down the side of his cheek under his eye. One of his hands looked broken, the fingers all askew and swollen. Nazir had taken out his wrath on him for her disappearance, no doubt.

"Feryar—you are hurt. He beat you. He was angry because of me. You didn't have to let him do this. You could have told him I magicked my way out or something. I never meant for you to be hurt."

Aylith touched gingerly at the swelling under one of the elf's eyes, which looked very much as if the delicate bone beneath had been crushed. His face was cut in long strips, like he'd been whipped with a switch. He made no move to back away, letting her prod and search the tissue for deeper damage. It must have been excruciating, but he only breathed deeply, never once calling out. Her heart swelled with compassion for him, and she began to see his face the way it had been before the beating, each damaged area coming into sharper and sharper focus until she could not believe in the hurts anymore.

And then a very strange, unexpected thing happened. The swelling subsided, the skin regained its proper color, and the cut seamed itself over, as though it had never been.

Aylith caught her breath sharply as she watched Feryar's face slowly change to match her inner vision. She could feel the bone under her hand realign itself and knit together. When his face had returned to normal, he smiled and kissed her hand, the tiny points of light still glowing upon her fingertips. Aylith remembered the broken hand then, and set to work on drawing out the heat, the fingers straightening easily—all but the little one. It refused to unfreeze, the bones seeming to have knit wrongly in a tight curl. Aylith tried again, but could not see the finger straightened.

"That's . . . old, child," the elf said sadly, and his voice sounded like a cold winter wind in bare treetops.

Feryar remembered when he had broken that finger. It was the last night Malvos had come for Thrissa. The apothecary had prescribed "music" for the crazed Crephas. Thrissa was to sing to him from the elven ballads, to help him sleep, as he often could not. Thrissa had frequently answered such a summons; all of the Felonarchs had had the same problem. Crephas had raised the call for her some hours past the last glass, and Malvos had taken her from Feryar's warm bed to the master's cold study once again.

Only this time, the master did not really want her to sing for him. Malvos stood guarding the door, even though Thrissa had not fought Crephas, knowing he would punish her chambergirls and her errand boys, indeed, all the tower inhabitants, if she resisted. But Feryar could not sleep that night, too. And when there was no music, and he heard his wife crying, through the stone walls, through the tapestry folds, through the long years of knowing her heart so well that he could hear it breaking, he had fought with Malvos and stormed in upon the old wizard king with death in his eyes and hands, intent on ending the Nohrish line despite the prophecies that had shaped the service of his entire life. The old king was caught by surprise, vulnerable in his nakedness, thinking he dreamed, and it would have been a simple thing to pierce his heart and leave him. But Thrissa had stayed Feryar's hand—sharply enough to break his little finger. That pain had made him remember the other beings, the ones they had saved alive for years at terrific peril, the ones who waited for the light, the restoration of day, for their own healing. The ones who awaited the Mender.

The prophecy had to play itself out. He could not end the line he had spent his life protecting. Feryar's hand had tightened on the poniard, his little finger wrapping itself crookedly into submission. He turned, walked over the unconscious Malvos, and left Thrissa weeping and Crephas alive. It was the hardest day of Feryar's service.

But when the old king died years later, he had left a son. He was Crephas's only male child. The last of Nohr's line: Nazir. Outside those in the bedroom that night, and the tongue-cut Albion midwife who had delivered the boy, only Malvos had ever known Thrissa was Nazir's mother.

On Nazir's coronation day, Thrissa had had a mysterious vision, and she had gone to Loch Prith, saying nothing, and leaving Feryar to continue at the tower until the vision manifested.

Feryar's finger had been forgotten by the time the child was born, but never had it straightened, the bones remembering too well their own break and that of the old elf's heart, which had never healed, either.

He closed his eyes upon the withered memory.

"Thank you," he whispered to Aylith. "And do you now see? You are the Mender. You must save yourself. Wait outside in the cleft of the wall just opposite the cellar. They will change the watch soon. You can leave then, and return to Inys Haen with the acorn. Take this cloak and the food; it's very cold outside."

"Feryar, no. I am no Mender. Please stop saying that. Remember that Jedhian is here. He's my cousin. Nazir has him and will kill him if I don't give up the Memories. I heard him say so. In fact, it may already be too late," she fretted, remembering that some time must have passed since she had overheard Nazir and Malvos.

"No, it is not too late. But it would be better if you would go without him. However, I believe there is someone else who will help. We can find a way to mend this, too."

CHAPTER
12

LORRIS STRODE QUICKLY FROM HER QUAR-
ters to the place by the tower where the Haenishman
had fallen into her life, and searched vainly for the
weapons she knew he had dropped. The last watchman
had told her the news: Nazir would behead the
Haenishman if the girl did not offer herself up. Lorris
knew Nazir would kill the man anyway. When nothing
turned up, she realized Jedhian's knife had been
dropped, probably in the secret cellar. But going back
there would arouse Malvos's suspicions, should he
have anyone watching the place from the outside, as he
most surely did. And the only other entrance to the cellar was halfway up inside the tower. Nazir himself now
sat brooding within yards of the secret stair, and what
reason would she have for going up there? The knife
would have to remain where it was. Only now, the
Haenish would have no weapon. And when she sprung
him from the pit, he would need one.

But what was this? A flash of bright metal caught her
eye as she gave the area one last inspection. She moved

into the shadows of a pile of stones at the tower's base, where an old sword was stuck obliquely into the marshy ground, like a skewer. She retrieved it, thinking it must be of Haenish make; no one here could do that sort of finely chased work. Snakes ran all the way around the hilt and down the blade's center. The blade itself looked dull and round at the edges, like it had never seen battle: a dress weapon, for show and pageantry. The pommel was made of silver snakes that had been plaited together to form the handguard, and two pommel stones hung from a thick silver cord drawn through the hilt. The fine swirl of different shades of mixed metal reminded Lorris of waves on the sea. She brushed the dirt off the sword and then wrapped the weapon in a cloak that she had brought for the Haenish.

This will have to do, she thought. *I hope you can show some skill with it, my friend.*

She pressed close to the rugged tower wall, placed the bundled sword inside a long gap between the big wall stones where some smaller stones had fallen away, and slipped around to the area marked out in her regular watch . . . outside the pit.

Aylith had waved Feryar off into the shadows and up the secret staircase; he had been gone too long from his duties already. Now it was up to her.

She munched the last of the morels he'd somehow managed to bring despite his beating and finished off the jug of water as well, thinking about their plan to get Jedhian out of the pit and then the both of them out of Inys Nohr and back home. It was a very long chance, but the only one they had right now. If Lorris could change places with the pit guard, she could get Jedhian away before the executioner came for him. Then Feryar would make sure the Albion miners were

one man short of their complement on their daily
trudge to the coal mines. Lorris and Jedhian would
meet with Aylith there, and then be off for Inys Haen.

When Lorris passed the widowweeds on her way to her
regular watch, their voices called her name this time.
She stopped but did not look down. Then she pretended to examine the fastening on one of her greaves
and spoke quietly to the ground in front of her.

"Who calls?"

"Aayliithhh, Aayliithh."

"Stay there. I'm off in another glass."

"Noooo time . . . "

Lorris got up and walked on, then turned her corner
just before the pit's only grating and stood still for a
moment.

"Are you alive, Haenish? Do you hear me?"

Jedhian jerked his attention back to the grating and
again raised himself up the chain.

"Yes. I live. Thanks to your father. He gave me word
for you."

Lorris never blinked when she heard the catch in
Jedhian's voice. She knew. They'd already flogged her
father and he was dead. She snapped her next words
off like dry twigs.

"We have no bargain now, Haenish."

"What? No bargain? What about Aylith? Will you
not get us away?"

"I did not say I would not. I said we have no bargain. What I will do, I do now for myself. I will see
Nazir at the other end of his own lash if it takes my
dying breath. Now stand clear of the grating. Be quiet,
or better, talk to yourself like you rave or have a fever.
I will bring Aylith, and we will get you out. Somehow."

"Lorris?"

She paused, not looking at the grating.

"My name is Jedhian."

"Jedhian," she repeated, and moved on, walking the line with the same measured pace, never once feeling the tears that streamed down her face under her closed visor.

Jedhian backed away from the grating. "Bring Aylith? We will get you out?"

Jedhian didn't need to talk like he raved. He thought he truly did; Lorris couldn't have meant that. Aylith had been at the mercy of Nazir the last time he'd seen her, caught in a spell like a bird in a cage. And now she had escaped? He was turning these possibilities over and over in his mind when the great door rattled, and the guard hollered in at him.

"Oy, Haenish, yer gonna lose yer capper if the girlie don' come back! I heard it from upstair maid. I'll be havin' that fine shirt when yer done for, too!" He giggled, pounding on the heavy iron door.

The man was drunk, likely from the upstair maid's stolen mead, but her information made Jedhian wish he shared the guard's tankard. So this was Nazir's plan, then. Use him to catch Aylith. So she had indeed escaped!

"Hurry, girl. I can't save you from down here." He smiled weakly.

When Lorris passed by the widowweeds the next time, she whispered to Aylith that Jedhian yet lived. On the next pass, she gave her instructions as to where to wait until the watch was done, and that Feryar would bring her clothes.

The third pass Aylith was out and gone from the cellar, and into the shadows of the wall, waiting. She settled in, glad for the fresh air, even if it did have the stink of the moat about it. But it was cold out here. She hoped Lorris would not be long.

As she backed into the cleft in the wall that Lorris had indicated Aylith should wait in, she found that it was already occupied. Shoved far back, and covered in a leather wrapper and a lot of dead, dripping fungus, was a sword. Aylith smiled and drew the weapon from its ignoble sheath. The tip was broken, but the rest, as far as could be told in the cramped nook of the wall, was sound and true, though it seemed a bit off balance. One of the pommel stones felt lighter than the other. Aylith replaced it in its wrapper; the glitter of the coiling silver snakes could have alerted any watcher to her presence even in the dark of Inys Nohr. But this was comforting. Lorris had meant what she said.

She felt very sleepy again, and then startled awake, remembering the last time she had given in to that feeling. *Well, this cloak is a cloak,* she mused, glad of Feryar's forethought.

Aylith wondered what the elf was doing here, serving old Nohr's tyrannical progeny, taking beatings for strangers, moving in and out of the dark world of Inys Nohr in silence and patience. What interest could he possibly have in all this?

It reminded her of a story Logan had told her once about a shepherd who had given his life for another when a boar, crazed with pain from a hunter's spear, had charged them. Aylith had turned this over and over in her mind, trying to make sense of it. Finally, she had asked Logan about it.

"They were shepherds," Logan had said gently. "Dangerous things can happen away from the clanhold. The man had chosen long before the danger arose. He just loved his friend. That's all."

He just loved his friend. That's all. But how can you love someone you don't even know, Feryar? she wondered. *How can you love me?*

CHAPTER
13

THERE WAS NOTHING TO BURY, LORRIS knew, but the last worried look on her father's face.

Traitor or not, I go now, she thought ruefully. *I have not taken the oath for life. My loyalty is sworn solely to my blood, and I have only one question for Nazir now. And an answer for RoNal's death.*

Lorris had made up her mind. When they were safely away, perhaps the Haenishman would be good enough to let her stay at Inys Haen until she could find her own way in the world, maybe to hire as a paid soldier, maybe to lay down the sword forever once she had killed Nazir with it.

That insane fiend had no idea what sort of man he had killed when he put her father to the lash and the pit. Nazir, whose troops hoped never to see him or speak with him, for that surely meant only punishment, thought his forces followed *him*, followed his grand dream of bringing the light. But Lorris knew that it was RoNal who made sure they were fed, who stood their watches himself when they had to bury family who'd died of the hack or starvation. It was RoNal who protected the children of the prostitutes when the women went to the wharves to ply their trade. It was those children who became his soldiers if and when they grew to age. RoNal's troops, easily half of Nazir's marching force, were loyal only to RoNal.

Except for Thix. Though the young man had not suspected his uncle, Nazir must have been waiting until he could make everything seem just right, she thought. Not that Thix hadn't long deserved to see the point of someone's sword at his throat. Lorris remembered the day, and always would, that Thix, far too easily riled in a mock fight, had purposely given her a foul cut with his double-hooked dagger. She had lost a month of her training over that encounter. Her hand and forearm now bore that lightning strike of a scar forever. Her father, though he knew what the boy had done, only told Lorris to expect the unexpected, to move more quickly, and to never let it happen again.

Nazir had never even touched Thix.

Legendary for their inventive parricide, the Felonarchs before Nazir would have applauded him. His weapon had been the sword of RoNal's honor.

Lorris made her way to her father's little room off the side of the main barracks, a long stone building with a slate roof. A frozen rain colored the dark rock even darker. Lorris entered, but did not bother to take off her muddy boots. There was no time.

The room had no candle, but she knew what she was looking for and soon had the brace of dress daggers, their edges kept razor sharp, and the locket with her mother's likeness in it, the heavy brooch with the dragon head and its ruby eye, and the tiny piece of chamois with the map of Cridhe delicately burned into it.

Lorris had already packed it all into her scrip when she heard a footfall outside the door. She moved quietly, deeper into the darkness, one of the daggers drawn and ready.

The intruder edged into the room slowly, almost reverently, carrying something rolled in leathers before him. His diminutive form and bent shoulder instantly gave him away. Lorris sheathed the dagger.

"Arn."

"Ah! What! Who . . . ?" the boy choked out, more afraid even than usual.

"Arn. Come over here. It's only me. What is it you have there? Why have you come here?" said Lorris, stepping away from the wall.

"I'm sorry. I'll go, please don't tell the master. I just wanted to say good-bye to 'im. He was good to me, sir. He set my arm when, ah, 'twas broken. I didn't come to steal, I swear it."

Arn was almost out the door again when Lorris caught hold of his ragged tunic and hauled him back in.

"It's all right, Arn. I loved him, too. He was all I had. All a lot of us had. You can stay."

The boy settled a bit, and she took her hand away from his sleeve. Then he started to tell his story, his voice cracking miserably.

"Sir, I saw him be flogged. The master read him, in private, from a charge scroll I held, and your father just nodded, and then they cut his hair and stripped off his shirt. They took his sword and broke it, and that went hardest on him, you could tell. And then they set to flog him. They tied him to one of the gates and gave him the lash thirty times. That would ha' killed most men on its own right then, sir. He took it brave, never called out, never passed his water. He stood up best he could when it was done and shook the soldier's hand that had to do it to 'im. I never saw nothin' like it, sir. He just looked the master straight in the face when they took him to the pit, and the master, he wouldn't meet his eye, and—"

Arn lost his words. Then found them again. "I didn't say nothin', sir. I think the master had your father lashed because he thinks he was a traitor. But I'm the traitor. I know who leads the rebellion, and who follows it. And I just let this happen." Arn shook from head to toe, miserable and guilty.

Lorris looked down at him from her considerable height. "He would have been glad you came. Here, I want you to take this, Arn," she said, leaning down to give the boy the glittering brooch. "You can take that and bribe your way out of the tower, make your passage through the city, maybe to the Southern Isle, where it might be just a little warmer, better on that shoulder."

He shook his head at her, but she knelt and faced him, insisting. "Arn—you can't stay here. Look, RoNal would have been proud of you for not giving away your cause, for not bringing death to hundreds of other people. But you're in as much danger as my father was. Pretty soon, Nazir will realize he didn't get his man. And he'll go looking again."

He met her wide gray eyes and nodded. "I found this when it was all over. I wanted you to have it."

He quickly gave her the rolled up leathers, reluctantly taking the brooch. Then he was gone. And Lorris was alone again.

With her father's broken sword.

She carefully rewound the leather wrap and laid it on his thin pallet. She closed the door to RoNal's room softly and quickly made her way to the mess, where she hoped to gather some food without being noticed. Inys Haen was a long way off. And there would be three traveling now.

Lorris moved to a table where several of the younger

soldiers had gathered, a dice game in progress, and their night fairly far gone in perf.

"Who is to wear the hood for the Haenishman's death?" She slapped one of them on the back in greeting.

"Um, BiDrun, I heard," said the man, his eyes never leaving the spinning dice.

"Oh, can't be," said another. "He came down with the hack last night."

"Then that would leave Merco," added the third man. "Lorris—it wasn't right—what happened with your father. We know—"

"It's all right. Thanks," she murmured, turning quickly aside, toward the serving line. It was nearly morning and breakfast was underway. She took her tray, its gray contents even more unappetizing than usual, and moved to a table a little farther down.

Merco. The whistling axman. He liked to whistle sea songs for his victims before he worked, to try to calm them, but the effect was usually that they met their deaths a bit more gladly and in greater haste. Lorris checked the glass-counter. Merco always ate at the same time every day, coming up from his torture chamber, which was located directly next to the cell where they held Jedhian, to pass conversation with his comrades.

She sat casually picking over her food, her eyes alert for the entry of the executioner. This would be simple. Just a matter of waiting. Merco should be in at any moment, and then she would have a clear shot to the pit, buy off the guard's duty—he would do it gladly and without question—and get Jedhian out of that miserable hole before Merco could return and hear them escaping, or worse, begin his preparations.

When another glass had passed and Merco had not shown, Lorris rose from her cold food, stuffed several rolls into her pockets, and slipped out of the mess hall.

She made her way toward the pit without incident and faded into the doorway and down the steep stairs, hoping she was wrong about her suspicions.

But, just as she rounded the last turn, an offkey whistle broke the silence and echoed up the staircase.

Nazir paced.

He could not stop pacing, and he knew that he would do it until he dropped from sheer exhaustion. The birthmark on his chest screamed with fire and he could not hear for the roar of his own blood in his ears. The anger had taken him again. The spells were coming closer together. The first one had been when he was barely walking, old Feryar had told him. He'd thrown a tantrum that had lasted four days and driven two of his nurses to collapse. The next time, when he was twelve, he'd burned down one of the barracks. Then at nineteen, Nazir had found himself wandering the moors, with blood on his hands. Days later, a few yards from where Feryar had hauled him out of the snow, a tinker had been discovered with his throat crushed. A year ago, he'd killed fifteen men under the lash in one day. It was always like that; once he passed a certain point, he had no control.

He wondered if he'd killed Feryar this time; the old elf had fallen badly and Nazir had not seen—had not been able to see—what damage he had suffered. When the anger took him, all Nazir knew was the red waves before his eyes and the blue flame upon his hands.

He took another huge gulp of the newest batch of foul, chalky potion Malvos decocted for him. It tasted worse than usual. He gagged as it went down. The internal fire receded.

It had been nine years since Nazir had left the confines of Inys Nohr. The last time, he had ridden forth with the spring raiding party to take the Keeper himself, to show his people that at last a ruler sat the throne who had enough courage to face the Haenish in person. But the closer he had come to the place, the worse the birthmark had burned, until the torment had become unbearable, and the young ruler, newly invested, had to turn back in shame for the comfort of the mountain stronghold, and to Malvos's elixirs.

As had every other man of the house of Nohr before him, though he couldn't know that, for they all had found other reasons for the journals to record why they stayed in the tower. Nohr had never given credence to the power of the curse he'd brought upon his family when he rent the Clan Tree, and he'd died raving, thinking he was in another world, walking about with imaginary friends and discussing the virtues of a peculiar liquid metal in the service of weatherwatching.

Nazir needed some exercise.

Swallowing the last of the potion too quickly, he dissolved in a coughing fit and dragged on the shabby blue cloak that he'd used to greet Aylith. The people of Inys Nohr would never suspect the garment clothed their illustrious ruler.

He pulled the hood down over his damp hair and took off the eagle-emblazoned ring on his left hand. It had most recently belonged to Thix, as it always belonged to the youngest male member of the bloodline. The family crest: old Nohr's pet bird Atalanta. RoNal had put it into his hand the instant Nazir had heard the commander's report of Thix's death. Then, without further inquiry, Nazir had had him flogged. Well, that was only necessary, even though RoNal had been his best officer, his most loyal man in arms. His troops had loved him, Malvos had said. And the Sifter knew the truth, even if he didn't always tell the truth.

What is it to love someone? Nazir wondered as he

left the tower and moved through the gate, the Haenish girl's face strangely appearing in his mind. *I have never felt what that is.*

He thought about the dark depths of his heart, where the madness beckoned, where there was no wondering, no need for love. No need for anything but the fire of the anger, the all-consuming revenge. Nazir drew back from the thought, dizzied at its power even in the abstract. That old revenge, that old anger—it wasn't even his. It belonged to a madman who'd passed it down to every one of his progeny. It was the only part of the old man that had never completely died. And now it lived in Nazir and came closer to taking him into its permanent darkness every day.

Sometimes Nazir wondered if Nohr had really ever gone. It seemed the old man still struggled and raged and whimpered inside Nazir. And he got stronger, more demanding about it, all the time. There had to be light here soon. There had to be an end to the curse. If he could find the Keeper again. Take from her what was rightfully his. What should have been Nohr's. The light in Aylith's eyes. The Memories of the Clan Tree.

A fog moved in off the inlet, obscuring the filth and squalor of the lean-to's and fisher shacks. Ahead lay Inys Nohr's only publican house, with a smoking torch marking its doorway. Nazir moved inside, already feeling the creeping damp of the Nohrish night.

Inside the cramped, crudely built greatroom, several fishermen sat drinking perf, a drink Nazir loathed, and eating their day's meager catch. Eels. Ugly purple-skinned, long-jawed, razor-toothed eels. They swam in the moat at the tower, they infested the river, and they ate most of the game fish left in Cridhe. They had come up from the depths long ago, when the Parting had caused the Long Winter, and they had adapted to the new darkness and cold of the waters with zeal and proliferation. And they stank, their flesh full of inky vitriol. Nazir hated eels.

He ordered ale, but got perf. The publican had laughed, thinking the shabbily dressed man at the long slate bar was making a joke.

"We got the drink o' the ill sorts here, sir. Good mushroom sour mash. Only up the tower do they get ale. Have to steal that," the publican had said.

Nazir took the jar of dark syrupy liquid from the publican and sipped the bitter brew slowly. The fishermen gave him a long stare, but no one came to talk with him. He sat for a moment thinking of Aylith, of the sound of her voice, the shape of her face. The anger began to rise again, and he felt his hands quicken with the searing heat that came before the fire. He finished quickly, paid the man, shorting him by a half decca, and left, feeling the need to continue walking.

A sea fog had moved in quickly, covering the city with a thick white blanket, like a shroud, thought Nazir. And just as deadly; there were fogs that killed in this place, he knew. They carried the hack in them. Those miasmas settled in the lowest parts of the city, where the air never moved. You could always tell a pestilent fog, though: the mist was tainted the same pink as the froth on a dead man's mouth.

He turned into a side street and stopped. Bearing witness to his thoughts, before him lay a pile of corpses, their faces obscured by the pinkish foam of their death throes. Nazir wondered why the wagon hadn't removed them, but then he saw. Atop the pile, greedily guarding their hideous find, seven or eight enormous shield bugs hunched, their wide mirror eyes glinting in the darkness, picking up the light from torches down the alley and reflecting it. In the "day," they took to the rooftops, flattened themselves, and turned the polished surface of their eyes to black to capture any heat that radiated from the weak, cloud-diffused twilight that seeped through to Inys Nohr. But in the total darkness of night, their mirrors gleamed silver.

The fisherfolk had a legend. If you saw your reflection in a shield bug's eyes, he would eat you the next day. Nazir backed away. There could be something to the fishwives' tale; the shield bug was a vicious creature. The drivers of the body wagons would often just leave them to their dreadful work, never wanting the chance of a slash from their wicked, serrated pincers. If the pile of bodies had been laid out for pickup in a remote part of town, the wagoneers would simply toss a torch into the midst of them, carefully averting their eyes. All along the waterfront, and outside the wall, such corpse fires burned daily.

Nazir turned around and walked on. A few more steps took him to a brothel. He passed it by, knowing that a great many of the customers and the girls, too, would be part of another pile of bodies in the morning, also dead of the hack. Nazir caught his scarf up around his nose and mouth, thinking he saw just the faintest tinge of pink in the air outside the brothel, and walked a little faster, heading unconsciously toward the Albion slave colony.

Nazir's father had created these people. Crephas, in the early years of relative sanity he had before the experiment that took his life, hated the cold of Inys Nohr more than the darkness. In his efforts with the Clan Tree's magic, he had altered a rare, delectable fungus, called ardré.

At first, Crephas expected the new plant to make him less sensitive to the cold. But after consuming vast quantities of ardré in tinkering with both its energies and taste, he discovered that it had different properties. The original experiment failed, but Crephas found another way to use his magic mushrooms. He determined to engineer a master race of workers for the coal mines, so that he would never be chilled again. He gave the best men in his army the altered fungus in their food, thereby increasing their capacity for work and their ability to see in near darkness.

It had worked beautifully. Coal production tripled, Crephas lived in rooms hot enough to make him sweat continually, and the miners became so addicted to the ardré that they could think of nothing else. But Crephas soon found he had a new problem: the men died when deprived of increasingly greater portions of their new food source. They turned blue after awhile, too. The mirke, they called it, after the mines' ubiquitous gray-blue clay. You got the mirke by taking the ardré. But then, more and more ardré kept you from dying of the mirke, too. So Crephas set aside a large area of one of Inys Nohr's northern mountainsides to grow the necessary substance for his new race of workers, thinking that it was enough until he was gone, that the Albions would also eventually die out, and Nazir could warm his own feet in his own way.

Alas, the workers passed their new capacities and their addiction on to their children. Suddenly, Crephas had a much larger group of people to manage, and to grow ardré for.

For lack of a better solution, he simply enslaved them. The Mirkalbions, as they called themselves, were bound to Crephas more surely than if he had chained them to his own person. Though the Albions tried and tried, they could not grow ardré anywhere but in Crephas's craggy, vertical, north-face fields, for the level of darkness had to be constant, and there was some peculiar white mineral there that fed the magically altered fungus, maintaining its special properties.

The new people were never quite accepted by their normal-skinned neighbors—their blue-gray markings and odd eyes, often white or of two different colors, terrified the general population. There were stories about how they could make you sick by looking at you, how, from a distance, they could cause the ground you walked on to collapse under your weight.

The rumors were good for keeping the public from finding any sympathy for the miners, but the slave colony had lately found a focus for its incredible energies. One day, several months back, Morkin, a mining crew mess captain, discovered that strong torchlight withered and eventually killed the precious fungus. Rumor spread that the ardré would not grow if light came to Inys Nohr.

Ever since Nazir had announced that he would bring the light back to Cridhe, Morkin and the other Albions had stirred and talked and plotted to make sure the Felonarch never kept that promise. Once or twice, in his tower room, Nazir thought he had heard rumbles echoing up through the hollow walls from deep below the structure. And Morkin had a strange new interest in the rocks and soils of the area. . . .

Nazir passed through the gate at the edge of the colony, the guards receiving the day's password without looking to see who spoke it. He strolled down a ramshackle lane, the dwellings made of cast-off materials from the fisherfolk. Here and there, three or four old boats bound together and covered with rotting leather sails served as shelter, their prows lashed and pointing toward the dark sky. Nazir saw a blue-skinned woman, weeping and bent to the task of a small burial.

"What . . . is your grief, woman?" he asked.

She gave a start and turned to see the Felonarch himself standing close enough to spit upon. For a moment, she hesitated, then answered, pretending not to know him.

"What do you think? I bury my baby, sir. And those are the graves of my man and other children. I'm all that's left in my house." She gave him no more than that, her eyes, one palest blue, one black, fixing him in their unequal stare.

"What if I told you that Nazir would bring the light very soon? Even within the next days. What would you say of him, and of your new life?" he fished.

The woman could not contain herself. "Sir. You speak to one who hopes never to see light come to this place. Our very lives will be taken if that snake dares to make good on his ridiculous promise. The ardré cannot grow anywhere but here, and under these clouds. There will never be a way out of the dark for the likes of us. We are close already to starving, and the Felonarch works the blue skin off our bones just to keep that heap o' stones of his warm. We die in our sweat, in the dead air of the mines, in places that have never seen a candle. There's a rumor that the Keeper at Inys Haen is dead."

Her gaze bore into him, her eyes searching his. "And if that's so, there'll never be no more light at all. For all the world. I'd give half my ration forever to see it so! That's what I would say if you told me such as that," she finished boldly, her thin frame shaking.

Coldly furious, Nazir pulled a glove on, reaching to strike the woman for her insolence, but thought better of it, the shadow of doubt staying his hand. What if the rumors were true? And he was alone, inside the colony, the guards too far away to hear him. Nazir backed off, turned and walked purposely and indelicately over the graves the woman had pointed to. Nohr's curse had moved to the streets and wore hobnail boots, too.

He passed through the gate again, the guards sleepily saluting. It was nearly morning. He had begun to make his way back to the tower when a crowd of angry, drunken townspeople, out long past their curfew, rose out of the fog before him. A man in a red cap, four prominent bluish white streaks falling through his long, glossy black hair, stood at the rear of them, motioning the group to silence. Nazir stopped to listen in the back of the perf-besotted crowd, the sea fog now swirling around his feet. Among the other listeners, he noticed the fishermen he had seen earlier in the tavern. Could the Albions have friends among the townspeople? It seemed unlikely until Nazir heard the voice of the speaker.

"The Haenish Keeper is dead! I say we take that tower down! I say we leave him tangled in his own bitteroots and feed him to his own frog. And that giant buffoon that's always with him. He don't make no medicines for us! We die every day of the hack and he don't see, don't care. All he wants is raided dainties, while we starve and can't feed our children but for the stinkin' eels. We'll never see daylight again. I say we burn the tower now. What have we to lose?"

The voice ahead, misted and hidden in the fog, ceased. Nazir strained to see who spoke such sedition, but the man had dissolved into the crowd like the fog.

Another took up the cry, and another, and another, until the whole mangy group was calling for Nazir's ruin. The crowd began to shift and move toward the tower, and Nazir knew he had no time; they suddenly produced nets and gar hooks, miner's picks and shovels, and worst of all, the sickle knives used to harvest the ardré.

He raced down another side street, through a seldom used shipyard, his heart pounding. Nazir found the bailey's wall. There was a garbage heap that reached fairly high up the stones and he jumped upon it, sinking to his knees in the tower's refuse, but catching hold of the jagged rock face, and hoisting himself to the top, looking over his shoulder to make sure he hadn't been seen. He threw back his hood as he dropped safely to the ground inside.

"Close the gate!" he shouted on the run at the hosteler, waking the young man from his nap just before the mob reached the portal. Zell, the terrified gateman, slammed shut the heavy iron grates and stood shaking as Nazir saluted, red-faced and panting.

CHAPTER
14

AYLITH HAD PRESSED HERSELF INTO THE wall's cold embrace when Nazir landed a mere few feet in front of her, clutching his chest and stumbling momentarily. Then the roar of a mob broke the silence and he ran several yards, shedding his old blue cloak. He clambered to the top of the bailey wall again, this time in front of the jeering crowd, and somehow pulled himself into a semblance of angry majesty. The crowd, stopped short of their mobbing, was struck more or less silent by the sudden display of the ruler's bravado.

"Where did he come from? Can he hear us plotting against them from the tower now?" someone whispered.

The fog became thicker, mingling with the darkness. The red-capped man tucked up his hair and faded even further toward the back of the crowd, nearly tripping over a boy with a dragonhead clasp at the throat of his hooded cloak.

"I am delighted that you have come," Nazir improvised brilliantly. "You are just in time for the proclamation

that I wished to make. This day at the third glass, just
a little while from now, I will either bring you light or I
will bring you the head of a Haenishman. Yes. But you
must help. Through the mistake of a servant, I have
lost a prisoner. She is small, she is Haenish. She is the
Keeper." A murmur rose from the fog-enshrouded cot-
tars. Nazir went on, his confidence rising.

"You must bring her to me. I know she is yet with
us."

He brought the Clan Tree to mind, and held up his
hands, rimmed with points of blue light. The stunned
crowd drew back, making various warding signs and
murmuring prayers. From her place by the wall, Aylith
felt an odd pull at her mind, like someone catching at
her cloak. Nazir then turned and looked behind him, his
head pointed straight at her, but his eyes missing her in
the deep darkness of the tower's shadow. Aylith felt for
all the world like a rabbit gone to ground, the fox close
enough for her to see his teeth. He swept the crowd
again with that probing gaze. She was close, he knew
it—but where? The potion was wearing off. The birthmark felt like a firebrand.

"If you harbor her," he continued, returning to the
crowd of fisherfolk and enjoying his pun, "and bring
her to me, I will give you the reward of seven fine
ships. By the sixth glass!"

He jumped straight backward, down inside the wall,
leaving them to think he had magicked his way out of
their sight.

Malvos listened to the speech and looked on with
satisfaction from his crumbling balcony on the second
floor of the tower. Nazir had found himself a little bit
of unexpected drama, it seemed. But the boy always
could work a crowd. This was going just fine now.
Should flush the pigeon smartly and have the ceremony
wrapped up by midday meal. He would open that old

bottle he'd been saving and have it with custard tarts. Yes. It would be a lovely way to leave.

Ah, Tempé, it has been so long. And I have grown so idle sitting here in your little backwater punishment cell. But when I get out, you will reckon with me. Finders can be Walkers. You promised to teach me when I was a child. But instead you marked me with your serpents, and dragged me with you wherever your whims took you. You promised so long ago, and you will keep that promise very soon, or I will trade the sources of your mana to Platon or Krim, or whoever is the highest bidder. And they will take these wretched snake shackles from my hands for that bargain. Yes, you will teach me to use the mana, and then I will Find for no one but Malvos.

He picked a bitter seed from his teeth and was out the door, heading for the kitchen, in a swirl of orange and purple silk.

Lorris crept the rest of the way down the staircase to the pit quietly. Obviously, Merco had already come for Jedhian. The guard, drunk again, lay snoring loudly beside his post. Lorris hoped he would not choose this very moment to wake up. She sprang for Merco as he was about to launch into a particularly heartfelt rendition of another drinking song, going first for his throat and then for his head. She dispatched the crooning axman with one hard knock, and laid him out his entire length along the doorway to the pit. The guard still snored on; but then, if he could sleep through Merco's serenade, he could sleep through this. Lorris found the key quickly and opened the door to the pit.

"Thank the Maker it's you!" came a relieved voice from the wall. "I thought he was going to do me in even before Nazir could."

"Hold still. The same key works on your chains as the door," Lorris replied. In a second, she had him free.

"Merco? Bring him up. He's nearly ready and wants him out here now. He's waiting." Malvos's impatient voice floated down the staircase.

Jedhian met Lorris's eyes. "Is there any other way out?" he mouthed silently. She shook her head, frowning.

They heard Malvos's footsteps move down the hall a bit.

"Then we'll have to go along for now. There'll be some kind of break once we're in the open. It'll be all right—you did your best, I'm sure," he whispered. Then he whistled up a bit of the same tune Merco had been rendering, his best imitation still a little too true, hoping the echoes would do the rest.

No one slept in all of Inys Nohr for the next two glasses. The crowd that had been ready to pillory Nazir a couple of hours before had spent the next ones looking for his bolted prisoner. Every hovel, every shack, every barrel had been searched. And still, no one had found the elusive Haenish girl. There was talk that since she was the Keeper, she was a wizard herself and had made herself invisible. So it was a sleep-starved, irritated group who gathered in the tower's inner ward to watch what Nazir had promised. Light or death. The better part of the city, especially the Albions, given their choice at this point, would have taken death. At least that was a surety. And possibly entertaining, as long as it was someone else's. Especially a light-lover's.

Aylith had spent the hours wide-eyed and waiting for Lorris and Feryar. Who never came. When the gates were thrown open at the first glass, and the drums began an hour later, she knew something had gone wrong. When they marched Jedhian out from the pit, she realized she would have to do the best she could alone.

As the bailey gates were closing, the last of the swinish crowd pushed through, the heavy metal portal nearly swinging shut on the last person in, a bent-shouldered boy. He moved slowly, and the guards hurried past him to get a better view of Nazir's promised spectacle.

That's Nazir's page, my fisherboy, she thought, making quick changes in her plans.

Aylith rose stiffly from her hiding place and whistled softly to him. The boy stopped and looked around, his eyes going wide as he found her emerging from the wall like a housemouse. She silently motioned him over.

"You!" whispered Arn, fading easily into the deeper darkness of the wall. "They're looking all over for you. How is it you're here? I thought you'd be flown nearly to Inys Haen by now. Look what Lorris gave me." He proudly showed her the dragonhead clasp on his cloak.

Aylith smiled appreciatively. "I have need of your clothes, boy," she said, pulling at the stretchy wool in her dress to make sure it would accommodate Arn's larger size. "Will you help? Will you trust me?"

Arn nodded. In all the time they had shared the river, the young woman had never betrayed him to the Haenish. A moment later, the brooch adorned Aylith's shoulder as she made her slow, bent way toward the open area.

When the stoop-shouldered boy finally edged his way into the torchlight, Jedhian was being pushed toward the large wooden block, indelibly stained a dark reddish black from great age and much use. He stood bravely, though he limped a bit, and a tall soldier steadied him at his left.

The executioner.

The tall soldier had his black visor down and his sword drawn and at the ready. The blade caught the torchlight and its edges gleamed sharply—something of a kindness, under the circumstances. Jedhian's hands had been bound, thick chains biting into his wrists and turning his hands blue. The soldier hastened Jedhian onto the block.

Nazir, bedecked in a cloak of purest white, a blazing yellow orb worked in gold embroidery on its back, with radiating arms of reds and oranges, stood upon a group of boulders piled before the block and surveyed the crowd with pleasure. The clouds tumbled above his head, threatening snow or sleet, but he unfurled the cape in a sweeping, grand gesture and saluted his people.

This would be his moment; he knew someone would give up the girl. He felt her presence too strongly, despite Malvos's potion, to believe she was really gone. He had felt it on the wall, before the reckless villagers. It had seemed to envelop him, strong but directionless. She had been there then, waiting, hidden. And she was here now.

Jedhian felt that presence, too. He looked for Aylith's face throughout the milling crowd, but did not find her anywhere in the sea of coughing, scabious, unsavory Nohrlanders.

These poor folk, thought Jedhian, *look like walking death.* The names of herbs and poultice recipes flashed in his mind, along with cures for the coughing sickness and something that might have worked for RoNal's walking plague: speedwell. Some older Albions, no longer fit for the mines, now attending to Nazir's personal needs, had gathered in a tight bunch at the edge of the crowd. One of them held a majestic crown wrought in golden oak leaves upon a white pillow. Their bluish faces and white eyes stared hopelessly at the Felonarch.

But Jedhian's attention was brought back to his own health rather suddenly. Nazir cleared his throat to address the crowd. Silence dropped like a stone.

"My people. Thank you for your faith in me. I have come this day to receive from you the captive who will set us free from the darkness her wretched clan has forced upon us for centuries. Today is a new day, a new beginning. We are the Nohr—we will rule all of Cridhe in the full light of my power. This day I will give you what has been promised."

He stopped and brought his hands to the sky, to the canopy of roiling clouds beginning to drop piercing darts of frozen rain upon them all. A thousand pale, poxed faces followed his gesture.

"Who will hand up the Haenish woman to me now, and stand with me for the bringing of the light as reward for your loyalty?"

"'Ay, your Holiness said we'd get seven fine ships," came the hidden reply, somewhere off to the right.

Scanning for the insubordinate, Nazir gave the jeering mob his best and sweetest smile, the burning mark on his chest making it difficult to maintain.

"Yes, that's true. But who could possibly think that inferior prize more worthy than to go down in Nohrish history alongside the one who brings the light?"

He looked skyward again, and completely missed the covert spitting that was his answer.

Beside him, the executioner pushed Jedhian's head down onto the block. He was turned uncomfortably to the side, the executioner's hand directly in front of his face.

The hand had a jagged, lightning-shaped scar running down it. Jedhian kept his eyes on it, his face pressing into the block, which smelled vaguely of cedar, of old blood and sweat. He could understand why. His own collar was wringing wet just now. And where was

Aylith? Still waiting for them? Not if he knew his cousin.

A few rows to the left, the late-coming, stoop-shouldered boy pushed his way through the crowd. For the most part, they ignored him completely. Only the old elf, attendant upon the king's apothecary, took notice of the child's ferreting movements to gain a place at the front of the crowd.

He quickly looked away from the boy, lest Malvos follow his stare, and surreptitiously inched a long, thin foot directly in front of the big man.

When Nazir's question got no response, he asked again, and when that produced only a rising murmur in the crowd, he frowned and gestured toward the Haenishman.

"So you would have death over light? Are you all dark-dwelling Albions now? You would harbor the only person who can help me lift the curse? You would rather have the pitiful death of a weasely Haenishman than the glory that I have promised you? Will no one come forward with the girl?"

Nazir's face had turned the color of a death fog. He fought to control the fury he felt rising to take him again. Jedhian's quiet, if uncomfortable, position at the block further irritated him. Why didn't the man resist? There was no fight to him at all, and that was ruining the show. When the crowd grew completely silent again, he could bear it no more.

"So be it! You will have death. The foolish Haenishman's first, and then your own. For Inys Nohr will surely die of this infernal darkness, this diabolical Haenish curse. Without the girl, there is no light! Without—"

But he could not finish; the words froze in his throat as he saw Arn, hooded by a red-and-blue bhana, his shoulder seemingly healed, walking into the courtyard, carrying an old, broken-tipped sword.

CHAPTER
15

"I AM HERE, NAZIR. AND I COME TO RANSOM Jedhian, the Haenishman you hold at the block. You may take the Memories from me, only let him go. Now."

Aylith dropped Arn's cloak on the hard-packed courtyard and pulled the bhana down around her neck. A gasp went up from the bloodthirsty crowd, and a few of them even put down their perf jars as she faced them and they saw who really stood before Nazir.

"I give up my weapon."

And she held it out by the block, in front of the executioner. Who extended a familiar, scarred hand to receive it.

Aylith caught her breath, but quickly recovered. She searched the hood for Lorris's eyes and got a quick wink.

Nazir smiled wickedly down at Aylith and folded his arms across his chest. She was so close that the burning of the mark had nearly toppled him from the rocks.

But now he had her. She had fallen to her own family's curse: love. Nazir found Malvos in the crowd and smiled knowingly. Had he not predicted this very moment? Was he not destined to give the Haenish their miserable due?

Aylith took the opportunity to glance once at the executioner and once, tenderly, at Jedhian, as if to say good-bye. The crowd began to stamp and whistle.

Malvos, casually watching the scene from his cushioned panoply, had dropped his tart and lurched forward, not in response to Nazir's self-congratulation, as the Felonarch supposed, but at the sight of the old sword that lay on the block—Tempé's sword. He gestured in the air, just to be sure. Yes, it was Soulslayer, and still with the invisible mark of his Finding upon it.

Malvos gathered himself to retrieve it, to take it back to his safekeeping, until he could get Nazir to perform his part in his long-awaited escape. But as Malvos took the first step, Feryar's bony foot blithely tripped the giant, and Malvos came down on the five men in front of him with the force of a falling boulder. Feryar smiled secretly and rapidly made his way out of the arena, on the pretense of running for Malvos's apothecary bag. The big man scrambled to regain his feet, but the tangle of mashed grooms trying to help him had made that impossible.

Nazir, oblivious to anything but himself and his imminent transcendency, raised his hands in triumph at Aylith's announcement, urging the grumbling crowd into a weak cheer. Looking skyward, hoods raised against the pelting rain, they still couldn't quite believe he would bring light. And now they had begun to think they might not get to see an execution, either.

Undaunted, Nazir hopped gracefully down from the boulders, his white cape blossoming around him, and Aylith circled slightly to face him, moving just out of range from the executioner and Jedhian, covertly signaling them to bolt when she made her move. She could only hope they would take their cue and run when she gave them the brief moment of Nazir's distraction.

As Nazir moved toward her, she lifted a hand and stepped back.

"First let Jedhian go."

The crowd roared at that, and it took Nazir several moments to settle them enough for Aylith to hear him speak.

"Surely you can see that these good folk will not have that, my dear . . . they came to see a Haenishman die today. No, when you provide me with the Memories, and return what you have stolen, I will bring them light. In their celebration, they might forget about your cowardly clansman. But not until then." He chuckled.

Aylith ducked her head and readied her hands.

"As you say."

Nazir stretched out his arms and spread his fingers wide, their tips glowing with the blue fire of his pain. He moved slowly near to her, until he stood within inches of touching her head. His mind churned with rage, with confusion, with desire. And then Aylith looked him straight in the eye, smiled her biggest, and threw back her head, screaming her high-pitched Haenish war cry. In the stands, Malvos clutched his ears and doubled over in spasms, onto the grooms again, just as he was untangling his foot.

Nazir stumbled at the shock to his own concentration, the focus in his eyes giving way to the blindness of the rising fury, and he lunged at her. The pain in his chest throbbed and hammered at him until all he could see was the red haze, the madness about to overwhelm him. Aylith whirled away, snapping her hands in front of her and drawing fire from her own fingertips, weaving her light spell into a mantle of warding, the Nohrlanders agog at the glorious display.

At the familiar war cry, Jedhian raised his head and held his hands to the block. Lorris cut his chains with one swipe of her sword, and threw him the broken-tipped blade as he rose. Jedhian reached for the weapon, trying to see what was happening to Aylith at the same time.

And missed the sword. It skittered across the hard earth and into the side of Nazir's boot. The berserk ruler instinctively, gracefully, caught it up and went for Aylith, his reason and his sense completely given over to the rage.

Horrified, Jedhian watched as Aylith danced away from the broken blade, whirling and spinning in her cloak of light, her hands high above her head. Nazir relentlessly ran her around the courtyard. Lorris finally had to grab the Haenishman's collar to get him to move.

"Will you not use the time she has paid for, you idiotic light-dweller? I myself wish nothing more than to go after him here and now, but you would be killed if I left you to this mob. Come away, while this gang of butchers is otherwise entertained. Hurry!"

Lorris fairly lifted him along as she dashed for the inner bailey's gate, where the twins were gawking, slack-mouthed and transfixed, at Aylith's brilliant dervish dance.

Nazir swung the old sword with all his weight behind it, the blue fire arcing in great bolts all over the courtyard. Again, and again, he came at her, ignoring Malvos's bellows to stop, to take his tonic, to put down *that* sword. The Nohrlanders' hysteria now matched Nazir's, and fights broke out all over the mob's fringes.

Tiring, Aylith fought for her concentration to keep the magical weavework aloft, and moved steadily

toward the gate that Jedhian and Lorris had bolted
through. So far, Nazir had not so much as touched her.
Just a few more feet . . .

Nazir missed his mark yet again, and then gave a cry
of desperation and hatred. He closed his eyes, brought
the Clan Tree into focus in his mind, and charged one
last time, with every ounce of strength left to him, his
face a bestial grimace.

In that fierce blind rush, the power of Soulslayer
came to its fullest brilliance in his hand. He drove the
firesword directly through the bright green mantle,
shearing the glowing threads into blue sparks. As the
light mantle broke apart, Nazir bore down on her,
plunging the sword into Aylith just above the heart,
running her completely through. As the last bits of the
light-woven spell fluttered to the ground, revealing
what had happened, the crowd grew silent.

Nazir put his foot on Aylith's chest and pulled, free-
ing the sword, and shuddering in his red fury as she
swayed but refused to fall backward, to be dead.

Before blood could flow from the wound, before
Aylith could gasp for a breath, before the Nohrlanders
could utter a sound, a small barn owl alighted upon
her shoulder and dug its talons, one of them oddly
crippled, into the red-and-blue bhana. With ease and
silence, the owl took to the air and carried her up into
the night, past the torches, past the tower wall, past
the tower itself, over Lorris and Jedhian's heads, west-
ward, beyond Nazir's astonished, unseeing stare.

The tyrant froze for a moment, Soulslayer still glowing blue in his bloodless grip and outshining the torchlight, its slight humming the only sound in the silence.

Then Nazir threw back his head and howled, and the
crowd's frightened dumbness broke into a thousand
shrieks and quarrels. Malvos uttered an inaudible
curse, pulled on his gloves, freed himself of his helpers,

and waddled into the open area. The old Albions in the crowd, seeing their chance, quickly and easily overran the guards, their strength still far greater than the younger soldiers'.

Nazir swung the sword again and felled six of the mob, then on the backstroke took it through four or five more. He whirled around and around, like Aylith had, his anger continuing to wield the flame of the sword in great blue swathes all over the yard. A man in a red cap fell, and the Albions suddenly stopped their charge and ran to see to him. It was a massacre, and when at last Malvos could get close enough, he seized Nazir by the arm, stopping the next wave of death, while at their feet, more than thirty men and women—many of them slaves—lay dead amid a cold white brume, their bodies already frosted over with rime.

Malvos, with Nazir and Soulslayer in his formidable grip, teetered in midstep—even as two hack-ridden sailors bore down on him—to pick up something he saw from the corner of his eye: a glittering acorn lying on the flinty surface of the ground.

CHAPTER
16

AS THE OWL ROSE AND FLAPPED SILENTLY
into the deep darkness over Inys Nohr, Aylith lost consciousness, her wound bloodless from the freezing touch of Soulslayer, and drifted on the currents of troubled dreams. The owl flew her into the high thermals that would take them to Loch Prith. As they left Inys Nohr behind, the red-and-blue bhana fell from Aylith's shoulder and drifted down to the frozen moors. Feryar could not stop for it; he prayed she would not freeze to death before he could reach their destination. It was a journey of moments and a journey of years when Feryar flew, time twisted in upon itself somehow.

Aylith sank into her visions and watched as Nohr parted the clan; as Hankin, fifth from Nohr, brought forth the tower; as Jermin, seventeenth, sought the counsel of Malvos for the attack on Inys Haen that breached the first earthwork, still not completely repaired in Pamid's Reign of Blood, the twentieth, when all the prisoners of his taking swallowed poison in one afternoon.

She saw Quid, twenty-fourth, take his wife from a rebel Far clan where he left only the women alive, and only those with blond hair. She looked on as Belieal the Bald used Malvos, clean shaven, to set up the laboratory in the tower attic, and saw Crephas, Nazir's father, hunt down elves with an ancient longbow and create the first shroud from a spoonful of the moat, a patch of lint from a Haenish cloak, and the erratic, broken heartline of mana from the Clan Tree's crown.

And as they flew west, into warmer air that smelled of fish and deepwater kelp and thick salt mist, Aylith saw Thix viciously kill her mother, ignoring the woman's pleas, and set fire to her cottage. She watched as Nazir coldly ordered RoNal's flogging, and then whirl into his great sweep of destruction upon her rescue, the frozen faces of the Albion slaves staring up beseechingly.

Aylith started awake with a mighty jerk and nearly tore them from the sky, the owl's wings faltering, but not its viselike grip, a thousand feet above the craggy shoreline over Loch Prith, only a moment before they would need to land. Miraculously, he maintained his altitude, and they sailed into the gray dawning day without further injury. When his tawny wings touched the earth, the owl released the thrashing, feverwrought girl upon hard, clean sand, and regained his regular form.

Despite the rising tide, and the oncoming fury of a storm, Thrissa stood waiting, her long, white hair whipping about her shoulders, one hand pointing to a shimmering cloud rising from the beach a few steps away. She kissed him, and handed him a rain-spattered tunic, and kissed him again. A bolt of winter lightning crashed close enough to them to light the beach with its fire, making sudden, bubbling glass from the pure, white sand.

"She is come, Thrissa. The Mender is come. Now we must find a way to mend *her*," he said.

He quickly picked Aylith up and ran for the whirling, sparkling cloud, the only door to Loch Prith, Thrissa at his heels.

"Yes, my darling, we will," she shouted over the wind. "Nazir and his Sifter will soon be at work, searching for her, for the Memories she carries. I have seen this in my pools. My son is nearly taken by the curse already. We cannot save him without first saving her."

Thrissa looked around at the dark, cold world she rarely visited anymore. "Indeed, we cannot save anything." Another brilliant bolt flashed overhead and she dove through the glimmering portal before the thunderclap followed. Feryar shook with cold in the storm, but surrendered his cloak for the sky again. There was work yet at Inys Nohr.

Lorris kept running in the direction they had seen the owl take Aylith long after she thought they were safely away from the bloodthirsty crowd. Jedhian, several steps behind her, was having a bit of trouble keeping up, and when they rounded a corner, where there was an overhang large enough to shield them from view, he bade her to stop.

"We can't. The gate guards will be aware soon of what has happened. And don't think that crowd won't still want to have your head on a pike outside the gate."

"Lorris—it's not that I *want* to stop. I must."

He slumped to one knee and peeled away the bandage, now days old, from the wound he'd received fighting the Nohrish war party—Lorris's unit—and revealed what he had hoped was just a suspicion. The cottony plague fungus clung to the lifted bandage and stretched between it and his leg, *writhing*, walking, as RoNal had said. With his other hand, he touched behind his ear, torn while falling from the tower, but it felt clean.

"Ah, no . . . no. Not you." Lorris gasped as she examined the festering wound. "How long?"

"I began to feel it just before you came for me."

"Then there's still a chance. And it hasn't spread to your hurt ear," she said, pushing back his hair to see for herself. "But first, we must get out of the city."

She tore a strip of cloth from beneath her mail shirt and rewrapped Jedhian's infected leg. He hoisted himself upright, despite the pain, and hobbled after her as they slipped along the wall. There was only one sentry at the gate, Zell, a young man known for his exaggerations, and fast asleep at his onerous post; everyone else had drawn a better duty to see the show in the inner bailey. Lorris made sure that since he would wake up with a headache, he'd have a fine story to tell his commander for his unwilling cooperation.

She threw open the gates, and they hurried down one of the wharf streets, passing only a couple of old women haggling over a day-old eel, and found an over-turned fishing boat, in drydock for a scraping, by the looks of the hull. Lorris kicked the boat to scatter its complement of sea roaches.

"Get under here," said Lorris, checking constantly for followers.

Jedhian, beyond caring about the filth on the street, lay down beneath the old shell, the smell of eel grease and freshly dead kelpweed nearly finishing what the plague had started.

"Bring speedwell," he told her as his head disappeared under the battered craft.

Lorris made for the tower again, hoping that no one had seen her, or missed her, and that the real execu-tioner had yet to free himself from the leather bindings that secured him to Jedhian's cell door. When she passed the young sentry, he was still sleeping peace-fully. Lorris fairly ran, her chain mail annoyingly singing out her every stride. It was no wonder someone heard her approach.

"Hsst! Over here." A small voice called to Lorris from the dark shadows where Lorris and Feryar had meant to meet Aylith much earlier. Lorris drew her dagger and waited just beyond the darker cleft in the wall.

"Show yourself."

"I can't, sir. I'm wearin' a dress. I was hopin' you'd find me real clothes."

Lorris felt her expression go soft for the first time that day. "Arn, I'll get you some clothes. But first, come on out. Your masquerade isn't over."

"All right. You know what to do. Be quick, don't linger and get all ensorcelled by the things you see up there. You know how you are. Keep your head low and your voice high. Go. And grab some packs, too."

Lorris gave the boy a sharp pat on the back and sent him into the tower, hoping fervently that it wouldn't be the last time she saw him.

As he tried his best to walk like one of the serving girls, she suppressed a laugh and became aware of the knot of tension she had been holding in her shoulders. Shoulders. Arn's shoulder! It was straight—how in the name of Nohr, she wondered, had that happened? Aylith? If so, she wished with all her heart that the strange Haenish girl were here to help Jedhian now. She had acquitted herself well with Nazir; maybe she *was* a wizard, thought Lorris, remembering her half-joking question to the girl on the way to Inys Nohr. For someone so small and frail looking, the girl had proved to be nearly indestructible. Lorris feared she had gravely misjudged Aylith.

Her thoughts hung on the last word, and she cast a look toward the door where Arn had disappeared.

•   •   •

Up the great bleak staircase, tripping frequently in his
cumbersome new identity, tiptoed Arn, with all the
grace of a kirtled ox. But no one had paid him any
attention; most were still caught in the press outside.
Only a few older servants haunted the lower floor,
spinning wool and stories about things Nazir's grandfather had done to Haenishmen.

Malvos's room was on the right at the second landing. A large, ornately carved wooden door loomed over
Arn, and the boy never passed it without marveling at
the richness of the expensive, warm walnut and the
way it felt under his hand.

Someday, he would think, *I shall have a whole
house made of wood. And every bit of its furnishing
will be wood also. And I shall burn wood in the fire-
place!* Arn would send himself into hysterical laughter
at the prospect of such wealth.

There was a keyhole under the latch, the key, of
course, always on Malvos's belt. Arn pulled out the
bent eelhook that fastened his shoe and easily tumbled the lock. He slipped inside the vast, dark room
and took a deep breath of the only sweet air in all of
Inys Nohr. With a quick turn of the mechanism, the
lock was reset, and Arn could wander freely among
the batches of Haenish lavender, cords of rosemary,
clove-studded fruits, dried prickleberries, and sage.
All this and several things nameless to Arn hung from
rafters and spangled the walls in glorious colors and
scents.

Arn could have lost himself in this room, and had
nearly done so once. That was the day Nazir had found
him hiding in the barrel of thyme and the ruler had
thrown him up against the bare stone wall and broken
his frail, birth-twisted shoulder. Arn rubbed at the

slightly sore, newly repaired joint and swore by all the wood in the world that he'd do whatever it took to help Lorris and the sick Haenishman. For they were looking for Aylith, whose magic hands had healed him.

He walked straight over to the cabinet where the precipitates were kept, noticing several bottles of Nazir's special tonic easy to hand on the top shelf. Malvos always kept that stuff in stone jars. Arn suspected it would eat through anything less sturdy. The boy wondered what the tyrant would be like without regular dosing with that foul brew. Maybe worse, but he couldn't see how.

He grabbed several of the same tiny jars marked "speedwell," as Lorris had made him memorize the letters, and dropped them in his ample sleeve. Just then, he heard the massive walnut door swing open, and as he cleared the windowsill, saw Malvos, his concentration fixed on dragging Nazir, shaking, dazed, and still clutching the broken sword, into the room.

Lorris had already counted several times as high as she could go, and was now about to follow the boy into the tower, when he dropped quietly to the ground below Malvos's room, the wool dress billowing in blue folds about his ears.

"I got them. And Malvos has got Nazir. He didn't hear me. He wasn't lookin' for my noise. There was Albions behind him."

"Let's go," Lorris said, and Arn gathered his skirts up to run for it.

When Zell, the young sentry at the gate awoke, his story of what had transpired during his watch had improved. And so had Arn's wardrobe.

CHAPTER
17

NAZIR, THOUGH A BIT ON THE TALL SIDE for a Nohr, was never heavy, or at least had never seemed heavy, thought Malvos, until now. The apothecary hauled him into the room most unroyally and dumped him just inside the entry. He quickly threw the bolt on the wooden door, and not a moment too soon. Several straggling Albions had seen them in the bailey, and had followed, tearing through the hands of the guards to rage at the ruler for the deaths of their families.

While they banged hopelessly on his door, Malvos wondered, irritated, why the guards didn't already have them out at the block—and where in the name of Nohr was that speedwell? Nazir had taken a couple of scrapes as Malvos had hefted him through the hallway, and he wanted to get the skin closed on them immediately. Couldn't have the only man who could get him off Cridhe die from the walking plague.

All Malvos came up with was a bit from an old jar in the bottom of the case. But it would have to do. He could have sworn he'd put a new batch up a couple of weeks ago. And here was the tonic, too. He poured a generous draught of that and fed it to Nazir, who then came out of his fit coughing and gasping for breath.

In a few moments, when he could speak, Nazir focused his eyes and winced.

"Where am I? What happened?" he mumbled.

"Um, you are in my humble and unworthy quarters, most gracious, athletic, and daring of monarchs."

Nazir frowned at the apothecary, obviously not feeling any of those attributes at the moment.

"We are having a bit of medicine for you here," Malvos continued, his tone not quite so patronizing. "Some of your subjects are not appreciating you much at the moment."

"Why?" Nazir looked at him innocently.

"You remember . . . nothing?" Malvos said smoothly, his gloved hand easing the old sword under a pile of Haenish fennel.

Nazir shook his head; he obviously had not fully recovered from the rage.

"Well, my wondrous ruler, you—uh—killed some of their families and such. Mostly the older Albions, though, no loss, really. Fewer mouths to feed. I believe you even took down that troublesome Morkin." He grinned capriciously, showing too many of his foul, rotten teeth.

"Oh. Oh, very good." Then Nazir clambered hastily to his feet, remembering Aylith. "Where is the girl? What happened to her? Did you see her leave? Was that a bird that took her, or did she fly out of there herself? Does she still have the sacred seed? What happened to Merco? Where is the Haenishman?" He rapidly ticked off the questions without waiting for Malvos to answer any of them.

For once, the apothecary held his tongue. At Nazir's mention of the acorn, he had suddenly become distracted by the power of the prize he had picked up from the

courtyard ground. The Clan Tree's seed seemed to hum
and glow in his belt pouch. Its mana made him want to
hold it, let the fire course through his hands and body,
let his hungry heart feed upon it. But Tempé would
know instantly. Not yet, not yet. He couldn't touch the
acorn, but he had it. One more piece of his plan to get
out of Cridhe. And if he could get Nazir to leave this
tower and go to Inys Haen, he had the rest of it handily
tied up, too. Malvos violently tore his thoughts from the
acorn's power and made himself pay attention to Nazir.

The Felonarch sway back and forth on unsteady feet,
then caught his balance, and taking another long drink
of the tonic, he strode to the window.

"I know I saw her fly out of here. Where is she now?
I can't feel her presence at all. What if she's dead?" he
said to himself, touching the birthmark as he surveyed
the decaying city below.

Malvos cleared his throat and finally offered a reply.
"Would Your Excellency like to send troops to follow,
or shall you go yourself?" Malvos noticed absently that
the Albions seemed to have been removed; they no
longer pounded on his door.

Nazir hesitated a moment, searching the streets and
the bailey visible from Malvos's window. He seemed to
remember a riot of sorts, and Malvos had just said that
the Albions were openly up in arms, but he now heard
nothing from behind Malvos's door and outside: no
sight of anyone; no noise, either. Perhaps Malvos had
exaggerated most of the killing. Surely there would be
more reaction from the discontented populace than he
could find from this vantage point. If the city were this
quiet, maybe the guards had quelled the minor upris-
ing; perhaps now the Albions were afraid of him too
much to react openly. He seemed to remember killing a
man in the red cap . . . and, of course, they were angry
about RoNal. Yes. That was it. He had killed their

secret leader, beheaded the entire movement, and now they had run to hide. The Albionic rebellion was over in Inys Nohr.

Another thought then struck Nazir. Maybe they would never notice if he went on the search party and left no one here to keep the tower. After all, if Malvos, with his phenomenal sense of hearing, led the search, then everyone would assume Nazir naturally to be back at Inys Nohr. Perfect.

He checked the far horizon for evidence of activity, for fires, and for the snarl of a hungry mob. Nazir blinked and turned to Malvos, finally answering.

"March toward Inys Haen. It's the only place she could be. And my guess is, we'll find the Haenishman there, too. Have somebody find Merco. Use his own instruments to find out what he knows. Get Feryar to call troops together, if he can find his face."

"As Your Eminence prefers. Only, could I not stay behind here and prepare the medicines, keep order in the city, and so forth for you until your joyous and triumphant return?" Malvos was positively twitching at the thought of his plan working so perfectly.

"No, you will go also. I have need of you, and so may that girl. If she lives." Nazir had also recovered enough to realize the peril of leaving Malvos anywhere, in charge of anything. Nazir would never get the hulking slug out of his chair if he left him in the city alone.

Malvos pretended to sulk, but unlatched the door and made for Feryar's quarters. He had not seen the old elf since the riot. He complained gloriously to himself all the way to the end of the hall, swung open the door to the elf's sparse room without knocking, and called distractedly for him.

There was no sign of the addled old fool. How very inconvenient and how very typical. The elf was profoundly dense, especially for one of his kind, and

Malvos hated having to explain everything again and
again. Over several hundred years, it got to be tedious.
Even to a Sangrazul. And then there was all that nasty
business with Thrissa. He hoped the old fool didn't
think he'd forgotten the broken nose.

Malvos caught his breath at another sudden intru-
sion of mana in his senses. Oh, to have it, to have it in
his very hands, to touch the power and absorb its
energy.

Malvos closed his eyes and tried to regain his purpose. Feryar. Yes. Now where was the idiot, anyway?
Probably down in the pantry, Malvos reasoned. The
pantry was the answer to most of the more important
questions, he continued to himself, and promptly
decided to go there.

The acorn sparkled in its velvet pouch. It would be a
long journey home; *longer even than you suspect, my
perfidious puppet of a prince, my manipulated man-
nequin,* he mused. Malvos was positively starved.

On the ledge outside his window, Feryar finally
breathed. The Albion he had found listening at
Malvos's door, Sims, looked over to him gratefully,
and dropped back into the room. Feryar followed, his
long finger across his lips in warning. The Sifter was
not yet out of range. Sims just smiled and slipped out
the door, disappearing into the tower's stonework like
secret water.

CHAPTER

18

LORRIS THREW BACK THE BARNACLE-
encrusted hull of the small boat and found Jedhian
passed out, part of his shirt clenched in his teeth.

"So he wouldn't cry out," she said to herself, inter-
preting the scene. She knelt, raised him to her shoulder
and braced his back.

"Jedhian, come you now, sit, and take this. You
know what to do with it, and I don't."

She gently shook him, and his eyes, wet with tears
and bloodshot from the pressure of his silence, blinked
open. He gasped and released the shirttail from his
teeth, taking several huge, controlled breaths, still trying not to make much noise. Not that it would have
mattered. All around them, people shied away, hugging
the sides of the buildings and moving quickly, some
with torches—having come from the inner bailey—
some with nets gathered up from the wharves, some
with nothing in their hands but their anger. No one
seemed to recognize the Haenishman as he worked the

medicinal paste into the cut on his leg, the soldier tending him and the boy, also dressed in mail shirt and greaves, standing by with a broadsword as big as he was. Too much else was afoot in this part of town. It made Lorris a bit nervous, and she hailed one of the fishermen passing and asked him what was his urgency.

"Nothin' at'all, sir. We're making plans for a great many burials," he said cagily, his eyes never meeting hers.

Then she realized she must look like she still served Nazir, and that he would tell her nothing. She let him go. But it gave her another thought.

"Jedhian, we have to leave right now. I don't like the smell of this place; there's too much business here and nothing seems very normal to me. If these people are about to try something against Nazir, we'd better be gone. We'll be taken as his loyal subjects, and that would mean they'd see you lose your head today, after all. And ours with it. So finish there, and Arn and I will support you."

"Lorris?"

She looked into his fevered eyes. "Yes."

"Where are we going? I can't walk yet, and we have to find Aylith. Before Nazir."

She hadn't quite thought it through that far, but when he spoke, she knew instantly what to do.

"Arn, help him to his feet." The boy did so, and then Lorris overturned the boat, checking for holes in the bottom. "We'll go as far as we can upriver in this, if we can find an oar. When the Sobus is frozen beyond moving, we'll walk, you with the oar. Your leg will be better by then, anyway. That should give us a bit of a start on Nazir. I know he'll send troops out to Inys Haen again. It's the only place Aylith could be."

Jedhian smiled and scratched at his scruffy beard.

"That will do nicely. And I think the speedwell is starting to work. I can't feel the plague walking anymore."

He rubbed more of the green goo into the cut on his leg and wrapped it with a cloth strip Lorris had torn from the dress Arn had gifted to the unconscious gateman.

They moved nonchalantly out from the alley, Lorris and Arn portaging the old boat, Jedhian, his face covered with his cloak, limping alongside it, his hand upon the upturned hull for support. They almost made it to the wharf.

"Hey! That be Donnon's craft, eh? Whar ye goin' wiv it?"

Jedhian slapped the hull, and Lorris and Arn took off at a full run, leaving him to explain. He turned toward a puzzled fisherman and shuffled painfully up to the doorway of the nearby shack.

"Yes. Donnon has lent it to us for a bit." He smiled, but the soot-faced fisherman eyed him the more closely, scowling.

"Donnon be dead three day now. Whar ye going wiv his boat? Hey, ain' you that Haenish—?"

"Yes, I am," Jedhian said softly as he suddenly closed his grip on a nerve in the old man's thin, outstretched arm, the ensuing pain dropping him unconscious in his doorway. "That won't hurt for long, I promise."

He rolled the slack form into the hovel and started slowly off in the direction the boat had gone, down to the river.

Lorris had found an oar and had the craft in the water when he got there. Arn had met up with him several yards into his awkward journey and hastened his progress.

Jedhian smiled engagingly at her. "I have never sailed before."

Lorris helped him into the boat while Arn held the

side of the craft steady. "Neither have I," she said, grinning back at him.

"I have," offered Arn timidly from his place at the dock. Clearly, he hadn't supposed they would take him along.

Lorris leaned forward and touched his hand. "Please hurry, Arn. Hop in and push us off."

The boy's smile seemed to drape both his protruding ears. He deftly boarded the little boat, poling them away from the wharf and past the weathered fishing shacks, then rowed them along the mouth of the Sobus with all the expertise he had promised.

In an hour's time, they had navigated the river up to the narrows, a winding passage that hardly ever froze, its current too strong and its depth never plumbed. Two or three people a year drowned in the narrows while fishing, but their bodies were almost never recovered. Lorris thought there must be trolls or some sort of spirit under the gray, racing waters, but Arn told her it was caverns.

Jedhian took a chill there, and both Arn and Lorris had to give him their cloaks. Arn bumped the little craft off a sharp granite boulder in midstream, and Lorris caught a bit of spray.

"Whew! That's really icy. How much farther do you think until it's all frozen over, Arn?" she gasped.

"I don't know—another mile or two at best. It's turning to slush very fast," he replied, frowning as he held up an ice-shackled oar for her to see.

Lorris nodded and pushed the cloaks up around Jedhian's chin. She brushed back his tawny hair and touched his face gently. He opened his eyes and looked up at her for an instant, then shook violently again with a chill.

"Arn, we've got to stop and get him warm. Us, too. Find a place to beach and I'll find something to burn.

We have to risk the fire, even though Nazir will be scouting for us. Maybe some of these rocks will help hide the light and smoke," she said as she glanced around at the imposing granite that formed the Sobus's banks on this part of the island.

A light snow had begun to fall when they finally found a suitable landing and beached the boat. Lorris struck out alone and scratched up some fairly good kindling out of a bit of dry grass. Also, to her great surprise and profound relief, she found some very old, dry driftwood in an eddy wash upriver from their camp.

She had had a gruesome time of it picking through the mingled, gnawed bones of mountain lynx and ribworm, stray goat and sheep that had been beached in the wash. The river gave up her dead with no respect to species. There had been a human skull, too.

Lorris looked at the long tooth marks on a sheep's leg bone. Makana. The great lizardlike creatures, oblivious to cold, ghostly white, and able to move underground like eels in the ocean, had also been the creation of Crephas. Like the shrouds, makanas now roamed the lower elevations unchecked, no natural predator taking down their populations. Though they ate mostly carrion, they preferred anything that moved, homing in on the prey's heat with their acute sense of temperature.

Warily tossing down the sheep's bone, Lorris shifted the driftwood in her arms, gathered up the human skull, and set it up in a hidden cleft between the rocks, out of reach from the makana. They could tunnel, but they could not climb.

"Rest, my friend. Be hidden in your death, and be glad you do not live under the tyrant any longer." She sighed, then trudged back to the camp.

Arn had spread himself over Jedhian in order to share his warmth, and when Lorris arrived, he gave her the duty and instead tended the small fire that would keep the Haenishman alive through the night. Lorris lay behind Jedhian, with her arms around the shivering Haenishman, holding his icy hands in hers.

He is so well made, she thought as she fitted her chin over his shoulder. She traced the hollow of his scruffy cheek with her eyes and noticed with alarm that his face had grown thinner; in fact, it now very much resembled the skull she had found in the eddy wash. The plague was eating him alive, taking his flesh in the fever, and there was nothing to feed him. Arn's stomach, used to catching its fill only now and then, had made no complaint, but Lorris now began to feel the pinch herself, and knew that Jedhian would not survive without nourishment.

The hollow eyes of the river-drowned skull suddenly stared back at her. She longed for the food she had stashed for her original plan. She had even had to leave RoNal's sword behind. But enough of what was not.

"I'm going hunting. Or fishing. We've got to have some food. Maybe I can get something to make him a broth," she said as she tucked the cloaks back around Jedhian.

She started to take her sword, but Arn shook his head. He bent down and gathered several of the smooth river rocks from near the fire, took out of piece of leather from his pouch, and offered the sling to her.

"You'll get more wi' this, sir. And I'll fish while yer gone."

Lorris smiled at him, thinking what a mistake it would have been to leave him behind.

"Arn, what about your shoulder? It's straight now," she asked curiously.

"Oh . . . well, the Haenishwoman saw it the way it was supposed to be. And when she touched it, this green fire burned into me, only it didn't hurt, and then my shoulder was fixed," he said simply.

"'Saw it the way it was supposed to be'? And it healed? Just like that?" Lorris marveled.

Arn shook his head and stirred the fire up. "No. The twisting went fast. But the hurt Nazir done me wouldn't go away right off. I wanted to be well bad, though, bad enough to stop thinking about how he enjoyed hurting me. And when I forgot that, she remembered my shoulder right. She done the magic, eh? But I knew I had to help with the last part. Somehow I just knew," he said, still looking into the fire.

Lorris nodded, and took the sling from his outstretched hand.

It had been a long time indeed since RoNal had denied Lorris supper until she knocked off the piece of bread he had tacked on a pole several yards away. Lorris had learned her marksmanship very quickly and very well. She did not like to be hungry.

Her hobnailed boots made odd tracks in the inch or two of powdery snow as she quietly made her way north from their camp. The clouds shifted and flowed overhead, a grayer version of the river's face. Cridhe had seen no moon since the Parting, except for when the Haenish made spring appear. Then the clouds rolled back over Inys Haen and exposed a glorious night sky, with stars burning brightly by the uncountable numbers. Lorris had seen them once, when they reached the outlying marshes of Inys Haen and had been a day or two late for the spring raid. She remembered some of the constellations: the wolf, the two fishes, the open book, and the hunter, her favorite. His bright bow gleamed with a green star and three red ones. She wondered what it would be like to use a bow. There had never been enough wood on Cridhe for archery since the Parting.

She made herself look away from the cloud-covered vault. Her attention needed to be on the ground, where there should be tracks. She saw some from a weasel, probably very far from here by now, and a few mice and thatch hens. Thatch hen stew would be very good for Jedhian. She turned in their direction and crept up to a mound of bracken, loosely covered by the new snow. *Two or three of the hens in this nest will do nicely,* she thought.

Lorris knelt, loaded the sling, and whistled shrilly. The nest exploded in a flurry of black wings as two small hens took to the air. Lorris brought down the first one easily and winged the second, thinking she could have done better with practice. She retrieved the first creature and trussed its four feet, hung it on her belt, and went after the second hen. She found its limping tracks, then sighted the hen and bounded over a small saddle between two hillocks after it. Another stone brought it down, and Lorris strode happily toward Jedhian's dinner.

One more foot closer and she would have been someone else's dinner. Out of its lair, no more than a furrow in the ground camouflaged by the snowfall, rose a snarling makana, probably the one who claimed the river eddy as its territory, its teeth snapping within inches of Lorris's feet, its great wedge-shaped head shaking off the snow to reveal two small red eyes. It fixed those eyes, even though they were blind, upon Lorris, and its reptilian claws lunged and scraped her greaves, leaving long bright gashes in the bronze. She nearly dropped the second hen, but managed to snatch it up again and ran crashing through the rock-strewn headland back toward camp.

The makana was in no mind to let her reach it. It powered under the ground, raising a ridge behind it, like a mole. Lorris swore as she slipped in an icy spot while rounding a large boulder, only yards ahead of the irritated beast. She found her feet just before the makana surfaced and closed on one of them, and finally made her way to some tall rocks, where the makana could not follow. It keened and grumbled below for awhile, but eventually trotted off after a mouse that had scurried out of hiding when Lorris had disturbed the rocks.

By then, Lorris had another problem. She was lost. The makana had chased her farther in from the river than she had noticed. Even from this height, the twists and turns of the nearly frozen Sobus were now hidden under the deepening layer of new snow and the tall headlands that banked the old rift. She sat for a moment, mentally retracing her steps, plucking the gray and black feathers of the thatch hens and listening for sounds of the returning makana.

When she had finished cleaning both birds, she hung them over one shoulder and began to descend the thirty feet of slick, snow-dusted granite that had saved her life and restored her bearings. She looked around one last time, thinking that it was now so dark that she might be able to see Arn's fire from that height. Off to the left, a mile or two behind where she had reasoned Arn and Jedhian to be waiting, something did seem to be burning, the red glow staining the darkness weakly. But as Lorris looked harder, she saw that it was not just one fire, but three.

Nazir's troops were upon them, and even more quickly than she had imagined. Lorris scrambled down the rock pile without heed to whether or not the makana had found enough to eat, and raced over the ground where her tracks showed faintly under the drift of the shifting, blowing snow. The wind had picked up and it looked like the snowfall was getting heavier. She lost her way once, but caught sight of the river and made for camp by way of its freezing course.

Arn startled only a little as she walked quietly up on their camp and whispered her news. He nodded and began to butcher the hens, having spent his time well, also—there were a couple of eels on a flat rock in the middle of the fire, roasted and ready to eat. Lorris peeled one of them off the slab and tried not to think about the flavor of the meat; it would keep her alive. When she had choked most of it down, Arn returned with the hens and added them to the bake stone.

Jedhian groaned in his fever, and Arn rearranged his cloaks.

"He does seem some better, sir. I think being still has helped. So will this meat, if we can get it down him. I couldn't find nothin' to make soup in," the boy apologized.

"Thank you, Arn." Lorris rubbed her temples and took off her greaves and gauntlets. The metal armor had become intolerable in the dropping temperature. "You did a good job."

Arn grinned back at her, his ears and nose gone red either from the cold or the compliment, Lorris could not tell which.

"We have to get moving in a couple of hours. Those troops will be on the quick march if I know Nazir, and we have to make it to Inys Haen before them. It will be very close as it is, but I think we have a little gain for now. Surely he won't be leading them himself—he never leaves the tower."

Lorris calculated, and Arn took in the details with the practice of listening to Nazir's once given, life-threatening commands.

"How much farther do you think we can use the boat?" she asked him.

"The river is fast gone to slick, sir. I don't know. Perhaps we can use the pole to break it up if it ain' too thick, and move that way. It's slow, but still faster than overland wi' the Haenishman," Arn replied.

"I can make it however I must," Jedhian's voice cut in, surprising both of them with its strength.

He sat up and yawned like he'd been asleep in his own bed, and gratefully took the hen leg Arn immediately shoved in his hand. Lorris could not conceal her relief and gave him a glorious smile, her gray eyes dancing. She really was rather pretty when she wasn't brooding, he thought.

"Jedhian, you—you are healed?" she asked, amazed.

"Well," he said, laughing, "not thoroughly. The speedwell has stopped the spread of the plague and broken the fever. I feel a little weak, but I'm going to live," he finished, pleased by her reaction. "Where are we?" he added, biting into the stringy fowl.

"We are too far from Inys Haen and too close to Inys Nohr," offered Arn.

"We've come a few miles," said Lorris, pointing to the beached craft. "Nazir's troops are close by, and we must be moving as soon as you can manage." She sighed.

"Aylith?"

Lorris shook her head. "You know what we know."

Jedhian finished the hen leg and gulped a great swallow from the hollow of a broken geode Arn had found and filled with melting snow. Its crystal lining gleamed purple and blue in the firelight as Jedhian drained the odd cup again and again.

"Let's go," he said, rising unsteadily.

Arn broke camp and had the area detailed by the time Lorris had Jedhian situated in the boat. They cast off, poling through the rime-frosted, thick-skinned water, Arn breaking their path more often than not and taking the turns in the widening Sobus with ever more difficulty. It became obvious, three miles up, that they would have to abandon the boat and walk.

Lorris beached the craft, turning it on its side to shelter them from the falling snow. They huddled under it together, making themselves as warm as possible, hoping the small gain they'd made by going on was enough to arrive before the Nohrish army. They decided against a fire. The headlands had dropped their elevation and the moors spread out from the river in open land. If Nazir's army had sent scouts ahead, they would spot a fire in no time.

Tomorrow would be a hard push. But for now, they had to rest. Lorris took first watch, her arms around Jedhian, and her ears pricked for any odd sound. She passed the next three hours fighting to stay awake and fighting to put her feelings for the young healer out of her mind.

He was Haenish. She was not. It would never be possible. And the last thing she needed was a distraction. After all, their safety depended on her alertness.

That was the last thought she had before Arn, who had not been able to sleep anyway, tucked the cloak more snugly around her, loosed the sword from her hand, and took over the watch.

CHAPTER
19

OVER THE NEXT TWO DAYS, JEDHIAN CON-
tinued to improve, and his wound was closing well, the
cottony plague all but gone from his leg. He thought
that perhaps it was the kind of thing you could wear
out if you lived through it and had a bit of help. And
the right place to be. Inys Nohr had all the wrong
humors about it for recovery. No wonder everyone
who contracted the plague there died.

They managed to stay far enough ahead of Nazir's
troops to make Lorris more comfortable about their
progress. The time had passed without further trouble;
the driving snow had obliterated their tracks behind
them. She had come to raid once before via the Sobus
and knew how long it should be taking them. The
evening before they should see the clanhold, she called a
halt and made camp early, and Arn hauled out another
thatch hen he'd brought down earlier that day. They dug
a pit in the peaty soil, which never entirely froze there,
thinking they could chance a fire long enough to cook.

"What will you tell them about me when we get there?" asked Lorris as Jedhian applied more of the speedwell to his leg.

He smiled up at her, his blue eyes searching her face. "That you saved my life. That you brought me home. That you hate Nazir as much, or maybe more, than they do."

She dropped her eyes and bit the edge of her full lower lip. "But I was part of the war party that killed the Keeper and some of their kin—and burned their homes. And took Aylith. Won't they want to put me to the sword on sight?"

"Some of them might. But you are the only person, besides me, who might be able to find Aylith if she isn't there already. You know this country. Most Haenishmen have never ventured beyond the light. They would not risk her life by taking yours. And now, sweet Lorris, you are also a deserter of the Felonarch's finest, so that will help," he answered.

She sat dumbfounded for a moment at the warm affection in his reply, but then the plainer truth of it struck her. "Yes, I suppose I am a traitor. My father would not be proud."

"Your father told me that you owe the Felonarch nothing."

She nodded. "It is true that I have not yet pledged. But won't your people assume I am a spy? There are many lives at stake if they trust me."

"Lorris. Remember when I had climbed the tower and it was your watch, I was not 'already dead.' You had a life at stake then, too. Your father was a brave and honorable man. He gave himself up to that monster in order to save me, and told me to take you from Inys Nohr if I could. Well, you took me, it turns out. There are good people in every clan; bad ones, too."

Finally Lorris smiled back at Jedhian, and he took her scarred hand in his.

Across from them, Arn turned the hen on the rock in the fire pit and eyed them, chuckling. *They don't even know*, he thought. *But plain as yer old gray shirt, they're in love.*

The gradual, faint lightening that was day brought an end to the snowfall. After a couple of hours on the trail, Arn smelled the peat fires of Inys Haen, their smoke rising on the wind.

"Phew! What do you folk burn there?" He gagged.

Lorris cuffed his ear and bade him hurry on. Jedhian had become more and more able the closer he came to home, hoping desperately that Aylith would be there. He had thought again and again what he might use to treat her wound once they arrived.

Jedhian would never forget the look on her small, pale face when Nazir's sword had slashed through her magical ribbons of light and caught her on its blade. Her eyes had gone unfocused, as though she saw something from within, not the enraged man on the other end of the magical weapon. Jedhian had nightmares about that moment. And the healer in him warred with the hunter whenever he thought of Nazir.

Lorris touched his hand as they climbed over the last hill before the clanhold, and Jedhian silently motioned for them to stop. Something was very wrong. By now, someone should have seen them coming and skated across the Sobus, well frozen here, and greeted them. A chill creeping up his spine, Jedhian instantly dropped to the ground, dragging Lorris, who dragged Arn down in succession.

She sought his eyes with a question in hers. He shook his head and listened.

The thornwall looked exactly like it had when he left; the gate still wide and gaping. The burned huts were draped in snow, their charred sides mercifully covered in white. But Jedhian could see no movement

inside the clanhold. And no footprints. It had been
snowing for days, but had stopped long enough for the
new fall to be marked with the daily activity of a village.
A great tension surrounded the place, and he could feel
it in the pounding of his heart. He squeezed Lorris's
hand, silently telling her to stay with Arn, and was
about to go down alone, when suddenly Arn gasped
and pointed to the northeast, where a column of Nazir's
black-clad troops marched toward Inys Haen.

Malvos rolled his eyes and plodded onward, the young
man at his right yammering incessantly about the time
before when he raided Inys Haen, and what had really
happened the other day when his commander had
found him wearing a dress in the gatehouse, the fugi-
tives having escaped under his sleeping nose. Zell had
guessed that was why they'd given him this duty, and
on and on.

Malvos had long since ceased hearing the words, the
man's voice a drone like the swell of Plavian bees. It
had been several hundred years since he had walked
this road, the last time just after the Parting had
occurred, and he had gone with old Nohr off to found
the shelter that had eventually become the stronghold.
He had been fit and healthy then. That trip, though
uphill, had been as nothing to him. Not so now. The
pain of bearing his massive weight was telling on him.
His feet hurt to the point of numbness, and yet Nazir
insisted, from his position back in the company, that
they push forward "with all due speed and resolve."

The tyrant had chosen to march as one of the common troops, putting Malvos in the vanguard. And
Malvos knew why. This cumbersome little army would
have to move through the territory recently plundered
by Nazir's raiding parties. Several of the clanholds,

made up of refugees from Inys Nohr and the occasional
escaped prisoner, had been torched and rifled, but their
inhabitants had run off in advance or hidden without
putting up a fight. And so they were primed for a bit of
silly revenge, having nothing left to lose, and thinking
that, if they survived the attack, they would be remembered forever as the ones who brought down the great
Nazir, Felonarch of all Inys Nohr. Fame was a powerful
prize for the nameless, the homeless, the hopeless. So
Nazir was safe while Malvos was leading the army.

This very uncomfortable revelation had made
Malvos think all the harder about the precious acorn
safely tucked into his belt pouch. One thing saved
Malvos's humor: they were marching toward the only
place, according to the Haenish prophecy, where the
Mending could occur. And who knew when the
equinox would be upon them again? It could happen
any time.

As they met a bend in the Sobus, at the end of the
high road the raiding party had taken just weeks
before, Malvos halted the weary troops, waddled out in
front on a promontory, quieted his mind, and listened.
He did not like what he heard. Which was nothing
much at all.

Below, Inys Haen lay curled in the hollow of its glen,
smoke rising from one of several of the chimneys
where the huts were still intact and habitable. But
there were no children laughing. There was no group
of elders gathered and shouting about retrieving their
Keeper's daughter. Perhaps the thickening blanket of
snow muffled the sound. Perhaps.

"Command the troops to halt and make camp," he
said as he returned to the loose-tongued soldier.

Zell was now a courier. He called out the order
immediately, never bothering to turn his head, catching
Malvos's ear directly in his strongest volume. Malvos

clutched his head and bellowed at the man, and Zell turned around this time, unfazed, and shouted his command again. He ran down the long line of men, stopping only to pick up a red-and-blue bhana that lay partly covered in the snow.

When the young man reached Nazir, the ruler pulled up his hood, threw down his pack, seized the bhana from Zell, and made his way forward to see why the apothecary had called for such a strange action; it was early in the day, and they were nearly upon the place. What could possibly make the Sifter stop now?

"They're not there," came the reply inside the quick shelter thrown up for Malvos.

"What do you mean, they're not there? Of course, they're there. Where could they have gone?" Nazir snapped, his words collapsing into a coughing fit.

Malvos took out a small stone bottle from his pouch and offered it to Nazir, who snatched it violently and poured its contents down his throat. He sat back, his face red, and his hands clutching at the birthmark. Aylith was not near, to be sure. The pain he felt from the mark now was normal, merely aggravated by the cold. In fact, the closer they had come to Inys Haen, the less it had burned in that particular way that told of her proximity. He had not wanted to think about the reason that could be. If she were dead, then so were his chances of retrieving the light spell. And so was he, for that matter. He pulled his cloak tighter. There was nothing much to burn out here; the boy was probably still looking for the fire.

"We have encountered no resistance so far, most honored campaigner, and it may be that the Haenish have likewise fled before us, our showing is so mighty," Malvos purred, trying to distract Nazir's attention from trouble. The potion was dwindling, and it looked like there would be greater need for it later, when and if he encountered the girl again.

"Yes, I have considered that. Malvos, is it always this cold out here?"

He shivered, his face turning a little blue now that he wasn't marching, or quite so angry. He examined the red-and-blue bhana in his lap and stroked it, examining the weave. Clouded images of Aylith's hands appeared in his mind, her long, tapered fingers at the loom, her quick pass of the shuttle to and fro. But there were no clues of her whereabouts on the bhana. It was as if it had dropped from the sky. He ripped it to shreds in frustration and pushed it into Malvos's pack.

"You are asking me? But of course you are, you have only once been out of the stronghold." Malvos pointedly did not add, "that you would recall," thinking of that throttled tinker from long ago. "Yes, they tell me it is, when the Haenish allow the winter."

Nazir rubbed his hands together through the leather gloves and stared out the leeward side of the hastily erected shelter. Nothing but snow. As if there was no Inys Nohr, no Inys Haen, no curse, no past.

No future.

CHAPTER
20

JEDHIAN EDGED BACK DOWN THE HILLOCK;
Arn and Lorris waited at the bottom.

"Now what?" she asked, brushing the snow from her cloak.

"Well, there's someone down there, keeping that peat fire going. I'm going in. You come one at a time when you see me wave. Something's not right down there," said Jedhian.

"Be careful." Lorris winced.

After a dream that followed another and another, Aylith heard Feryar's song blending and mingling with the swell of the Memories' own music. In her fever, she saw Jedhian at Inys Haen, and walked and talked with him in the sunlit days of their childhood, and there Logan appeared and silently smiled at her before he joined a sandy-haired man with the bushy white brows of a Keeper, and then faded from her sight.

She saw the budding of branches and the bursting of

bloom, and the mighty rush of plum blossoms on the high spring winds. The salmon had leapt in his urgent mating and the crookspider had spun webs of gold lace in the deep forest, where iridescent moths tangled themselves in death dances that created new life. Wispy purple motes floated in the lavender-scented breeze, the castoff flowers of the forest's greenest season. They lingered on the still, warm air, whirling at the slightest current of breeze, finally falling to earth, lightly frosting every bush, every stone, in what looked like a summer snowfall.

Then Aylith woke up. The ripple of a small stream invaded her thoughts and she raised her head, only to bring on a pain that nearly made her black out yet again. Slowly, with every movement taking her utmost concentration, she turned her head to the side where the stream gurgled, and then rested for a moment before trying anything else as taxing. She brought her hand up carefully and felt the wound on her chest, where Nazir's unexpected lunge had driven his sword through her, leaving her impaled for a moment on the unbearably cold blade, suspended between heaven and earth, like a broken puppet. She remembered Nazir's enraged, distorted features, his glowering anger erupting from hard eyes—eyes that despised defeat.

Just now, she felt the wound beginning to close under her lightly probing fingers, the flesh covering the sundering of bone and blood, skin beginning to stitch itself over the gaping hole.

And sealing in the poison that Nazir's sword had borne. The pain in her head abated, but a new one in her chest, just above her heart, where her fingertips lay, drove into her with astounding power. It felt as though something heavy, with cruel claws and a slavering mouth, were sitting on her rib cage, hungry and impatient for her to give in and die.

"Jedhian? Are you here? I need your medicines," she whispered, the breath to speak costing all her energy, and the sudden surge of raw hatred she felt for Nazir making her gag. Black bile roiled in her stomach and the searing injustice of her plight leapt before her eyes in all its acute and horrible detail.

She should never have been given the Memories. *Logan did this to me,* she thought. *I hurt all over now because of him. I am not, not the Mender.*

And there was more, the words she found for her pain seeming to drag out a heavy chain of linked injustices. Logan had betrayed her, but so had all the rest. Her mother had deserted her, choosing what she must have known would assure her death instead of staying with Aylith in the cottage the day of the equinox, when Nazir's raiders had come. RoNal had saved and then enslaved her. And where was Jedhian? He had run off with Lorris, and now she'd probably never see him again.

Lorris. Her "sister." What folly. The woman cared only for her own skin, and had probably sold Jedhian back to Nazir. Lorris and the elf had let her face Nazir in the bailey alone. They had as good as given Nazir their consent to do this to her. And what about that owl? He had crushed her shoulder, had taken her against her will in a terrifying flight she had never consented to. All of their faces rose up before her eyes, mocking her in her pain, laughing at her peril.

She pitched forward and clawed at the air, trying to summon substance to all their images, to tear them to pieces, to rend them as they had rent her body and her heart, destroyed her life, despised it, abandoned it. She hated them all, but Logan's gift was the worst of all.

"What treachery do fathers breed?" she tried to howl, her lips never forming the words.

Thrissa heard her scream and came to her side, a

warm cloth in her hand. She dabbed at Aylith's fevered face and hushed her raving with sweet elven tones.

"No, dear, be easy. I am Thrissa, the Prophetess of Loch Prith. You are here with us, brought by Feryar, my husband. We will heal you if we can. You are safe; Nazir cannot see you here, nor can he find this place. Not even Malvos can find you here." The elf woman bent low to Aylith's ear, speaking in music, in harmonies no human voice could produce.

Aylith came out of her rage and slowly sat up; immediately, there came two attendants to help her.

"We must begin the baths, now. There is no time to lose," said Thrissa gently. "This is Ruka. And to your left is Portis."

Aylith thought for a moment she was still in the fever dream. Her two attendants were the oddest looking creatures she had ever encountered. Ruka seemed to be human, but she had wings, the same color, Aylith realized with horror, as the giant moth body hanging in Nazir's tower room. Portis's delicate elven features were green, her hair replaced with tiny heart-shaped leaves.

"They were brought some time ago from Inys Nohr, Aylith, like you. They are some of the survivors of Crephas's experiments with the torn magic of the Clan Tree."

Aylith recalled what Lorris had told her about the owl in the night sky, always flying west, with strange creatures in his grasp.

"I thought Lorris was making those things up. Where am I? Is this . . . ?"

"Loch Prith. You had come to think this place was imaginary, too, I know," Thrissa said, laughing. She noticed the unspoken questions forming on Aylith's face. "What else, dear? You may ask."

"Is Feryar . . . a bird? An owl. Was that Feryar?" said Aylith.

"Yes. Some of us have more than one form." She smiled. "It is a shape that suits him well, don't you think?" Thrissa said, humming.

There was something very, very familiar about the prophetess. Aylith studied Thrissa's oval face, her silvery hair, the arch of her brow. There was no guessing her age. It seemed that same face had smiled upon her another time, long ago. And the voice . . .

"You are the elven woman who visited our village when I was a child, Aylith remembered, suddenly recognizing her.

Thrissa's blue eyes danced. "Yes. And I told you stories of this place. And you and your cousin, of all the children who heard my songs, believed. I knew who you were even then, child. I had a dream when I was at Inys Nohr, when my—when Nazir was crowned. I had to come and see you for myself, and then make my way to Loch Prith to prepare for this time. I read the Maker's sacred words and pictures as they appear on the Gwylfan's loom. That is where, so long ago, I read of the Mender. It has been a long wait."

Aylith let Ruka and Portis take her arms. The prophetess was compelling. Aylith saw no reason to resist.

"All right. I believe you. I'm ready for whatever is next."

Ruka and Portis led her to a high, vaulted cavern, filled with a bright, soft light. She was immersed in warm seawater, made to float in it for some time, despite the incredible sting of the salt upon her healing wound. They rinsed her, and then moved her on to another bath of fragrant oil, and another of cool fresh water. The gash on her chest began to further draw, the smaller one on her back to knit even more quickly. Aylith felt sore, as though she had used her arm too much, like at spawning time, when she helped Logan lift the heavy nets, or haul the baskets of produce in from the fields during harvest.

Ruka clothed her in a soft, warm tunic, made of a fabric that Aylith had never seen before.

"Cottonum," answered Portis, seeming pleased that she had asked. "We grow it here. It is soothing to the injured flesh."

They fed her. Constantly. Fruits and breads made from many grains, things Aylith could not figure out, drinks the color of berries, tasting of sunshine. She passed what seemed like one long day in the company of the elves and their companions, in the warmth of their fires and the peace of the community.

And the wounds closed magically. In a bit, she came to Thrissa, amazed that her flesh now bore only a scar, a clean white line that bespoke no semblance to the horrid gash Nazir had given her.

"Yes, you feel well, I'm sure. And you look well. No doubt. The magic has worked. Our herbs and waters have done their job. And most importantly, you have let them."

"But . . ." Aylith began, sensing the hesitation in Thrissa's voice. Aylith knew, all on her own, that something was still wrong. She could feel it, dark, and sinister, moving about inside, taking root in her heart.

"Give yourself a little more time. Pass the night, at least."

Thrissa glided off with a man who had the face and claws of a rock lizard.

Aylith spent a horrific night, waking several times in cold sweats, her ears ringing with vivid dreams.

The next morning, she sat barefoot in a great mass of purple clover and sweet cirlian that bordered the stream. She turned the dreams over and over in her mind, trying to sort them out. The dreams had ended with the equinox burning its imminence into her consciousness, making it plain to her that there was little time left. One last chance to bring the light.

She would have to find a way to fulfill this call soon, but Loch Prith was a place no one would ever want to leave. Aylith had never been made more comfortable, or shown more attention, anywhere else. She dreaded the thought of going back into the freezing blast of wind that waited at the surface, the dullness of the landscape, the lonely harshness of her life. Even now, she could imagine the storms outside, above, the constant waves crashing against the rocks, the wind howling. Inland, the snows and the same wind waited with bigger teeth. On the surface, everyone struggled in winter's bondage, just trying to find enough food and shelter. It would only get worse. The island would not be long in dying. And though Aylith could stay here in comfort forever—and never even see what her choice wrought for the Haen, the Nohr, the poor Albions and the squatter clans, and all the animals and plants that needed the sun—*she* would always know. That seemed a far worse burden than the Memories, a seed far more deadly to plant and let grow in her heart. Would that choice also not make her just like Nazir? So selfish that she lost the ability to love?

Aylith looked around herself. The walls of Loch Prith were cleverly planted and carved and draped, but they were still the walls of a cavern. The light here came from other odd life forms, like the lumini, that Crephas had experimented with. Bright as those brilliant balls of light were, they were not the sun. Loch Prith was a waystation, a holding place. They waited well here, but they waited, nonetheless. The prophetess, the lumini, all of them—they waited.

For the Mender. For her, they all said. "But I am not the Mender," she insisted to herself. "Only the meantime Keeper."

But why did they wait? Why did they ever have to leave? This place was pleasant, warm, full of beauty.

"But hollow," she added aloud.

Aylith moved her hand across the place above her heart, where the sword had entered and the poison had never been lanced away. Today it felt hot to her touch, the throbbing anger always only a thought away from reopening the awful wound.

The insidious poison demanded darkness, and silence, defying exposure, commanding attention away from her real task, making her want to protect it, serve it, coddle it into quiet. With every passing moment, it became more difficult to trace the Memories. The poison was spreading.

She got up to find the prophetess. Two places in the short ground cover lay brown and dead, perfect outlines of her bare feet.

Back inside the great cavern, Aylith's eyes grew accustomed to the brighter light, and she was able to discern colors and shapes. Above, spanning hundred-foot stalactites, hung mosses of every shade of green, their lush growth seeming to drip down the alabaster walls. In several small grottos, cool blue and yellow light flickered, outlining the translucent beauty of the cave's natural formations, some of them surprisingly like statuary. Butterflies darted in and out of the grottos. Butterflies? How long since she had seen them? Their colors rivaled the flowers they danced around: bright golds and oranges, outlined by bold blacks and blues. Some of the insects were several inches across at the wing, and reminded Aylith of the ones she had seen in pictures on Nazir's walls at Inys Nohr. But these glittering jewels were very much alive.

She put her hand in the gurgling waters, the underground stream Thrissa said never froze and always
flowed pure and sweet. This was the stream Aylith had
heard upon waking from the fever dream. Its soothing
song brought some peace to her troubled mind. In a
blue-green pool, its depths untold, but its waters perfectly clear, floated several large white blossoms from a
tree Ruka had shown her. Their scent flavored the air
like sweet cakes, but with a tang of sharp freshness to it.
They rode down the gentle slopes of the stream and collected in the pool, swirling away after awhile down into
another part of the stream, hidden from view. She almost
knew their name, the secret word slipping just beyond
her recall. How tempting it would be to join them, simply
float away, bathed in warmth and fragrance.

She moved into the brilliant hall of the orbs, where
tiny fireflies clung together in giant balls, flying in perfect order and cooperation, hovering over the tender
seedlings that would be Loch Prith's food in several
months. This was Aylith's favorite room. It almost
seemed like summer in here, and reminded her of
Jedhian and the carefree days they had so swiftly run
through, never thinking they could disappear, never
taking time to love the moment they lived in.

Feryar, back again from Inys Nohr, moved among the
lumini, raising and lowering them, adjusting the
seedlings under them, turning the plants to the best
advantage, making sure they did not grow up weak. She
watched the old elf, his little finger still crooked despite
Thrissa's latest efforts at healing, and Aylith's own
attempt the night before she had been hurt at Inys
Nohr. She wondered what it would take to heal that
particular wound. Feryar moved out of sight.

From the hall of orbs, she passed the orchid chamber, the prophetess's receiving hall, and had to close
her eyes against all the splash and show of color there.

It was simply too much after the dreariness she had known aboveground, especially at Inys Nohr. But gradually, when she had sorted out most of the different perfumes of these exotics, she could open one eye at a time, and concentrated on one bloom for awhile, seeing the intricacies of shape and tone and hue.

Music filled the air at Loch Prith. Aylith had grown up with tambour and harp, with gittern and pipe, but never had she heard such symphonies of the human voice, the elven voice, the rhythms of the cavern stream mingled with the incredible harmonies of the insects. From glass to glass, the music changed, keeping the workers active during the lighted hours and rested during the nights. There seemed to be industry here: the growing of food, the making of clothing. The animals were cared for and the sick folk Feryar had brought in were under the constant attention of the healers.

Aylith truly believed at least one person never slept. The prophetess always seemed to be about, well— inhabiting the place. Her presence was the heart and soul of Loch Prith, the genius of it, the love for it. And her prophesies were the words the residents of this strange community lived for. Most often, Aylith saw her with written scrolls in her hand, sorting out the ancient writings of the Maker.

As soon as Aylith thought of Thrissa, it seemed that she would appear. And now, the tall, thin elven woman parted the curtain of vines that overhung her private chambers and stood smiling at Aylith.

"What would you ask of me, child?" she said, and Aylith heard the shifting of sand in her voice, the rise of the tide.

"Thrissa. You have done all you can for me, haven't you? I am not to be healed here, am I?" asked Aylith, finally putting words to what gnawed like a rat at her thoughts.

"Yes. We have done what we can to mend you. Your body is whole. But your heart is in great danger. You still carry the poison of anger, and if it reaches the precious Memories, already dimmed by their long disuse and many passages, when you try to bring the spring, it will not appear rightly. I don't know what will come, but it will be very terrible, and misbegotten, and tangled. For anger will unravel the best of patterns, and the spell you weave with it carries its own thread of death. No matter how well hidden in the fabric, no matter how beautiful the design seems, that thread of anger will cause the whole design to fail. It pulls, and tangles, and shrinks, and frays, making holes, making rents; the divided pieces just keep on dividing. Soon the whole garment is useless. You will weave something horrible if you invoke the light at equinox the way you are now, Aylith. Have you seen it in your dreams?"

Aylith nodded, her head down. She could not stop the tears. "I have seen such horror! The world is green again, but the Clan Tree is ugly, and has thorns, and foul, shriveled fruit, and it grows crooked and black into the sky, like the vines I saw upon the tower at Inys Nohr. And the other plants do not know their names, and never wake up because I do not know them, either—I am forgetting and I shall lose the Memories altogether if something doesn't change."

"Nothing will change for the better," said the Prophetess, "until you are ready to surrender your anger." Thrissa paused, her voice passing into a lower register. Her bright blue eyes fastened on Aylith's as she continued. "You must free the prisoners of your heart."

"The prisoners of my heart? You mean . . . ?"

"I mean all the people you are angry at, especially Logan, and especially Nazir."

"How did you know about Logan? And how will that help me to heal?"

"You are their jailer. And if they are not free, you are not free. You are spending your precious energy in hating them, blaming them, even though you believe you are right, even though you think you are justified. There is no energy left over to begin to heal your inner wounds. When a snake bites, waste no time in killing the snake."

Aylith fumed at the prophetess. How could the elven woman simply expect her to rid her thoughts of Nazir and his venom? Why should that snake go free to bite again? It would give her such completeness to destroy him. . . .

"It sounds like you are telling me to forgive them, Thrissa, after all Nazir has done to me, and to my people. After all his family has done to our clan, how can I forgive him? The only reason I didn't die on his sword was because I wanted so badly to have the chance to turn it on him. What will I have left?"

"I am not telling you to do anything. I am telling you what I think will help. Will hurting Nazir bring back your family? Will any good come of it? You are welcome to stay here as long as you like—for all your life, if you want. We have done all we can for you. Only if you can have the strength to let go of your most desired revenge will your heart heal. I know how hard that is, child. Believe me. I know. It is the most heroic thing anyone can ever do.

"Aylith—it is not Nazir you fight. You must believe me. He has good in him. Only one of his parents was cursed. He is not your enemy. In fact, he is necessary for the prophecy to come true. It's the curse that you have been empowered to destroy. Look for Nazir's true nature. Do not worry about having anything left inside once your anger is gone. Nature abhors a vacuum. You will see what grows there, unhindered, when the evil is rooted out."

Aylith nodded, tears welling in her eyes again.

"What is the difference, Thrissa? I suppose I will take whatever chance there is," Aylith muttered.

"Every gift is its own blessing or its own curse, my dear. Right now, your vision is very confused. That's largely what anger does. It makes you forget the right way of things. But you can learn to see your gift in its own true light. It is a blessing, if you can rid yourself of this poison. To do that, you will have to leave this place. You will have to take your journey. We will call a counsel of the Gwylfan. They are the World Weavers, the original residents of Loch Prith, placed here by the Maker when the world was very young. The ones who sent Feryar and me, so long ago, to watch over Nohr's family and make sure the prophecy came to fruit."

Aylith gave her a startled look, quickly calculating the elves' age.

"They will advise you. There is nothing more," Thrissa whispered, the music in her voice lingering in the air.

CHAPTER
21

AYLITH PASSED INTO CAVERN AFTER CAVERN as Thrissa held aloft the glittering curtains which separated each space.

"The World Weavers have worked their magic loom since the beginning of life on Cridhe. This cave system goes back miles and miles. They have filled every cavern in the chain with their weaving, and now they work the loom in this next one. All of the patterns of the Maker's words have been woven upon it, all of the pictures of life," said Thrissa as she drew Aylith through the last cavern before the Gwylfan's grotto.

They arrived at the majestically arching oval door, and inside, Aylith could see the enormous tapestries that lined the high-vaulted room in marvelous pictures, full of the colors of life, the stories of the races flowing from panel to panel in sequence.

The first thing Aylith fixed upon was the panel of the original Clan Tree, the face of a sandy-haired man, the same one from her dream, peering bleakly from its

branches at a small, angry-looking man who must be
Nohr, she realized. He held a sword, pointed at the
sacred oak. And by his side, she noticed with a chill,
stood a large man, draped in gaudy red silks. Though
he looked far younger, and his weight had shifted from
his chest to his waist, it was distinctly Malvos. In the
background of the panel strange animals gathered,
feeding in the sweeping fields of tall grass.

"Horses," said Thrissa, watching Aylith take in the
Weavers' work. "They . . . gradually became extinct
after the Parting occurred. They are grass-eaters, and
since they produced no wool or meat, the cattle, goats,
and sheep got preference with the available grains.
They're beautiful, aren't they? There are more of them
on the other wall, in the older work."

Aylith's glance wandered to the side of the huge room
where the panels of the time before the Parting hung.
These were dark and fading from age, but she could still
make out the various birds and flowers in them, most
of which she had never seen anywhere but in the nurs-
eries of these very caverns. The ones in the weaving
looked far larger in scale, more lush and verdant.

"Parrot. Sunflower. Daylily. Bullfrog," Aylith whispered their secret names as her gaze moved over the
weaving of the lost species. The Memories seemed
more clear to her in this room.

"Cridhe . . . was the garden of the world," said
Thrissa wistfully.

She turned Aylith's attention to the center of the
room, where three women sat at a loom made of radiant red rosewood, its shuttle in constant motion. The
bench was so long that it took all three of the women
to pass the shuttle. Upon the frame hung a nearly finished piece, the pattern of which lay hidden in the
great folds of the silken fabric, piled upon the cavern's
gleaming crystal floor.

"Antistita, Vestira, and Praetis are the Gwylfan. Praetis is the one on the far left." Thrissa pointed to the youngest-looking of the women, a girl of about Aylith's own age. She had long, flowing red hair and a supple body, her hands making the most intricate of passes when the shuttle was handed to her.

"The next one, in the middle, is Antistita." Aylith saw a brown-haired woman in her middle years, fuller in form, hard of muscle, with a determined set to her lean jaw. She set a rhythm expertly with her feet, straightening the heavy cloth when necessary.

"The one on the far right is Vestira." Where Thrissa now pointed sat a woman of great age, her hair thinning and white, her blue eyes merry, her hands knobbed and stiff. She was thinner than straw, but sat the bench straightly, her backbone completely visible through her shift.

"Thrissa," Aylith whispered respectfully, "how does she still work? Her hands seem locked and tired."

"It is she who knows the pattern, dear." Thrissa smiled. "You may ask only one question of them after they speak to you. Choose wisely, Aylith. Do not worry. You will see me again. I will wait for you outside, and Feryar flies now to help set things right above. You shall have as much help as we can give," whispered the prophetess as she withdrew.

The sheer curtain fell back to its place, and Aylith entered the sacred chamber. The Gwylfan looked up at her as one, but did not stop their work.

"Hello, Aylith. Please sit with us. We would know your mind. You have been in great turmoil," said Vestira, her large blue eyes seeming to look right through the girl.

Aylith settled on a soft pillow at the foot of the loom's bench, Praetis closest to her.

"Gwylfan, I know that I must leave Loch Prith. I

have to go back to Inys Haen. The equinox is coming very, very soon. I can feel it. I must bring the spring as best I can. Thrissa says there is one way I can be healed before that happens."

Antistita paused before passing her shuttle through the warp. Then she spoke. "Aylith, do you know what you risk?"

Aylith nodded. "I would suppose I risk my life. But I have no life here. I can survive nicely forever here being warmed by your baths, anointed by your herbs, fed by your hands. I could pass all the time the Maker has allotted to me being taken care of. But my heart is being eaten away. If I do not attempt this thing, the land will die. People will starve. I have already chosen."

Antistita resumed with the shuttle, and Praetis caught it with a practiced hand, drawing tight the one golden cord in the dark tapestry.

"The threads have shown that you will have several labors to accomplish, Aylith. The first one will be to look upon your internal wound, and if you survive that, the second task will be to find your way home. The path is hidden. You cannot leave Loch Prith the way you came in. What you encounter may surprise you. It may look impossible. You can pass through it if you do not believe more in what challenges you and its power to hurt you than you believe in the words you speak. Words are eternal, you are eternal. All else is changeable. You are the Mender; remember that it is your right to pass through. The last labor . . . you will know it when it is upon you. It will be the hardest thing you have ever tried to do, and will take more compassion than you think you have. The Prophecy of Haen says that the lines of Haen and Nohr will merge when the Mender comes. That is all there is. You may ask a question now, and we are bound to answer it."

Frowning, Aylith puzzled for a moment before

producing her question. "And just these things, when I have done them, will heal me so that I may heal the land, remove the curse? I do not see how . . ." She had expected something more dangerous sounding, with swords or battles, somehow. Maybe dragons.

"Yes, you will be healed when you have done these things. You said you had already chosen. If we gave you hard words, impossible tasks, you would receive them and try, would you not? All we tell you to do is discover the nature of your wound, leave this place, and wait for the Great Prophecy to manifest. Is this too simple?" said Antistita.

"No . . . I will do it. I just thought . . . "

"There is a kind of thinking that deceives the thinker. It makes you go round and round trying to conjure for yourself, to control the journey, know your entire path all at once. Just do the next thing."

Aylith could not help but recall those moments in the secret cellar at Inys Nohr, where her memories of Logan's words, those same exact words, had produced the fire in her hands when nothing else could.

"Do the next thing," repeated Vestira. "Just believe. Your healing is already there, in your heart and in your words. Aylith of Inys Haen, are you not the Mender?"

Aylith wanted more than anything to shake her head, to turn from them, to run back into the warm caverns, with their beautiful flowers, and simply lose herself among them forever. But in spite of it all, she found herself nodding.

"Yes, Antistita, I will be the Mender."

The Gwylfan stopped their weaving as the last word left her mouth. The silence in the great cavern stunned Aylith with its power. It felt as if all the sound in the world had ceased.

Praetis tied off the weaving, snapped the final knot, cut it from the loom, and pulled a long cord that slowly raised the new tapestry to the one unoccupied place on that wall. The folds fell out, and the tapestry shook loose into a picture of a huge oak, its branches wide and protecting. A thin, green-gold thread passed from the roots to the crown, but a great vertical rent parted the panel, and thereby, the Tree, from top to bottom, the two halves barely hanging on by that glowing thread. Beside the Tree stood a small, sandy-haired woman, the green-gold thread in her hand. . . .

"We can weave no further. The rest is up to you. Take this thread. It is spun of magic and will stretch as you need it, and it will never break. When you leave us, it will become invisible. Still, though you cannot see it, you will feel it. Do not let go of it," said Vestira, her words frighteningly loud in the sudden quiet.

"What? Why?" Aylith took the green-gold thread in her hand, absently looping it around her wrist in a butterfly pattern like the other threads looped through the shuttle on the magical loom. The Gwylfan smiled back at her, their silence deafening. Aylith's one question had already been answered.

After a long look at the new tapestry, she walked out the cavern door, trailing the magical thread behind her. Immediately, it winked out of sight, though she felt it still securely wrapped around her hand. Though she could not see it, with every step she took, the rent tapestry stitched itself together a little more.

"Morkin. Morkin, do ye live, man?" rasped a voice rough with years of breathing coal dust. The man in the red cap stirred, his hand coming slowly to his head.

"I do live, Sims. I do. But I think I wish I didn't." Morkin tried to sit up, and made it halfway.

"Morkin—don't—" Sims caught him as he toppled over, his other arm shooting out to steady himself.

And missing by a very long way, because his limb now ended at his heavily bandaged forearm.

"I was gonna tell you in a minute, Morkin. Yeah, the Felonarch's took yer hand in the fight with that fancy sword. Just clove it clean away."

Morkin grimaced in distaste at hearing the details of his maiming, and held up his arm in the dim torchlight, his face a great, sad question.

"But it feels like it's still there . . . I don't understand," he breathed. The missing hand felt like he had clutched fire and still held it.

"Neither do I. But it's a clean cut and already sealed, just a little frosty around the edges. You didn't lose no blood to speak of. Does it hurt very much? Do you think you can travel? We got to move you out before we take the tower down. If we take a couple o' crews away from the mines, we can have it down in a few days. Now's our best chance, while the Sifter is hived off after that Haenish girl. He leads a unit marchin' right now. You can go before them, warn the third Far clan. If yer up to it," said Sims.

"If I'm up to it? If I'm up to it? They'll have to run to get ahead of me," said Morkin, his many white teeth shining in a sinister smile. The Albion leader stood, something still not clearing in his head. He felt very different somehow. Like every nerve was on edge, like his skin didn't quite fit right anymore.

"And you, Sims—stay out of the sappers' way. You can direct from back in the tunnel. We need you. Don't get yourself killed by the Felonarch's downfall, eh?"

Sims grinned, crinkles forming beside his white eye. "You know I can't leave it, Morkin. I'll have to be the one what says 'Let 'er rip!' Only thing is, after all this time and work on the tunnel, I'd sure love it if you could see this pile of cursed rocks fall on that cursed tyrant. And I'd love it if I could be on the outside and

inside at the same time. It's a sight I've been dreamin'
of all my life. But I'll try not to eat too much dust. Not
that it would matter all that much now." He coughed.
"I just got one regret, Morkin."

"What's that, my friend?"

"The Sifter won't also be in this rock pile when we
cave it in."

Morkin laughed and clapped Sims on the back.
"Pack me up, my friend. I'd be obliged if you would
spare some of your own ration of ardré. I'll need to
travel fast and hard. Use the spores; they're stronger.
I'll need all the start on Nazir's boys I can get. The
Sifter can still move fast when he wants to. No sleep
for me."

CHAPTER

22

THRISSA HARDLY LOOKED AT AYLITH AS SHE hummed the sleep song. Aylith relaxed under the balmy words and let herself be calmed. Thrissa covered her with a bhana and moved a step away to the circle of three healers gathered by the stream.

"Her internal wound is yet grave, Thrissa," said Portis, her hands weaving a circlet of thyme and clover. "She raves. I can feel it. Her mind and her heart are flayed by the sword of anger, and the poison is working strongly now. The pattern of the Clan Tree will be lost forever if she fails."

"Yes," said Thrissa, "I know. And so does Aylith. Though the wound is invisible, it is deadly. We will have to wait and see what can be done."

From across the circle, a man missing his eyes and speaking through lips that looked like an orchid's petals added, "We may be able to slow the poison, and that will give the girl a bit more time. She is brave, if nothing else, and I believe she can do it."

Thrissa nodded and looked over at Aylith. The girl was staring at her, again wide awake, her blue-green eyes steady and a small smile on her lips. She had wrapped the magical thread around her hand in an intricate knot, so that it would stay firm in spite of whatever she encountered in her sleep.

Thrissa turned back to the circle and smiled. "I believe she can do it, too," she said, and the words fell like soft rain on Aylith's troubled white brow. She turned to Aylith.

"I will give you the passage potion. You will sleep. When you encounter the poison, you will likely thrash a bit."

Thrissa addressed the odd group of healers again. "My friends, there will be an awakening."

Thrissa closed her eyes for a moment and then spoke to Aylith again. "You must seek the internal wound. You must discover it, enter it, know it, and then return before you are tempted to stay forever. The call will be strong at a certain point—it is always more difficult to live than die. But you must resist, for if you stay there, you know that all Cridhe will die with you. Do this for yourself, so that others may live. Come back. While you sleep, you are safe; we can guard you and keep you."

Aylith nodded. Thrissa's reminders felt unnecessary. The pains of the equinox fired through her bones. The time was all but upon them.

Ruka moved to Aylith's side and bound her hands and feet in soft cottonum so that she would not hurt herself in the dreaming. The night would be long and tortuous for the girl as she passed from one dream to the next, down, down into the depths of her soul, fleeing the poisonous revenge that stalked her every thought.

When Thrissa offered her the bitter draught, Aylith hesitated, but then drank it down in strong swallows.

Aylith thought of Logan, of Jedhian, of Lorris. She thought of all of Cridhe, and how the green life called to her from its painful sleep. How it would never wake unless she did. And down, down, down she dropped, into the darkest, coldest pit she could ever imagine.

There were no walls, nothing to walk on, no sense of space at all. Aylith wandered in the freezing blackness, her hands reaching all around for something, anything, to touch, to make contact with, to provide bearing and direction. A small light appeared in front of her, and she moved toward it, unsure of just how. The light then exploded into a wash of color and noise, and she found herself in a forest when it passed.

The trees around her bore no resemblance to familiar ones, and they fascinated her with their tall, spiral limbs and silver trunks. The leaves shimmered with golds and blues, and the buzzing at her entry slowly calmed to the sounds of a healthy glade. She wandered further, drawn by a sense of urgency, and came into far more sparse country, where there had been fire and ruin, a path of blasted heather marking some terrible passing. She moved down it, cracking the blackened bushes under foot and smelling the sulfuric steam and vapor of violent rending. Down this charred furrow she ran, faster and faster, until she came upon a clouded, molten bubbling, and stopped just short of falling into it.

Aylith stared down into the gaping hole. She stood on the edge of the widening wound, more than somewhat confused. But she could do the next right thing. She closed her eyes at first, but then opened them. If she were going in, she would do it looking fully upon whatever awaited her. She jumped, falling, falling, until the bottom of the new chasm, so like the chasm the she had seen open up in her dream of the Parting, came to meet her with astounding suddenness. But when she hit, she did not feel any impact. There, yet another pit, another level to descend.

Aylith cautiously stepped all around the floor of the newest rift and saw that the earth at its sides was melting inward, drawn into the sparkling rupture with amazing speed, becoming magma and enlarging the pit with every passing second. She hopped backward several times to avoid being sucked into it, and tried desperately to see down into the bottom of the flaming wound. It was impossible. Again, she would have to enter.

She closed her eyes and jumped one more time, feeling the flame on her face, dropping toward the intolerable heat of her fever. When she came to the bottom, at least it truly was the bottom. All she could see was a huge ring of fire, but these flames were composed of darkness where there should be light, and they were cold, too cold to imagine, threatening to freeze her with every leaping tendril. She had come to the heart of the wound, the place where the poison hid and spread, the origin and new secret dwelling of the old anger. She was amazed. In the center of the ring of fire grew a tiny black vine. This small thing, all by itself, was the curse of Cridhe. It was only a root, a thing with no leaves, no fruit as yet.

But as she watched, it grew bigger and bigger, winding upward like the bitteroots around the tower of Inys Nohr. Since Nohr had spoken his betrayal, and placed the point of Soulslayer to the Clan Tree, this same bitteroot must have been at work in the heart of his every descendant, growing up hidden until it overtook their minds and, eventually, their bodies. And now its vile seed had sprouted in her own heart.

Aylith put out her hand to the root, like she had in the tower to the feeble Clan Tree crown. But instead of the answering luminescence of the forest mana, the black root curled toward her hand hungrily, wrapping its tendrils around her fingers in a death grip. Aylith cried out, knowing no one would hear her. The poison swept through her every sense, flooded her mouth with its foul, bitter taste, drenched her skin with acid. She coughed and choked and cried, but the black vine circled around her ankles, then her knees and around her body, until it covered her arms and shoulders and threatened to cover her head. The pain then miraculously left. She felt wonderfully protected and safe, the vine bowing itself to her every movement, worshipping her, raising her up from the fires.

It would be so easy, she thought lazily, *to let it cover me up. The pain goes away if I give in to it. It doesn't hurt anymore.*

The smallest tendril of the black vine inched around her neck, twitching, gently tightening. Aylith hardly knew when she slipped into unconsciousness. But suddenly, Thrissa's "unnecessary" warnings rang in her ears: "Come back—for all Cridhe."

She gulped air and fought the vine's caress, tearing at it with her teeth and hands. At last, she freed herself, only one last ringlet of the evil plant curled quietly upon her smallest finger, like a deadly ring. The rest of the vine shriveled, dried to the point of ashes, and blew away, sending black sparks up from the circle of fire.

"Don't stay . . . all of Cridhe—" Thrissa's words rang again in her ears. Aylith flailed her hand at the feathery touch of the dark vine, but it clung fast. Suddenly, she could no longer breathe, and fell exhausted to the hard, cold ground.

"She raves again, Thrissa," said Ruka.

"How is the fever?"

"Still there. She is inside, I believe, with it now. But

it could take awhile for her to come back. It took half
an outside year for Portis." The flower-faced man
sighed, then looked at the prophetess.

"We do not have that kind of time. I am sure of that.
She will return soon, " she answered.

Aylith could hear voices around her, but could not
determine what they said.

Then she floated again, the black root's seductive
caress forgotten. The pain had abated to a large degree,
but something was still not right. She fought to rise
from the drugged sleep, exhausted from the inward
journey and ready to leave the dream.

"Aylith. Can you hear me?" Thrissa's soft words fell
like rain upon Aylith's parched brow. The Mender
opened her eyes, and the prophetess smiled down at
her, obviously relieved.

"How long—?" Aylith croaked, her throat torn and
sore.

"A couple of days, as they measure on the outside.
But time is different here like when Feryar flies. You
can pass years in the space of moments. You are going
to be fine. Most with such a wound never reach the bottom, or if they do, they do not return. There are parts of
Loch Prith—the hives, we call them—full of those who
continue to dream. You are very brave, dear."

Aylith did not feel brave. Nor powerful, nor all that
well, even. She felt exhausted and thirsty. Ruka
brought water, and Aylith drank it all, the coolness of
it clearing her head as it slaked her throat.

"It's still alive. I got loose, but it's still alive," she
panted, looking at her hand for the vine. There was no
trace of it. All she could feel was the invisible thread of
the Weavers' tapestry.

CHAPTER
23

JEDHIAN CIRCLED AROUND THE BACK OF INYS Haen's thornwall, losing sight of Lorris and Arn in the whiteness of the drifting snow. But he felt that if he could not see them, Nazir's watchers would be having an even harder time doing the same. The Sobus lay more or less to his right, its undulating curves hugging the village in a cold embrace. There were no tracks on the ice. How long since anyone had broken the surface for water?

Jedhian peered in through a window of sorts in the thornwall, where the foliage covered it completely in the summer, but the thorns had grown oddly away from one another and now provided something of a view. When they were children, he and Aylith had played hide and find in this part of the massive hedge. Looking at the places where they had easily fit then made him wonder how he had ever been so small. More importantly, how would he fit through them again?

After a try or two, and several deep gashes to his shoulders and back, even through his heavy cloak, Jedhian found himself stuck in the living barricade, also remembering how well it served its purpose. Had Arn not disobeyed and followed him, he might have simply frozen there, caught between his memories and the eight-inch thorns.

"Hsst, Jedhian—don't move, I can reach you."

Arn had shed his borrowed armor, except for the tough leather undershirt. In a bit, the boy twisted Jedhian loose and took his place, darting through the maze of skewers like he had done it all his life. When he climbed out the other side, Jedhian looked through the opening and waved him toward the second hut, where the lone fire burned. Arn disappeared inside, and then came out again quickly, an old man leaning on his arm, the both of them staying hidden by the huts and the byre, walking a straight line to use their cover as long as possible. It was Harcher, one of the eight elders. When Jedhian knew they had come far enough to risk being seen by Nazir's watchers, he hailed them softly and bade them stop.

"They've all gone, boy. All gone. Said they were going to storm Inys Nohr. Make a good end of things. I'm too old. I told them I'd stay and keep the fires. Got to be somebody here for when they realize it won't work and they come running home. We're in for another Long Winter, boy. Best come on in here and be warm with me. You know the Keeper's dead. We won't see the light again. Pattern's broken. Best just try to stay warm and dry and make good company while we wait."

"Harcher, is Aylith back here anywhere? Did she come here? Maybe did you see something you think too strange to report? Like, say, she dropped down from the sky? Did you see that, and would she be here now?" His most important question was still unasked.

"Eh? The sky? You gone barmy? Aylith was kidnapped, boy. She been taken by the Nohrish pigs, dreckly after the raid. You been somewhere else. No, she has never been here since that day, and I would know it. I watched them leave, all of them, sometime after the soldiers packed up. Said they'd had enough. Keeper's dead."

Jedhian gestured for Harcher to keep his voice lower. "Yes, I have been gone. Gone to find her, and then lose her again, so it seems. Harcher, you can't stay here. Nazir's troops are scouting the village even now. Can you make your way through the wall?"

The question didn't sound so absurd when Harcher turned sideways to adjust his cloak and try. The man was rail thin. Had they left him any food at all, or had it just been that long since they'd gone?

Arn held the wall back, the woody thorns seeming to bend for him where they had stubbornly refused to do so for Jedhian. His hands took only a few new marks, and then the boy followed Harcher.

Jedhian found Lorris down the hillock, looking worried and coming toward them as fast as she could, but keeping very low. Jedhian dropped down in a crouch and threw snow over Arn and Harcher for further concealment as she arrived.

"They're coming in, Jedhian," Lorris whispered.

"Go. You will listen and spring whatever traps the Haenish have set. I cannot believe they would leave an open invitation to their plunder. Something is amiss down there. I will wait here and send in twenty men at a time, every hour, unless you signal, or a man from the last detail in doesn't come back. Find that girl, Malvos." Nazir stared hard into Malvos's flinty green eyes.

Something odd had happened to his salacious apothecary over the last several days. In fact, the man seemed to be someplace else nearly all the time. Treason? Betrayal? Illness? Whatever, if Malvos would not go, if he seemed to know too much about why he should not go, then Nazir would know his true colors. If there was a trap down there that Malvos had some-how fashioned himself, he would balk. After all, had not the apothecary desired to stay in the tower while his Felonarch risked his life out here searching for the girl and her precious light spell? Lately, it seemed his whole kingdom plotted against him.

Nazir shook the small stone bottle absently in his hand and drank deeply from it again, though the pain had become less insistent. The Keeper was still far enough out of range that he could not feel her pres-ence. But somehow, Nazir knew she still lived. When he had struck her with the sword, he had seen into her most hidden being, even past the warding. She was no one he could ever forget. He knew Aylith now. And more than ever, he knew he had to find her.

Malvos bowed decorously in a flurry of red and pur-ple cloth, and took the first group of men down the cliff to Inys Haen.

"Oh, yes, illustrious tactician, this is a great and wor-thy plan, and your battle strategies will certainly be pub-lished abroad when you have taken this little wart of a village by your astounding personal bravery," he mut-tered, slipping and sliding hugely down the steep bank.

Perhaps Nazir happened to be standing just in the right place for the words to strike his ear, or maybe Malvos had grown especially unwary, but Nazir cocked his head angrily and spat under his breath, "Lead on, O magnanimous Malvos. Your secret words do per-fume the very air I breathe. There will come a day when I need you not, old man."

He pulled his hood up and retired to the rear of the ranks, shivering and swearing at the boy who had yet to start a fire. He was surrounded by fools and idiots. And, by Nohr's bald head, he was cold.

Lorris, Jedhian, Arn, and old Harcher huddled together under the slim shelter of the hillock. The wind had picked up a bit, and they were grateful; it erased their tracks in the powdery snow. If they had not been seen before, they were safe enough for the moment.

"Tell me exactly where they've gone, Harcher, please. We need to know. Try to remember. Lorris is on our side—truly, she has risked her own life for mine," pleaded Jedhian when the old man had seen Lorris in her Nohrish leathers, shut his mouth, and refused to say more. The cold and the lack of food had addled him a bit, but Jedhian was sure he still knew where the village had gone.

"I'll say nothing in the presence of such filth! She'll betray us! She's Nohrish, can ya not see that, boy? Would ya have me give our people into her hands?" the old man objected again.

It seemed there was no moving him, but Arn touched Jedhian's arm, and the healer drew back in frustration. Then the boy sat down directly in front of Harcher and started to hum an old tune. The next time through, he added the words.

"Liana wept and Capin raised his hand,
A promise made, but never kept,
A curse lay on the land.
I'll be coming for you, love,
I'll be back one day.
Think of me, and bide the time,
Beneath these skies of gray."

Soon, Harcher was finding a note here and there

himself, forgetting to be disturbed and wary. Lorris fidgeted off to the side, thinking about Malvos's extraordinary hearing, but they were downwind of the army, and Arn seemed to know what he was doing.

"Sing us a verse, Lorris, please?" coaxed Arn.

Lorris looked at him like he had just asked her to eat another eel. Raw. Arn casually pointed his chin toward Harcher, whose face now beamed, the song having worked its magic. Then she understood. In a most pleasing alto, she softly sang the next verse in the long lay, and Harcher nodded in time, happily fumbling his stiff hands together on the beat.

"The years have come, the years have gone,
Liana waits and weeps.
Her wand'ring shade from glade to glade,
A silent vigil keeps.
Come back to me, my darling,
Or I will leap the rift.
For I am ever yearning
To see the Mender's gift."

When she had finished, Harcher turned to Jedhian and spoke so quietly and nonchalantly that the healer almost missed it. "They be hid up in the caverns of the first squatter clan to the east."

Jedhian found Harcher's distant, bleary eyes. Was the old man telling the truth? The first squatter clan was only a few miles away. They had carefully skirted it on their way in, having no way to tell where the clan's sentiments would lie.

Jedhian marveled at Arn, who burst into a huge grin, and patted Harcher gently on the back. The old man still hummed the song, his memories and his mind lost in his youth, in a summer on the bright Sobus with his long-dead wife.

Lorris and Jedhian drew apart to make plans.

"I had no idea there were caverns under the shelf

where the squatters live. No wonder they have been able to survive Nazir's attacks all these years," Jedhian whispered excitedly. "Maybe they have Aylith! Now, if we can just get word to them—"

"What are you thinking, Jedhian?" said Lorris warily.

"Nazir is marching straight into our hands, sweet Lorris. We just have to get his troops to close the door. Or gate, that is." He grinned cryptically. "And where did you learn that Haenish song?"

"Haenish song? That was the song my mother sang to me when I was a baby. That song is Nohrish, and always has been." She puffed out her cheeks.

Jedhian shook his head and threw his arm around her suddenly stiffened shoulders. "Easy, my darling, easy." He smiled and looked long into her large, gray eyes. She softened under his hand and smiled back.

Arn crawled over just then and uncomfortably cleared his throat. "Ah, sir, you want I should make the trip? That clan . . . well, that clan was the next one over to my home once, a long time ago. Someone might still know me. They'd drop either of you on sight, probably before your people—if truly they are with them—could make mention. I think it would be me I'd send. If I was in charge of thinking."

Lorris looked at Jedhian, and he nodded. "Yes, Arn, you should go," she said. "Tell them . . . "

The three of them squatted and drew lines into the snow, while Harcher rocked and hummed another tune.

A battle song.

CHAPTER
24

ARN CROUCHED BEHIND THE HILLOCK, HIS instructions firmly in mind, and threw off a makeshift salute, as much like RoNal used to do it as he could manage. The likeness was effective. Lorris noticed, and gave him a radiant smile and a wink. She pressed the small chamois map into his hands.

"My father's. Never failed him. Maybe the only accurate map of the whole island," she offered.

"Now, if you're caught—" began Jedhian.

"Jedhian, beggin' yer pardon much, but I'll not be caught. I know these parts better'n any o' that bunch o' toadmeat what follows Nazir now." Arn's face colored against the translucent snow. He was deeply offended.

"Oh . . . of course. I only meant—" said Jedhian.

"You were only about to speak me dead, again beggin' yer pardon. I won't fail you. I don't believe in me failin' you. All I can see is me makin' my orders, and makin' 'em in style. Please, Jedhian, don' be puttin' them bad pictures in my head. I got to be clear," Arn explained, his face turning even darker red.

Jedhian laughed softly and looked at Lorris, who raised her eyebrows in mild reprimand. It was more than Jedhian could take.

"I beg your pardon, Arn. And may you return with the entire Far clan nation in your pocket."

Arn grinned and said, "Now, that's what sort o' words a fellow can travel on. I will."

He was gone before Jedhian saw him leave, before his last word had died on the wind.

Arn moved on his belly better than most move on their feet. He had crossed the Sobus by building a snow mound in a sheltered cleft of the riverbank and pushing the heap of dry powder in front of him a little at a time, whisking away his trail with thrown snow, until he felt land again. Getting past Nazir's troops had been the easiest. Their attention lay solely upon the village of Inys Haen. No one had bothered to look behind.

He had watched Malvos lead the first group down to the thornwall and stop, the big man listening. But whether they moved in or not, Arn had not seen. He was a quarter mile away by then.

Standing up and stretching out, he brushed himself off, shook the snow from his hair, and ran for all he had, his newly healed shoulder feeling balanced and right for the first time in his life. He breathed the cold air in and out, his rhythm never breaking as he covered the icy, uneven ground in great long strides. Just short of the first Far clan, he slowed and walked a bit, cooling down in case he had to stop and hide for any length of time. A body could die from a chill otherwise, he remembered RoNal had told him.

Not ten minutes later, that and another piece of RoNal's offhand advice saved Arn's life. Three of the clan's sentries, roaming farther out than he ever dreamed they would be, spotted him and closed in, leaving him nowhere to run and giving him no time to explain himself. One had his sling loaded and whirling when Arn did what RoNal had told him to do if he ever got caught in a hard one. Something heroic and guaranteed to work. He fainted.

"Sit up boy, and tell us your name. Where are you from and what are you doing out on the moors by yourself?"

Arn opened his eyes to the gruff words of the bearded man standing over him. Baz. One of the men gone hunting when the Nohrish raiders had demolished Arn's clanhold a year and more ago.

When Arn had faked his swoon, the three sentries had pocketed their slings and brought him to the caverns, thinking he would not be able to find his way out or back in should he be more than the lost child he appeared to be. The hollow-sounding room he'd been taken to was much warmer than the moors, but the man's breath still made mist in the air.

"My name is Arn. You know me, Baz. My father was Drake," Arn said, feigning weakness.

Baz held the torch nearer and peered down at Arn's travel-stained face. "You be thinner than a rake, boy, but you say truth. I do know you. Thought you dead for sure, too, though we never found none of you after the raiders came. High Chief Odser here thought they'd roasted you, bunch of grimy cannibals. But here you be, whole and fine. But why?" Baz asked, the question hanging between them like a deadly spider on its silk. Nazir had sent more than one spy into their midst before.

Arn sat up, took the cup of hot stew someone offered him, and began spinning his tale. A few minutes later, Baz and the high chief, and the other man, whom Arn did not know, huddled in sharp short talk at the edge of the room. The echoes confused their speech, and Arn had to wait to hear what they had decided.

Meantime, Arn, glad of his full belly and the relative warmth of the cavern, studied the room well. By the far left corner hung a double stalactite. Overhead, a formation that resembled a star. He mentally measured the space, thinking it to be somewhere close to half the size of Nazir's great hall. But it was empty. He saw only the attendant who had brought the stew and the sentries. Arn figured this must be some kind of antechamber, the rest of the caverns connected to it. He got down from his pallet, pretending to stretch, and casually searched for a visible passage, but found none. Just then, Baz and the others came back and stood over him.

"We agree. We will take you to the Haenish leaders and let them decide if they will help you."

Arn smiled endearingly at them. RoNal had been right. Play to your strengths, even if they appear to be weaknesses.

Arn was blindfolded anyway. He moved through at least three different spaces, from what he could hear, the middle one much larger then the other two. When they arrived at the final chamber, Baz removed the blindfold and Arn looked out into a torchlit room, where he was introduced before seven white-robed old men, their faces stern and forbidding, who sat and considered him. Behind them, Arn could see row upon row of grim-looking people, their clothing far finer than anything the Far clanners wore. The hidden Haenish from the village. And from what Jedhian had told him, these men were their elders. They would be the ones he had to convince that Aylith yet lived, could be found, and that Jedhian's plan to cut Nazir off from his troops, and then offer him for ransom, would work.

Jedhian thought that by holding their leader he could
enlist the Nohrish foot soldiers in the search for Aylith
and guarantee her safekeeping if he could take the
Felonarch alive.

And if the Haenish and the Far clans would offer to
put themselves between Nazir and his crack troops,
holed up by now, he hoped, within the thornwall
fortress of deserted Inys Haen. Arn gulped, suddenly
overwhelmed at the importance of his mission and
painfully aware that time was running out. Lorris had
said Nazir's troops would be filtering into the abandoned village a few at a time, if they stuck to the regular procedure. Arn figured he had less than an hour to
get these people to commit themselves to his request.

He searched each old face for some sign of agree-
ment, some hidden trust. But these men had given up
their hope. Their mouths formed bitter scowls and
their eyes were hard. They had lost their Keeper. They
had abandoned their homes. All traces of hope had
vanished from the elders' countenances, and the only
thing Arn saw there now was revenge.

"What news do you bring that causes our neighbor
Baz and High Chief Odser to interrupt war council,
boy? Baz is not a man given to games. You have something of importance to say. Say out," the oldest-looking
of the seven Haenish elders intoned, his words echoing
through the large cavern again and again. He was obviously the Speaker. He wore the massive seal of the
Haenish on his hand, a great gold ring with an oak
engraved upon it.

Arn swallowed hard and turned to face the man,
looking him straight in the eyes, like he'd seen RoNal
do to Nazir. "I come to ask your help in retrieving the
Keeper. And in capturing Nazir. He waits at Inys Haen
even now, with a company of his best. I can lead you to
him. If you will gather the clans together, we can take

him. It will be the only chance you have to seize him outside of the tower," Arn hastily improvised.

A low whisper had begun when the boy had mentioned the Keeper and had grown to full-fledged talking in the ranks of Haenish and Far clanners who sat behind the council. The Speaker for the council turned around and glared angrily at the noise-makers, and silence followed instantly.

"What do you say, boy, that the Keeper yet lives? Surely you are addled from your harsh journey back from Inys Nohr. Tell us of your escape from the tyrant, and of his city. We have need of the plans of the wall and the tower's particulars. That is how you may be of greatest help to us. There is nothing left for us but to bring down the oppressor, take our noble revenge in Nohrish blood, and die fighting," the Speaker said quietly.

"Sir, I tell you true. The Keeper lives. She is Aylith of Inys Haen, and she was taken in the spring raid, after her father Logan was killed in a fire. He gave to her the Memories. She had been wounded by Nazir and we search for her here and in the Westlands. We thought she had been taken to Inys Haen, but she was not there. I thought you might know of her whereabouts. But Nazir is searching also. Please, sir, the battle lies at Inys Haen, not Inys Nohr. Please," he finished boldly, just barely containing his desperation.

With that, the Speaker rose from his stone chair and glowered down at Arn, his control of the noise in the cavern completely lost. "You say the new Keeper is *Aylith*, Logan's daughter? The Keeper is always a man! This is blasphemy. Logan has altered the pattern. This is an outrage—!"

"This is the truth!" shouted Arn, forgetting himself entirely, his voice miraculously not cracking.

The Speaker sat down again very slowly. The room had hushed and only the last echoes of Arn's voice could be heard. One of the other elders held up his hand to speak. He rose and looked at Arn, his face unreadable.

"I believe you, boy. I do. I have been thinking about this since the last raid. Something has not seemed . . . final to me about the Keeper. It is very difficult to bring to words. But I believe you. I believe the prophecy; the Maker would not leave us bereft. And you seem to know a great deal about that raid for not having seen it. Have you spoken to Aylith yourself?"

"Yes, sir, I have. And she has healed this shoulder with her power." Arn took down his sleeve and showed them. Baz caught his breath. Everyone in Arn's clan had known about his bad birthing. Now the bent shoulder was straight. Baz stepped forward, vigorously nodding his head.

"Sir, he speaks truth. The boy was born with a twisted arm," said Baz.

"It had been even worse than you knew, Baz. Nazir himself made it so," added Arn.

The Speaker rose to examine the boy's arm, still unsure Arn told the truth. The other elders waited for the inevitable test—Argile was Speaker primarily because he alone could verify such a claim.

"When a healing is done, there is always a trace. *I* can feel the path of the mana," the Speaker supplied pompously.

He reached out his hand, but before he even touched Arn, he jumped backward, as though stung. He looked at Arn as if the boy were death itself.

"Oh. Oh. Yes, it is true. The path is laid down upon his flesh. The girl is the Keeper! What has Logan done? He is the one who has brought us to this bad pass by giving the Memories to a woman. To *that* woman. The prophecy can never come true now," he wailed.

"Never mind what Logan has done," the second elder interrupted. "He did what he had to do, the same as you would have, Argile, if you had been Keeper and knew you were dying. The girl has always had the marks, anyway. He saved the Memories, saved his daughter, and now he has possibly saved us also, if we will listen to this boy and act on what we hear. Sometimes, Argile, the pattern needs to change. I beg you to be silent. Let Arn have his say. And he looks a man in a hurry, if I read him right. Arn, tell us more."

Argile buried his head in his hands, but Arn stepped up and relayed the particulars of Jedhian's plan. Just as he finished, another group of three sentries burst into the council chamber, snow still clinging to their cloaks.

"Nazir himself has been seen. He is outside Inys Haen. We were met on the moors by the third clan's watchers," the man panted.

"Are you sure it's him? You know he thinks he fools us with that ox Malvos," said Odser.

"It's him." The man grinned.

Arn jerked his head around to the elders and they in turn stood to address the rest of the Haenish. Within moments, Arn had been dispatched along with Baz to travel to the next clan, gather strength, and stir up the hope that the Keeper lived. Arn's blindfold was forgotten as they moved out of the chain of caverns, every Haenish and Far clan eye upon them, even Argile's.

"Wait, boy," the Speaker called after him. "Take the Haenish seal. It will help your case with the next clan."

Arn turned to receive the ring, and Odser pressed another into his hand also, bearing the mountain seal of the first Far clan.

"I pledge their safe return, sirs," said Arn. *Or my death in the attempt,* he added to himself.

CHAPTER
25

JEDHIAN AND LORRIS HUDDLED CLOSE TO old Harcher on the lee side of the hillock, trying to keep as warm as they could. Nazir's men had trickled into the village, just as Lorris had predicted, in small, cautious groups, the last man in always returning to the main group that waited above and then bringing down more men. Malvos, with his keen senses, had led the first trio himself. They could see him poking around, briefly visiting each hut, but not going inside. When he seemed satisfied that he heard nothing, he sent a man in and went on to the next cottage. Malvos was quite the brave one, thought Jedhian, his mouth twisting in contempt.

Harcher was becoming a bit of a problem. The old man would now and then loudly blurt out some bit of information concerning a council meeting he remembered from thirty years back, and either Jedhian or Lorris had to clap a hand upon his mouth to muffle the sound. Once or twice, Jedhian had seen Malvos look up, but then he went on, distracted by something in the village.

Lorris shook her head at Jedhian in frustration, not risking words. Jedhian nodded and gave Harcher the last of his share of the morning's thatch hen, hoping that since his mouth would be full, it would also be quiet.

That seemed to work, and gave Jedhian a moment to check how long it had been since Arn had gone out to "bring home the Far clans in his pocket." A glass, probably, and part of another, he judged, when he totaled his scratches in the snow that told his count of the Nohrish men inside the village. He would be to the first clan by now, and making his case. Jedhian smiled, his face raw and stiff. He was very glad Arn was on his side.

Lorris crept up the hill on her belly, the snow pushing uncomfortably into every seam and fold of her leather clothing. When she found a vantage point at the top of the rise, what she saw gave her a start. In the very last of the Nohrish company, waiting with perhaps thirty more men, stood a very tall soldier in a blue cloak, his hood pulled up against the cold. And against identification. It was Nazir himself, visible now that his troops had thinned out. Lorris set her teeth at the sight of him, and a thin smile pulled at her mouth.

Well, you have come out from your hole, you snake. And now you will answer a question I have for you, she thought. *He will be the last one in if he holds to his strategy. If anything goes wrong, he will plan to be able to run away up to the last moment.*

That moment will be mine, she promised herself, and edged back down the hill to see Jedhian applying more speedwell to his own wounds. The little jar, carried in his shirt to keep its contents warm and usable, was almost empty. Jedhian hastily covered the puckering slash on his leg as she came close and smiled a greeting, his eyebrows raised in inquiry.

She looked at him for a long moment, memorizing the color of his eyes, the configuration of his face, the way he looked back at her. She shook her head to signal nothing new.

It was the first lie she'd ever told him.

Arn and Baz raced across the frozen moors, dodging the widowweeds and the quickslime with the ease of long familiarity. In a short time, they were met by the third clan's sentries, who rose up before them from behind mounds of snow. Arn saw them first and tagged Baz's sleeve. They slowed their pace, held up their empty hands and moved cautiously toward the three sentries, who stood their ground and waited: the etiquette of approach in hostile times.

"Hallo, Baz!" one of the sentries called. "I am Senrick. To your left stands Paren and beyond him is Markam. You have come very quickly. What news?"

Arn pricked his ears at the man's voice—where had he heard it before?

"Take us in, Senrick. This is Arn. I vouch for him. We have great news, and much to tell. Make haste," returned Baz.

Senrick was a giant man, his black beard ringed with frost and his eyes bright with anticipation under his hood. He wore a thick bandage on one arm. He clapped Baz on the back with the other, and they all four followed him down a small, well-hidden passage cut in the ground near a patch of widowweeds, which began to sing at their approach, crying the song of abandoned women. Arn shook his head, trying to rid his mind of the sound—he hated widowweeds. Baz and the others seemed oblivious to the doleful music. But Senrick noticed Arn's reaction and lingered a moment at the door before coming in.

They moved into a large cavern much like the one where Arn had met the Haenish elders. Only this one, apparently, housed the third clan whenever the Nohrish raiders threatened. Arn could see that the clan was in the process of moving into the place on a permanent basis: churns and bright blue pottery, looms and other tools, not easily portable but vital to daily life, now occupied the recesses where swords and axes had probably been stored before. The loss of the Keeper, and whatever light the Haenish had provided through him, had caused some desperate thinking in the Far clans.

Arn pulled back his hood and breathed in the warmer air. The other men, one by one, did the same, the order going from youngest to eldest, as was custom in this clan, until it was Senrick's turn. The big man pulled down his hood, holding Arn's eye in his commanding stare, and revealed a head of glossy black hair.

Which was streaked by white in four places from the crown.

"You are—" was all Arn got out before the big man burst into laughter.

"Yes, Arn, I am also known as Morkin, and I am not dead at all. And you—you have escaped Nazir and his entire family curse to be here, I believe."

Lorris had needed a distraction, but nothing as big as the one she got when old Harcher had stopped his raving in midsentence, in midword, smiled sweetly at Jedhian, and died. Jedhian labored now at heaping a decent cover of snow over the old man, while she was supposed to be checking on the troop movements again. But when Jedhian turned to take care of Harcher's feet, Lorris grabbed her pack, slipped silently around the hillock, donned her mail shirt, and made her way through the same course that she had watched Arn take earlier. Only her destination was slightly different. She chose a path toward the Nohrish troops rather than away from them.

Nazir waited, nearly alone, at the top of the next rise. Lorris touched her sword, remembering the broken one she had left behind in Inys Nohr, her father's dishonor upon its blade. She climbed steadily, slowly, patiently toward her reckoning with Nazir, never thinking what Jedhian would suppose at her leaving.

"Lorris?" Jedhian whispered, anxiously looking around. He had just put the last of the snow on Harcher's body when he looked up to find her gone. Along with her sword.

Unbidden, the old man's words came back to him: "She'll betray us! She's Nohrish, can ya not see that, boy?" Jedhian squatted down in the snow, his arms around his knees, waiting for a battle Lorris may have given to Nazir, fighting down the echoes of Harcher's concern and his own worst fears.

"She wants to kill him, you know."

Jedhian jumped, imagining the voice to be Harcher's. But it was only the small bird perched on Arn's discarded armor.

"You . . . you've come back. I had begun to think I had imagined you on the tower, that you were a manifestation of altitude sickness, until I saw you take Aylith. Aylith! Where is she? Is she alive? What of her, tell me!" Jedhian demanded of the dun-colored owl, who had hopped closer and now sat on Jedhian's offered arm.

The owl blinked its amber eyes at him and twisted his head in both directions, sounding the air around them.

"Aylith lives, the last I knew. She is in the best of hands. She struggles to be healed at Loch Prith. She is strong, but she fights a hidden, internal enemy now. Nazir's poison has entered her soul and threatens her spirit. She walks her own path. Trust her. Nazir will never find her there, nor can Malvos hear through the limestone caverns."

"Limestone caverns? More underground caves? I thought Loch Prith was mythical, just a place in elven stories."

"Loch Prith is real, Jedhian. And it is not so far away. But Aylith will have to find her own way home; you cannot bring her out of there. But I can help you get to Lorris, though I suspect you already know where she has gone. Oh, fear not, she is loyal. Very loyal to you, I believe."

Jedhian thought he heard just the slightest echo of humor in the owl's voice, though the bird's impassive face never changed.

"Lorris is just a bit vengeful right now. If you hurry, you can reach her before she skewers Nazir on the blade of her own particular justice. You still need him. Remember, the prophecy requires both lines in order to come true," the bird whistled down to Jedhian as it took silent flight.

After following Loch Prith's small stream through several narrow caverns, the discomfort of being underground constantly plaguing her, Aylith found a gradual lightening in the cavern walls. She thought at first her torch was simply burning that much brighter, the air being richer. But now she stood before a curtain of softly wavering fire.

The prophetess had said there was only one way out of Loch Prith; it appeared she had found it. She steeled

herself to pass through the firewall, recalling all that
the Gwylfan had told her.

*It is only illusion. I can change it, unmake it. I will
not be fooled by what I see, what I hear, what the outside is telling me. It is temporal. I am eternal. It can
harm me only if I believe it can.*

But it was *fire*.

The Gwylfan's words had been burned into her consciousness, but now she would see which was more
real: those words, or this flame. Aylith took a step. The
fire seemed to surge and leap out at her, but she did not
back away. Another foot forward. Another. Then she
felt the heat upon her skin. She wavered a bit, doubting
thoughts flying to her mind. In the heart of the flames,
she saw again the day of the Nohrish raid, saw Thix
throw the torch upon her thatched roof at Inys Haen.
The hut burst into bright showers of sparks, the piece
on her loom, six months of intricate weavework, firing
in another instant. And she saw Logan raise his hands
to her head, about to transfer the Memories.

She flinched from the burning curtain and turned
her face, not wanting to think about her father, about
how he had betrayed her to this task, which should
never have been hers to take up.

Aylith shook her head and drew back, inches from
the wall of fiery glory, and calmed her thoughts, rid-
ding them of her anger toward her father, replacing
them with images of her childhood, when Logan had
brought her the first flowers of every spring, had taken
her to the Sobus to see herself reflected in its waters
after every winter, to remember her own face, and to
see how she had grown. He had brought her a baby
rabbit once and let her keep it in the cottage over the
winter. Finally, she felt ready to go on.

She put out a hand and closed her eyes. Expecting
the fire to burn terribly, like the one in the cottage, she

immediately jerked her hand back, tiny white blisters already forming on her smooth skin.

What was wrong? And then she remembered. *I believed in its power to hurt me, but I must believe more in my power to pass through it unharmed.*

She closed her eyes, thinking of how she had let the power heal Feryar and Arn, took the curtain of flame inside her mind, altered it, destroying its ability to harm her. Her hand stopped burning, and the blisters disappeared.

"You will not harm me." Aylith spoke to the fire. "I release Lorris. Jedhian. RoNal. Feryar. My mother. Logan. I am the Maker's own child, beloved of my clan. I will be the Mender, and for the good of all Cridhe, I must pass."

She put her hand back into the brilliant glory. And this time, there was no pain, only a slight tingling sensation. She opened her eyes to see her hand completely engulfed in the flames, and yet it burned not. Illusion. Temporal.

Aylith took the next step, holding the torch high, passing the real fire through the false, and never looked back.

CHAPTER
26

LORRIS HELD HER BREATH. SHE HAD EDGED
up to within a few yards of Nazir, who still paced in
front of a small shelter on the outcrop of rock, watching his men go down into Inys Haen. He was the last.
This would not take long at all.

Lorris eased her sword from its scabbard, dislodging
any ice that might have worked its way down and
frozen the blade in place. Valuable seconds had been
lost in sword fights that way. Then she stood to her full
height and tossed a snowball at Nazir's feet. He had to
face her—there was no honor in killing your enemy
from behind. Nazir startled, his head whipping back
and forth for a moment, and then all the way around.
For a moment, Lorris thought he would miss her altogether.

Nazir's jaw dropped. "You! Traitor!" was all he
could spit out. He fumbled for his sword, but his practice floor training, in the relative comfort and control
of the tower, had ill prepared him for a real fight. His
blade was stuck.

"Hello, Nazir. I have a question to ask you. And you will tell me the truth, won't you?" Lorris said stonily, her gray eyes never leaving his. In a heartbeat, she was upon him, like the big lynx she so closely resembled.

He dodged her first thrust sheerly by accident, his heel turning on a slick patch of snow. She stopped short of the overhang's drop and whirled to find him still tugging at his sword, the blade finally coming free in a mighty jerk and leaping up into the air, almost uncontrolled. She smiled at him and came on again, her lightning-quick hand flicking her blade through the scarf at his throat. It fluttered into two thin ribbons, and Nazir's white throat was suddenly exposed. He hunched at the shock of the cold on his bare neck and jabbed at her, but his arm was now unbalanced, and the stroke fell far short, and too high. Lorris danced around him, teasing with her blade, this time taking as her prize the brooch on his right shoulder. His bhana fell to the ground, tripping him, and he went down. She leapt in with a foot to his throat and one to his sword hand, and he released his grip on the weapon with a loud snarl and a gasp for breath.

"Different from your practice sessions, where you always win, isn't it? Where you always control everything. I always wondered what you would be like in a real fight. Now, Nazir, Felonarch of Nohr and all her principalities, I will make your throat my whetstone."

She picked up his sword and threw it off the cliff. "How about that answer, Nazir? Here is the question. Why did you have my father killed?"

She stood over him panting lightly, her face flushed and pink, her hobnail boots pressing painfully into his wrist and throat. She gently scraped the blade across several days' growth of dark stubble at his chin, and then touched it coldly to the throbbing vein at his neck.

"My . . . potion," he wheezed. Lorris shook her head.

"My answer. Or your death."

"RoNal led the Albion rebellion. He was a traitor. And now I see it runs in the family!" he rasped, his dark eyes full of fury.

Lorris made ready to deliver the coup de grace. "Oh, you have answered poorly, Nazir. My father was no traitor. And you yourself have made one of me for what you did to him."

Nazir's black eyes narrowed at her, then seemed to focus on something beyond her.

"Every soldier my father ever trained knows that one, Nazir. You have no help left here. I have watched your men all go down." Still, he stared behind her, a curious look upon his face.

"Lorris, do not kill him yet, I ask you." It was Jedhian's voice.

She hesitated at his words, and he came closer. "We need him. Come, help me get him tied and gagged."

"He owes me, Jedhian. I will have what I came for," she murmured.

He walked around from behind her and put his foot on Nazir's other hand, which was inching secretly toward a knife at his belt.

"I thought, for a moment . . ." Jedhian began, his head down.

"You thought I had betrayed you. And what else could you have thought? I knew you would not let me do this alone, so I just went when I had the chance. I did not think about how it would appear to you, I confess. And I am sorry for that," Lorris finished for him. And he nodded.

"I didn't know what I would find when I got here, and I am very glad for what I have seen." Jedhian smiled and let out a huge breath. "So. You have caught us a great, ugly eel. And someone told me the fishing was interesting in Inys *Nohr*."

"We tell everyone that," said Lorris. laughing. "All right, Jedhian. I owe you this much trust. If you say we need him, I will oblige . . . for now, at least. What do you think we should do with him?"

A little later, Nazir was bound, gagged, and on his way back to the hillock outside Inys Haen. The last man from the last group of soldiers came back to an empty command. He ran all the way back to Inys Haen, certain no one would believe him.

Malvos received Zell's news with disdain. After all, the young man had a penchant for telling tales; Malvos had had to listen to several dozen of them all the way from Inys Haen. The one about waking up in a dress was by far the most inventive, but did not come even close to the story he had just finished telling.

"He's what? He cannot be gone. There is no place to go, boy! Has he sent you on ahead with this prank to bedevil me? He heard me as we parted ways, didn't he?" Malvos fumed.

"No, sir, he is positively, actually, completely gone," said Zell, looking as though he were about to succumb to the hack. "I am not telling you a lie, and I have not all this way told you lies." Malvos narrowed his eyes and scowled. "Well, mostly, I have not. All right, I woke up in the dress, but I have no idea how I got there. Beggin' yer pardon, sir, but you are the Sifter—sift this one!"

Malvos studied the young man's ardent, flushed face for a long time, then nodded his head. Actually, he had already sifted the words, but because he did not want them to be true so badly, he refused to believe his own sense. Nazir gone . . . now what? What was the Felonarch up to? Malvos needed time to think.

"Post the gate. We have officially taken Inys Haen and do hereby occupy it," he bellowed.

Zell relaxed and ran to pass the order along.

Malvos pondered the situation for several minutes, entertaining possible reasons for Nazir's mysterious absence. Was this a Haenish trick, or had Nazir neatly made off with the girl after using the troops as escort across the dangerous moors? He leaned against the stone cow byre and fumbled in his pockets for something to satisfy his raging hunger. He seemed to remember there was one last cream tart left. When he found it, he pulled off his glove with his teeth and opened the packet, his nose already full of the tart's rich odor. Malvos bit into the pastry with abandon, his eyes closing at the touch of the sweet cream upon his tongue.

Had he been looking, he would have seen just how it was that Feryar appeared before him, stooping from the high clouds over Inys Haen, and gracefully, silently, arcing over the village. He alighted squarely in front of the big man and resumed his elven shape just as Malvos turned his head and the increasingly frustrated Zell ran up to tell him his orders had been carried out. The courier rolled his eyes, closed them, and turned around, already running for the broken gate, for a quick desertion and whatever chance he might have alone on the moors, this time not even believing himself.

Malvos choked down the last bite of the tart and grabbed instinctively for the sword at his belt.

Just as he remembered which sword that was.

His bare hand locked onto the hilt of Soulslayer with a shock that reeled the great Malvos back upon his heels, and the tattoos upon that hand took solid form and burst through his flesh, sending a dozen black, writhing serpents out upon the silver coils of the quillions, weaving together their scaly bodies, effectively denying Malvos's urgent wish to drop the sword.

"By Nohr!" Malvos shouted as he jerked at the sword. "Let go of me!" He pulled again at the sword, and only succeeded in slicing off his sash belt, the blue flame of the blade leaping at the touch of his anger.

Then he felt the surge of the mana, that glorious, sweet flame inside his very being, the fire of power running through every part of his body, setting every sense on excruciatingly wonderful edge. He could feel everything, hear the music of the universe, and see—

The topmost snake in the coil reverse its head and sink its fangs into Malvos's arm.

"Tempé, you foul witch! How could you do this to me? It was an accident! It wasn't time . . ." He moaned, sinking to his knees. He closed his eyes and began to weep silently, the mana rush fading rapidly from his awareness. For one split second, he had felt alive again.

"Tempé . . . please. I beg you," whined Malvos, forgetting Feryar for the moment. "Please. I am your best." No reply came. Of course.

Feryar walked behind Malvos, retrieved the fallen sash, and took to the air with silent, dun-colored wings.

Arn had ten thousand questions for Morkin, but he settled for one. "You lead the rebellion still, sir?" he asked hopefully.

"Yes, Arn, and you are yet loyal to the cause, I trust. I have never had opportunity to speak with you directly. Thank you for your help these last months."

Arn nodded earnestly. "By my last breath, sir, I would serve you."

Morkin nodded sagely. Arn looked around at the other men in the room, suddenly aware of their presence again.

"You speak among fellow rebels, Arn. The entire Mirkalbion rebellion is connected to the third clan now. Our goals are the same. We seek the same cause. You left the tower before our alliance was put into place. We had thought you dead before the massacre, that Haenish woman having done you in for your clothes. But why are you here now?" Morkin asked, sitting down on a carved stone chair.

Someone put a tankard of steaming Haenish wine in his hand while he waited for Arn to speak again. Before he drank the wine, Morkin took out a small pouch and spiked the cup with a generous portion of ardré. Its bitter smell reminded Arn of the mines.

"It is a long story, sir. Your farthermost sentries, closer on their rounds to the first clan than here, came there with sightings of Nazir and his troops on the moors. This I already knew, having seen him from behind Inys Haen with my two companions. If we hurry, we can contain the Nohrish troops, not allowing them to scatter. They have at best sixty or seventy soldiers, and they are Nazir's best and most loyal. But with the strength of the Far clans and the Haenish, we can cut them off from Inys Nohr. Malvos leads. And Nazir himself marches with the commons. The Felonarch has dared to come down from his tower. It may be the only chance we have to take him. I ask that you send word immediately to the other Far clans, and to Inys Nohr. We haven't any time to lose. Here are the seals of the Haenish and the first clan."

Morkin looked suspiciously at the proffered rings.

"Arn, what makes you think the other Far clans will have anything to do with this? They have made it plain that they want no trouble with the Felonarch. They are fearful of his hand against them in the raids. He is especially hard on the clans that seem the friendliest to the Haenish."

Arn shook his head, but said nothing while Morkin continued.

"We are on the verge of taking the tower, bringing it down forever, of making sure Nazir does not get his way. But you say he is here, on the moors himself, when he has never dared to leave his fortress before. How can we know this? Why is it not better to move as planned, bring down the tower upon him, and visit him with the kind of suffering he has doled out to us for years?"

"Why not leave him surely dead and out of the way, after he's served the purpose of making his troops search for the girl? It is she who will bring the sun back. He can do nothing without her, after all. It is the only chance we have to bring back the light," said Baz.

Morkin sipped his hot wine and considered. After a long while, and a study of Arn's young face, he answered. "Well, then. Why not, indeed? Sixty or seventy troops?" he murmured, still looking at Arn over the cup. Arn nodded. "You may have the afternoon to try, boy. If we do not hear from you again before the last glass, we will move on Inys Nohr as planned."

Arn finally exhaled. Baz shook his hand, and Morkin motioned for someone to bring him a parchment, so that he could draw a map. Arn almost refused it, saying he had his own, but thought better of it, honored that Morkin would draw for him, despite his missing hand. Morkin laid the parchment upon the table, Baz holding it steady, and made several marks upon it, drew some things in, and gave it to Arn.

"These, um, new areas are where you need to go. There are shortcuts through the higher places on the way. We've been at work there recently. You'll find your way easier," he offered.

Arn took the map and looked at it carefully.

"You mean there is a way to get from clan to clan

without using the regular pass? When? How?" asked Arn, his finger tracing the passage through the high hills that Morkin had drawn to the fourth clan.

"Only just of late, boy. We managed to connect with everyone a few days ago. Thought it would serve the rebellion to have a new route. One Nazir did not know about."

Morkin quickly diverted the topic. "Only the fourth clan is high on helping us with the tower, though. You should know that. You might not get much of a reception, but the promise of booty could speed your message along to the others. Tell the high chief at the Fourth clan what you know of the tower, and its riches, and that should be all you have to say," the Albion counseled. "You won't even need to go beyond him—he'll send runners of his own. And if you don't convince him, there is no need for you to go further anyway. The plan will fail without his help."

Arn thought of the carved walnut doors of Malvos's rooms and smiled. He could tell the chief of some wealth like no one in these clans had ever seen. He looked up at Morkin. The Albion's face seemed to contort strangely for a moment, as though he wrestled with some inner pain. Morkin rubbed at the bandage that covered the stump of his arm. *Of course,* thought Arn. *His hand pains him. As it would anyone. He is incredibly strong to bear it so well.*

"When can we leave, sir?"

"You. You alone. Remember to ask for the high chief. And right now is a good time, eh?" came the husky reply. "Some of these passages are very narrow, boy. All these men here are too big. We had planned to widen things out over the next several days, but you can't wait that long. Go now," said Morkin, his big face solemn. Then he smiled and all the teeth in the world shone in the dim light of the cavern's torches, the earlier discomfort seemingly vanished from his countenance altogether.

Arn held out his hand for the ring the high chief of the third clan offered, its three black corbies joining the other seals in his scrip. When Morkin made no motion to offer his own signet, a crude iron band with his initial scratched upon it, Arn shoved the new map into his scrip and unwittingly began his darkest journey thus far.

CHAPTER
27

NAZIR'S TONGUE KEPT GAGGING HIM. THE Haenishman and RoNal's traitorous daughter had tied the cloth too tightly around his head. He held up his bound arms and motioned this fact to them for the fifth time.

"Lorris, we need him alive, and it looks like that gag really is too tight. Could you loosen it just a little?" whispered Jedhian. They had gone back to the hillock and were waiting to see what Arn had managed.

Lorris nodded and moved around Nazir's back to slacken the cloth a bit. When she had finished, Nazir looked decidedly better, though not any happier.

He kept looking down at his chest and squirming. Lorris patted the front of his cloak and brought out a small stone bottle, very like the one of speedwell Arn had procured for Jedhian from Malvos's stores. Jedhian bent over and took the bottle, holding it up to try to read its contents. He unstopped it, smelled the medicine, then sneezed sharply.

"Some kind of bitter medicine. Put it back. He'll get to it soon enough. I don't see any kind of urgent condition upon him," muttered Jedhian, his concentration on the thornwall and the activity inside it.

Nazir's anger burned behind his black eyes, and his fingers, hidden behind his back, flared blue at the Haenishman's insolence. He glared out over his aquiline nose at Lorris with as much contempt as he could muster in the imposed silence. The Felonarch was clearly accustomed to having his own way. Lorris smiled back at him as she replaced the bottle, but her eyes were humorless.

"I'm going in," whispered Jedhian to her as she put her body between Nazir and the Haenishman. Lorris cocked her head at him in alarm.

"Got to—someone has to discuss the ransom," he said, his eyes dancing with danger. "If I'm not back in two glasses, as best you can reckon it, kill him."

He was up and off before she could make her case to go herself. A fellow had to prove himself at some point. And so far, Lorris had more points than he did.

Lorris slapped the ground where she sat as he disappeared around the hillock. From behind her came a deep, throaty chuckle. Lorris twisted around to see Nazir standing, gagless, his bonds burned through.

She gasped once before his fist clipped her across the jaw. In seconds, he had her gagged and her hands caught and cinched tight in the same cloth they had torn from his cloak to do the job on him.

"You are so very brave with a weapon in your hands, little girl. And not so brave at all when the big man is gone and you are surprised. Perhaps you recall the old Nohrish proverb: 'The last laugh is always the Felonarch's.' I do hope that isn't too tight," he sneered, shaking the snow from his ragged cloak, taking her sword, and moving away after Jedhian.

Nazir's punch lacked much power. Lorris awoke shortly and held up her hands to try to wriggle out of

the bonds, and then stopped, transfixed. The ends of
the cloth had been burned through. How could they
have forgotten about Nazir's firefingers? She silently
rebuked herself. Jedhian may not have even known.
But she was responsible for this one. And Nazir still
owed her a better explanation about her father.

Nazir moved with spite and urgency, staying just far
enough behind Jedhian that the Haenishman could not
hear him, watching Jedhian's graceful, silent descent to
the village. How assured this man was. How resource-
ful and confident. Jedhian had fought Nazir's troops in
the raid. He had made the incredible journey to Inys
Nohr alone. He had faced the frog and the fright of the
executioner's sword. And the plague, too, from what
Nazir could tell from the way he had anointed that
wound on his leg. Nazir's face began to burn with
envy. He felt inside his cloak for the small stone jar
and brought it out.

But the contents of Nazir's bottle would not have
helped him, unless he had the plague. It was only
speedwell.

Nazir swore to himself and threw down the stone
jar, making a small *thunk!* in the light snow. Jedhian,
two-thirds of the way to the village, whirled at the
noise behind him.

"Nazir! What have you done with Lorris?" he
snapped, charging the Felonarch instantly.

Nazir made no reply, but met the onslaught with a
drawn sword, and this time, his blade came away
cleanly from its sheath. Jedhian ducked, diving into the
snow, and caught Nazir around the ankles, pulling him
down on the sharp rocks that surrounded them. Nazir
wrenched his sword arm in a clumsy attempt to break
his fall, and Jedhian was upon him.

"No, by Nohr, you of all of them will not have the pleasure!" rasped Nazir, squirming free of Jedhian's headlock, and slipping away between two tall boulders to leave Jedhian winded and panting.

Lorris shook one of her legs above her head, dodging the dagger that fell from her boot by mere inches. In another moment, she had cut her bonds and was by Jedhian's side.

"He got away, Lorris," said the Haenishman, suddenly feeling the effects of the last days and his all too recent recovery from the plague.

"I know. But I will find him, Jedhian. I promise." She hushed his objections. "I should have known to bind him with steel. He has a certain power in his hands—"

"Like Aylith, then. I had wondered about the white brows."

Lorris nodded. "Can you make it back to the hiding place?"

"Yes. I'll be fine," he replied, and she was instantly off in the direction he had pointed out.

Jedhian thought he should be moving now, as the snow was making him sleepy.

A minute later, Zell, on his certain way to desertion, running from what he had just witnessed in the village, saw yet another astonishing thing. Now he came upon the Haenishman, blue and stiff and all but dead.

"Ah, no . . . what now?" the young man exclaimed, still reeling from his encounter with Feryar. He dragged Jedhian up, brushed the snow from his face, and gave a long, low whistle. "You'd be the frogbait that got away earlier. And the healer. Well, they'll have to believe my stories now. At least one of them."

He caught Jedhian by the collar and began to haul him toward Inys Haen.

Arn did not like the way this part of the trip felt. He ran the way Morkin had told him, but to his keen sense of direction, the path seemed to take him ever farther afield from the fourth clan. He found a couple of boulders that sheltered him from the wind, sat down on the tail of his leather shirt, and took out the map Lorris had given him, along with Morkin's.

Arn traced the way he thought he had come on both maps. According to Morkin's map, he was right where he should be, but the landmarks were definitely wrong when he matched them to Lorris's map. The group of hills that should be behind him was in front. He rechecked Lorris's map. Again and again, he saw that her map showed the mountains where they really were.

Arn had no time to sit and make excuses for Morkin. Whatever the reason the Albion leader had sent him astray, he had to warn Jedhian. And here he was, miles from Inys Haen. His allotted time would surely run out before he could make it to the fourth clan from here.

The only quicker way was over the Slicks, but that would take him through the biggest patch of widowweeds on Cridhe.

A slow, painful dawning came to Arn as he remembered how Morkin had paid such attention to his adverse reaction to the eerie, deadly plants when he and Baz had entered the cavern. Arn shoved the false map back into his scrip. Morkin had not meant to send him astray.

He had meant to kill him.

•   •   •

"You think the boy can make it in time, Morkin?" said Baz as he paced back and forth in front of the cavern's entrance.

By now Arn should be at the fourth clan, and there should be some sort of smoke signal appearing just at the top of those widowweeds. But Baz saw only clouds.

"Morkin?"

Baz turned almost in time to avoid the blow. But Morkin dropped him where he stood with the pommel of his sword, walked over him, and put the third clan behind him as quickly as he could. If Nazir camped somewhere on the moors, if he could make it in time, catch him out alone, Morkin could assure that the Felonarch would never bring the light and destroy all the ardré forever. And for that, he did not need the fourth clan, or anyone else.

"So he knows I know he doesn't want the light," grumbled Arn as he trudged over the last of the higher hills, toward Inys Haen, figuring it out. "And he didn't tell none o' them that. That's how he got 'em to help him.

"'Our goals are the same' and 'Our cause is one.' What hooey! He couldn't spare me tellin'. So he sent me out here to get lost. 'Poor Arn,' he'll say. 'What a brave little lad. Must have run afoul. There's so much can take a body down out there. Too bad we had to send him alone,' is what he'll say, and all of 'em will nod their heads, and ask if I had any family, and 'what about a song or somethin', to carry the lad's name.' But he won't get the chance to sing it, that Morkin won't."

Arn quickened his step and put another quarter mile behind him in complaint before he saw something red and blue in the snow up ahead.

He stooped over the bhana, its colors and patterns

sparking a vague memory, and then whistled low and
long.

"That be the Lady Aylith's. She had it on her head
so's they couldn't tell 'twas her, when she took my
clothes," he marveled, bending to pick it up.

Then the instinct of living on the moors for most of
his young life took over, and he paused, his hand just
above the cloth. Arn drew his dagger and pricked at the
bhana, trying to arouse any sort of movement from it
should it really be a shroud. But it lay still, even when,
with some difficulty, he pinned the dagger all the way
through. Only then was he satisfied that it truly was
Aylith's bhana. Arn picked it up and shook the snow
from it, then folded it up and tucked it inside his leather
shirt. When it was warm enough, after another mile
toward Inys Haen, he put it around his shoulders and
raised the hood, the thick weave of the wool scratchy,
but far warmer than the short collar on his leather shirt.

Several long, uphill miles later, Arn came to the
crest of the last hill before him. The dark twilight had
dropped into even darker night. Arn topped the hill
but kept walking, missing his footing every so often on
the steep slopes, but aware that he had to continue,
even though he had no doubt missed the chance to
alert the fourth clan. All he could do now was try not
to freeze to death and to get back to someone who
could stop Morkin. They had to be told about Morkin.
Whatever the Albion leader purposed, it could not be
what the rest of Cridhe needed, Arn now realized.
What had Morkin said? That Nazir "should not have
his way"? Arn didn't know how he had missed it. It
had been so plain. Nazir wanted light, even if he
wanted it his way. Arn shook his head, berating himself for how gullible he had been.

*All this time, I have believed Morkin to be working
to free the slaves. But he just wants to take Nazir's*

place. One oppressor for another. One darkness for another.

Arn slogged on, coming into the frozen marshes, lost in his thoughts, forgetting his caution, until too late.

The sound of mourning women rose all around him, the death chorus of the giant widowweeds, which had been obscured by the fall of night and Arn's self-absorption.

Arn was in the Slicks.

At the sound of his greatest fear, he startled badly, missed his step, and went down, down into the frozen embrace of the widows, their trilling, breathy voices the last thing he heard.

Until Feryar, his owl's ears pricking at the commotion of the struggling boy and the keening widows, dove sharply from his lofty circling and swooped down over the murky morass.

Owls, especially elven ones, have little trouble seeing in the dark. But were it not for Jedhian's gaudy red-and-blue bhana, not even Feryar could have seen what had already been swallowed by the icy swamp. The owl plunged into the tarlike swill of dead fungus and the rotting remnants of prey that the widows lived among, grasped the bhana in fervent hope, and strained mightily upward, flapping his small wings for all he was worth.

At last it was enough. The bhana tightened around the boy's neck and Arn broke the surface in a huge, angry gasp, flailing his arms, coughing up the foul murk he had swallowed in his underwater frenzy. Feryar managed to keep the boy's arms and legs from striking his wings out of the air only by letting him go again, this time over more solid ground. Arn hit the earth with a hollow thump.

Feryar floated down, pulled the constricted bhana away from the boy's throat, and perched upon a broken stalk of broom. He waited for Arn to regain his breath.

"Boy, you will freeze to death out here with no shelter and no fire. You are soaked through. Where shall I take you?"

"Ah . . . wh-where did you come from, and how is it you speak? Am I dead? If I am dead, how is it I am so c-cold?"

Arn's teeth chattered audibly as he wiped the filth from his eyes and face. But then, suddenly he stopped shivering. A bad sign.

Feryar fluffed and smoothed his feathers, preparing to fly again immediately. "Please, boy, just tell me where you are going. You haven't long before the cold takes you."

Though Arn's mind was working slowly, the cold turning him bitter blue in his wet state, he could still think well enough to sort out his destination.

"Sir owl, how far to the fourth Far clan?"

In the next heartbeat, Feryar took to the air, the freezing boy in his grasp again.

CHAPTER
28

ARMED WITH A SINGLE SMALL TORCH AND
the magical thread, Aylith moved through the dank
caverns with as much speed as she could muster. It
was more of a climb than a walk in some places. She
had no idea how far she would need to go, but the rise
of the cave floor told her that she was moving upward
all the time, and the surface had to appear soon.
Thrissa said that Loch Prith was under the Western
Sea's shore. How far could that be from Inys Haen?
She and Jedhian had sneaked off there several times
when they were kids, but had never seen anything but
craggy seashore and storms.

The way had not been too rough. The caverns were
fairly warm, though damp. And whatever lived down
there had retreated quickly whenever she came too
close. The rock formations, smooth and fluid,
reminded her of the surface with their hills and valleys,
their long flat fields. Aylith began to hum a bit, her
heart lightened since passing through the firewall. This

didn't seem so bad now. And the equinox would be fine.

I can do this, she told herself. I will be the Mender.

She moved on through the course of the underground stream, her own voice as company, until she reached a fork in the little river, where the water parted in two smaller streams, one going straight ahead and the other veering to the right.

"Thrissa, you did not tell me . . ." she began, her heart becoming suddenly anxious. She sat down on the cool stone bank, holding the torch well above her head, thinking. She began to notice that her torch sputtered and grew more faint.

Use none of your energy before the equinox.

She jumped at the clarity of the thought. Thrissa's voice seemed to fill the cavern. Aylith sat as still as the stone forms around her, the beating of her heart threatening to deafen her. The torch sent up a last curl of dark smoke and flickered out.

There is no darkness quite like the darkness of a cave. Aylith could not see her hand in front of her. And the darkness seemed to have substance, pressing upon her shoulders with its great heaviness. But after a short time, she began to see splashes of color on the face of the darkness, and the color took shapes, and suddenly, spring unfolded before her eyes, a radiant vision of green growing things. Aylith took a deep breath, put one foot in front of the other, faster and faster, until she was running, the magical thread trailing out behind her.

Through the caverns, blind but for the Memories, passing over the bottomless drops and sheer precipices that would have stopped her in her tracks had she seen them, her feet flew over the narrow, slippery rock bridges, never stumbling, never falling, the caverns always rising, room by room.

She moved through a cramped, narrow passage, picking her way over the increasingly sharp rocks. When the constriction became almost more than she could bear, when it seemed as if she was making no progress at all, from somewhere high above gray light seeped through, banishing the utter darkness she had grown accustomed to, the walls of the tunnel falling away sharply. This part of the cavern looked like it had been collapsed long ago, but not long enough for the edges of the split and harrowed rocks to be completely smoothed by the steady drip of the limestone-laden waters. She rubbed her eyes. This was no illusion.

"This . . . this is part of the Great Rending," she breathed. The island's heart lay exposed before her, the opalescent rocks gleaming dully, promising fire if ever light, true light, struck them again. When the path widened out, she stood in a vast underground room as flat as a field. It could have been any meadow on the surface, but the trees and bushes were composed of stone, unmoving and cold. She walked out into the underground plain, feeling more and more like someone was watching her.

And it seemed someone was. In the very center of the expanse stood the body of a man, strong in life, hands the size of shovels, a neck like a bullock's, now easily mistaken for a natural rock formation. His eyes, frozen in their eternal stare, seemed to look right through Aylith, into a time beyond—or behind.

Raphos the blacksmith, lost in the Parting, was found again.

"Oh . . . by Haen's own hand!" she blurted, the cavern amplifying and echoing her words.

Maybe it was something about the large cavern. Maybe the way Aylith's voice washed through the baffles of the stalactites. But the vibrations struck several stones around the edges of the plain and they shattered.

Raphos slowly shook his rock-encrusted head. His jaw creaked slowly open. "No. By the hand of Nohr," he croaked, his voice unused for centuries.

Aylith barely had enough time to duck as his massive fist tore loose from its limestone shell and slammed into a low-hanging stalactite behind her head. She whirled around, still shocked by the sight of the man, so long a prisoner of the icy touch of Soulslayer. Raphos's body looked just like the rocks he had fallen into so long ago, whitened and stiff. All this time, he had lain here in the deep earth, never quite dead, the steady drip of the weeping rocks slowly covering him with stone. Nohr had rent him of his mind, leaving only a body and a spirit consumed with evil. Evil bestowed by an old sword. . . . Aylith was beginning to remember now. Logan had told her the legend so many times when she was small, but like the stories of Loch Prith, she had believed most of it to be embellished and imaginary.

As Raphos awkwardly turned to come at her again, she slipped on the slick, smooth rocks and found her feet wedged between a couple of enormous boulders, probably fallen when the Parting occurred. Frantically trying to free her feet, she watched the unseeing, unknowing blacksmith bear down upon her relentlessly. Her legs would not move.

"No, Raphos—stop! Stop! I mean you no harm!"

But he was close enough for her to see the ugly, jagged wound still gaping upon his chest, right above his heart, icy crystals still clinging to its edges: the rime of Soulslayer, and the violence of Nohr's angry words.

Aylith closed her eyes as he closed his cold, stony hands around her throat.

His wound is just like mine, she thought. *This is what I would have become. He has lain down here all these centuries, hating, hating, hating . . .*

Just as she was about to lose consciousness, the unseen thread slipping from her hand despite the knot, Raphos loosed his grasp. Aylith opened her eyes and took a deep breath. The blacksmith crouched before her, looking at his hands in bewilderment. Where he had laid hold of Aylith, his hands had recovered their look of human flesh, warm and infused with blood under only slightly too pale skin. Slowly the effect spread through his body. His eyes regained their brown tint, and his hair began to turn black. The scales fell away from his body in small chalky showers whenever he breathed. The wound on his chest closed slowly and healed, a thin scar the only reminder of his battle with Nohr so long ago. Raphos blinked for the first time in five hundred years.

Aylith massaged her neck and watched as he rose, walked around a bit, his mouth searching for words.

"What happened? Where is this place? How am I come to be here?" he whispered.

"Will you help me, Raphos?" Aylith asked, the problem of her entrapped feet still very much on her mind now that the man was not trying to kill her. He quickened to her voice and found her face in the dimness of the cavern, as if seeing her for the first time.

He put his hands to the topmost boulder and pushed. She rolled from underneath in a smooth motion, the magical thread adjusting perfectly to the movement, her feet still intact and only a bit bruised. But Raphos had not fared as well. He turned to her, weeping, his strong hands quickly blackening and withering, his knees shaking beneath him.

He collapsed, his eyes upon her, his mouth open, and begging her ear.

"Thank you . . . it's all right. You have freed me. I have freed you." He smiled.

In less time than it took for her to nod, he fell into a

heap of dry dust. Aylith touched the thin scar upon her own chest. "Sleep well, Raphos."

She waved her hand lightly in benediction, and the dust scattered over the cavern floor.

Aylith turned and walked on across the wide plain. At the far side, a shaft of dim light spilled upon the tumbled rocks. The stream she had followed earlier pooled over a ledge, its current stilled and gelid.

Of course, Raphos Falls, she thought.

Beside the frozen stream lay the gaudy sash she had last seen around Malvos's vast middle, cleanly cut through, a small scrip attached. One tawny feather was pinned to the silk sash. Aylith smiled and opened the little bag, shifted its contents around, dug past old crumbs and the several oddly shaped keys, and brought up what she had known lay at the very bottom from the moment she had seen the yellow-and-red sash: the Clan Tree's solitary acorn, its surface shimmering slightly at her touch. She climbed up and out of the cavern, the frozen curtain that was Raphos Falls the only thing left between her and cold Cridhe.

Jedhian awoke with a Haenish roof over his head for the first time in weeks. Unfortunately, he was also on a Haenish floor. He thought he was still dreaming until the courier leaned over him and roughly sat him up. The young man waited impatiently for Jedhian to recover his senses and the use of his hands. Jedhian noted with some alarm that the tips of one or two of his fingers had turned a bit black from the cold.

"You the Haenishman from the massacre day. You'd be a healer, a guard told me. Said you spoke it to RoNal. The Felonarch's man here needs some help from you, then." Zell motioned to a huge mound occupying the only bed in the small hut.

Jedhian rose shakily and pulled back the red-and-blue cover—*just like my lost bhana,* Jedhian thought absently—to see Malvos, his arm swollen to gargantuan proportions and as black as the tattooed adders on his hands. The apothecary breathed in jerks and rasps, his face covered in sweat, and his other limbs twitching.

"By Haen's white brow! What happened here?" Jedhian whispered.

"All I saw was the bird turn into the elf, and then I was away. When I got you back inside, there he was, troops all over him, nobody knowin' nothin', which is what I know, too," quipped Zell.

"The bird—the elf?" Jedhian gave the courier a quizzical look and an odd smile, then shifted his attention back to Malvos again. "This looks like . . . snake bite. But how? It's the dead of winter out there," Jedhian continued, rubbing his cold, reddened hands. "Has he awakened? Has he told anyone what happened?"

"Well, I wouldn't be knowin' nothin' if he had," said Zell, and walked away, leaving Jedhian to deal with a very unusual patient.

He walked stiffly to the fire, brought down some crockery from the mantel, and began to thaw some snow he found in a bucket by the door.

Malvos stirred. Jedhian set down the bowl and bent over the big man, listening.

"Tempé . . . It was an accident. Please . . ." muttered Malvos.

"Wake up, man," said Jedhian in as strong a voice as he could manage. "What happened to you?"

Malvos's eyes fluttered open. "Her adders . . . they have poisoned me. I am dying . . . "

"No, you're not dying. Not yet, at least. We do have a little time, I think. But you are very sick. I need your help with this. Stay with me."

"My arm . . . "

Jedhian hadn't wanted to think about that yet. The arm was badly damaged, the tissue dark and dead looking already. "Tell me about your arm. What should I do?" he said.

"Pack it in ice, you Haenish fool. That will slow the poison. Have you seen . . . a woman with flaming red hair, dressed in silks, like mine?" Malvos queried.

"No, I have not," Jedhian answered, thinking the fever talked now, and emptying the rest of the snow in the bucket over Malvos's arm.

"Have you seen my sword, then?" A note of hope crept into Malvos's voice.

Jedhian looked around the room, and to his amazement, the sword he had buried Aylith's mother with— the sword he had fumbled in the bailey—stood in a corner, gleaming in the darkness. He brought it over to Malvos.

"The stones . . . I don't know if it's true," the apothecary wheezed, trying to remember something abstruse Tempé had mentioned hundreds of years earlier. "The stones might hold a cure."

Jedhian tried to pry the pommel stones open again, but had no more success than he had that day on the riverbank.

"Try . . . holding one of them and thinking about it open in your hand," wheezed Malvos.

Jedhian closed his eyes and concentrated, and when he opened them, the sword glowed blue around the edges and the stone had, indeed, popped open at its rusty hinge. Jedhian emptied the pale blue powder into a large ceramic pitcher. He tried the other stone, with similar results, except that this stone held nothing at all.

"What?" whispered Malvos, his eyes flying open. "There is nothing in the other stone?"

"Nothing," said Jedhian.

Malvos's memory had fully returned. He recalled with frightening clarity that Tempé had said one of the stones held a cure for the blade's wound, a saphirron crystal, to be used one time only, rendering the sword totally useless afterward. The other stone held a crystal that, when added to water and poured over the blade, would restore its powers. Malvos lay in his bed, the adder's poison crawling slowly toward his heart, trying to decide if he would use the blue crystal to live, or leave the sword in its magical state and try again to leave Cridhe with it. Jedhian, puzzled at Malvos's sudden silence, stood over him, helplessly waiting for further instructions.

"Feryar! That elf has killed me! One way or the other, he has killed me! He has waited all these years for his chance, and has seized it. Ah . . ." Malvos contorted under the blanket.

Jedhian wrested his head up from the pallet, preventing the apothecary from choking. "Come, man, stay with me. I don't know what you want here. Tell me what to do."

Malvos sputtered and coughed, his face a gray mask of pain. The healing stone was still there. There was little choice. "Do it," he croaked. "Mix the powder with water. Pour the mixture over the blade. Use the blade to prick the bite."

Jedhian quickly did as his patient said, and within moments, Malvos had regained some of his color, and the swelling in his arm completely receded.

As did his hopes of ever leaving Tempé's jail.

The sword, its snakes coiling hideously over the blade and hilt, turned black, blacker, and crumbled into flakes at Jedhian's feet. All that remained of Soulslayer was a pile of metal scrap.

Malvos wept silently, sat up in his bed, reached for

the ceramic pitcher, and brought it down upon Jedhian's head with a heavy thud.

When Malvos reached the gate, laden with the largest pack he could find, he shouted his last order to Zell.

"You are in command. Whoever comes to stand against you, do not wait. Meet them on the moors. You will probably triumph!"

Zell turned in astonishment, but Malvos had disappeared.

Across the moors, in the distance, marched several hundred angry Haenish, under the standards of the first and third Far clans, Baz at their command.

CHAPTER
29

ARN DROPPED INTO THE SNOW OUTSIDE THE fourth clan, its watchers never seeing his approach. The first sentry to him came in warily, circling the unconscious boy until the hooded man had assured himself that Arn posed no threat.

"Rallu, come quickly. Here's a lad nearly dead of the cold. We got to get him inside. I thought everyone had been brought in, but we must have missed one."

Rallu did come quickly, taking Arn's blue face in with one practiced glance. "Call the healer. He may lose some of those fingers. By the light, it looks like the boy's been dowsed!"

The two watchers rushed Arn into the secret cavern entrance, and Rallu called for the next shift to take their places a bit early. In the morning, he never would be able to explain to the man who took his watch over why the boy had left no footprints leading up to the clanhold. And the sentry never thought to look up, where the tawny owl circled and circled until Arn had been taken inside, and then flew with the speed of magic toward Inys Nohr.

•   •   •

Sims wiped the sweat from his eyes, the white one
beginning to give him some trouble in the constant
torchlight the delicate sapping required. They were
using all their complement of supplies in a mighty
push toward bringing the tower down immediately.
The men were tired, but they hammered and dug and
hauled continually, as quietly as possible, without so
much as a word from him. This was every Albion's
dream. To see the tower fall. To be free of the
Felonarch's torturous manacles and his brutish
demands. A man could turn sour from that kind of
treatment. He could become the beast that Nazir
treated him like.

They were almost finished. Just a few more feet, and
the tower would be ready, would practically fall over
by itself in the next high wind down from the mountains. Sims smiled. It felt good.

"Sims—there's someone here to see you." One of the
boys hauling buckets of rock to the surface came running through the narrow passage, his way dark but for
the torch at Sims's end.

Sims turned, expecting Henj from the outside crew.

When a small, tawny bird fluttered in behind the boy
and lit on his shoulder, Sims thought perhaps he
needed some fresher air. There were pockets of the
dead stuff down here, could skew a man's thinking
after too long in them.

The bird blinked in the strong light, the pupils in his
golden eyes narrowing to points. "I have flown above
the tower, and I see that you are nearly done with your
sapping. The rocks lean dangerously. They will fall
before you are ready. You will be crushed. Cease your
work here and come to join the Far clans immediately.
They seek Nazir himself. Your efforts will be more

wisely spent helping the clans to defend themselves and take back Inys Haen from its Nohrish occupation."

Sims took a deep breath and, feeling a bit silly, answered the owl.

"Who are you? How do you know this? And how do I know that you are not some bewitched spellcatcher for the Felonarch? He's right here, up in his warm rooms like always. But your voice sounds familiar, bird. I believe I know you." The Albion laughed.

"I am Feryar. Please, I tell you that Nazir is loose on the moors. Malvos is holed up in the Haenish village with Nazir's crack troops. The Haenish left it for the comfort and help of the first Far clan after the last raid."

Sims peered narrowly at the owl. "Show your true self."

Feryar hopped down and shimmered into his elven form. Sims smiled crookedly. "Well, I'll be frogbait. It's the Fool."

Feryar blinked at him and shimmered again, and the owl flew back to perch on the boy's shoulder. "Please. You don't know what you will bring down upon yourselves here. The structure is unsound. It will not fall as you think," he finished.

Sims cocked his head at the bird and thought for a moment. "Feryar. Tell Morkin, as I'm sure you will see him, that we will be along in a little while. We're up to his game here. Tryin' to make sure we wait for him before we drop the tower, that old shaft rat! I should have known he'd do anything to see it himself." Sims laughed. The Albion had no intention of giving up his sapping. Or of taking Feryar seriously.

Feryar gave him a long, sad look, and then flapped noiselessly back up the pitch-black tunnel. He had at least tried.

"Go on with it, men—and double yer stroke," shouted Sims when he was sure the elf had gone to the surface.

•   •   •

Wathel, the fourth clan's high chief, peered suspiciously down at the boy the watchers had brought in. The lad's fingers had turned a bit dark at the edges, but all in all, though he had certainly taken a cold shock, he didn't appear nearly as damaged as he should have. The only place he could have gotten that soaked was the Slicks, and that was miles away.

Arn's hand moved, and then he opened his eyes. A violent shaking began in his legs and traveled upward, his teeth threatening to bite through his tongue.

"Hanna, bring the cloth! The tremor's come on him," Wathel demanded, but the little woman was at Arn's side before he got the words out.

"Hush, you. You'll give him a scare. His heart's in danger of choking him and you want to yell in his ear," she scolded.

Wathel raised his brows, but stood back to let her prop the boy up and put the cloth in his teeth until the chill passed.

"I was only—" he sputtered.

"You were only about to kill him again. Now talk to him like you mean him no harm. See, he's quieted now." Hanna withdrew and left Arn, a rag hanging ridiculously from his mouth, facing the very rebuked high chief. They both pretended not to notice.

"Ah—harumph! Ah—who are you, boy?" Wathel began, pulling the badge of his office to the front of his bhana so Arn could not help but notice.

Arn spat the cloth from his teeth, trying not to gag on it, and said, "I am Arn of the vanquished second clan, sir. I have come to ask your help. My friends have seen Nazir on the moors. He hunts for the wounded Haenish Keeper, and means to do her more harm, and take her Memories so that he may control the light. I

want to ask you to bring yer best men, all of 'em, to
Inys Haen, where Nazir's best men are under the command of the Sifter and have been detained there. I have
come from the first clan, where the Haenish have gathered, and the third clan, also. We've all agreed. See
here, in my scrip are the signets of their chiefs."

Arn's stiff fingers shook out the large rings from his
bag, the mountain seal of the first clan chiming to the
rock ledge alongside the three corbies of the second.
The Haenish oak fell last from the scrip.

"If you will help, we can perhaps reach the Lady
Aylith before the Felonarch. Otherwise, the world
belongs to Nazir. And what do you suppose he will do
with the Far clans then, sir, I ask you? And there's
worse. Morkin, known also as Senrick, the Albion
leader, tried to lose me out here, thinking I would never
reach you. He has turned, sir. I believe he wants Nazir
dead so that the light may never come. I had once
trusted him, believing him to want only the liberation of
his people and no more killing." Out of breath from his
tirade, Arn slumped back to his pallet, panting.

Wathel stood over him gaping, trying to take all of it
in, when Hanna pulled him aside.

"The boy's telling the truth, I can tell it. I got the
truth chill when he spoke his piece. Do what he wants,
Wathel."

Wathel sighed, knowing that when Hanna got the
"truth chill," he would only come to his ruin if he went
against her counsel. Forty years with this woman and
he still had to rely on her for the really big decisions.
But she had never been wrong, he reminded himself, as
he always did right before he agreed with her.

"All right, Hanna. I'll ask him all my questions when
this is over."

Hanna smiled, dimpling at him, and patted his
broad, battle-scarred forearm.

"You'll not see grief for it, Wathel. Now, hurry and tell the captains. I think the boy has the need of haste about him."

Arn was stooped painfully over the rings, gathering them up again when Wathel turned around.

"While I ready my men, find some dry clothes, boy. We will need your guidance," he harrumphed.

Nazir saw visions. He wandered the moors again, just as he had those many years ago, staying warm by moving, the fire in his breast keeping his legs going when he desperately just wanted to sit down. His face had turned a ghastly shade of blue just under the skin. He looked like a dead man already. The mirke had come upon him far more quickly than usual when the ardré was withheld. One of his eyes had gone white, too, and he had a splitting headache from the twilight. Ahead of him there were big trees, and a grassy knoll. It looked so inviting. He ran for it, kicking up snow behind and slipping painfully several times before he reached the knoll, only to find that it was just so much more snow, and the trees were only a couple of big stalk fungi, their tiny spores now dusting him even more thoroughly blue when he crashed into them. He wiped the gritty particles from his face and hands, out of his eyes, and moved on, nearing Raphos Falls. The falls towered over him in a darkly glistening tumble of ice and rock. But Nazir saw great floating mountains in the air. He saw fire in the heavens.

He saw Nohr.

"Ahhh—" he cried, falling to his knees. "Father of fathers, you have come to speak with me."

Nazir bowed his head to an ice floe in the frozen water, which looked far more like a large pig than his ancient ancestor. The distinction was lost on the raving Felonarch.

His chest hurt miserably, and he fumbled again for the stone jar, finally remembering that he didn't have the tonic.

"Malvos. Where are you when I need you most? Where is your soothing potion? My chest burns like a furnace," he mumbled to himself, clutching at the birthmark.

Then he saw his hand. The blue mirke crept over it like the walking plague, covering his skin with its evil sheen. He removed the glove from his other hand and saw the same thing. He tried to rub it off, thinking it was just the dusting of spores. He looked beseechingly into what he thought were Nohr's eyes, but saw only his own altered reflection in the ice. He could deny no longer that the mirke had come upon him. Him, Nazir, Felonarch of Inys Nohr and all her principalities.

He was an Albion.

"How?" he mumbled. Slowly, slowly, he remembered the passage in the chronicles where the Albions had been created. Of course. His father had eaten the ardré, too. How could it *not* have happened? How had he missed this? And all these years—Malvos . . . the tonics. . . . He burst into a raw-lunged tirade.

"Crephas, what you have done to the last of our family?!" he screamed. "All my life I have worked to lift the curse the Haenish put upon us. And you, Malvos!" he continued, his voice rising with the wind. "I see now why your potions have been so necessary. What that foul taste must be—it's nothing but bitter ardré! All these years, you knew . . . why did you never tell me?"

Nazir slammed his fist into Nohr's image and broke into sobs, his dreams of bringing the light shattered along with the ice that had shown him his reflection. It was over. He would die here. Somewhere close by, he thought he heard fighting, but it could have been the wind.

Long minutes passed as he grew colder and colder, giving in to the snow's seductive offer of eternal sleep. The wind began to pick up, even his heavy clothing a poor match for its chill.

Aylith had heard it all. She stepped out from behind the gleaming curtain of the frozen falls and stood motionless before him.

"Look . . . and who is the fair lady who stands watching my demise?" He smiled vacantly, his voice small and tired. "Do you come to take me to the next world? Have I fallen to the curse so completely? Is this how it ends? I feel so strange. There is a dark thing strangling my heart."

Aylith watched as the man who had killed her father and mother swayed helplessly in the snow, covered in the mirke and grit, raving. The man whose family had destroyed the balance of life on Cridhe and had endangered every living thing in a wanton act of selfishness. All for the love of power.

The same power she held in her hands just now. Her face became stony as she rolled the Clan Tree's seed in her fingers. She trembled at the thought of what it would be like to simply strike Nazir dead with the fire in her hands. To unleash that magnificent natural force upon Nazir at his weakest moment, at the moment when there was no doubt that she would be able to finish him instantly.

Or drag out his death in small seconds, just to make sure he knew what was happening to him, and just who was killing him. How sweet it would be to see him suffer. . . . She thought of Logan and the fire again, and of her mother, struggling against Thix's cruel, random sword. And of Jedhian, his head upon that block, while Nazir mocked him and stirred the crowd with the prospect of his death. She thought of her own wound at Nazir's hand. The terrible pain, the unjust hurt. A bitter taste formed in Aylith's mouth. She would have to bring the spring tomorrow. Images of the twisted Clan Tree rose in her mind, the gall of her anger shaping them.

"Release the prisoner of your heart. . . ." Thrissa's words echoed in her ears, again and again.

"You will be healed. But the third labor will take all your compassion . . . " the Gwylfan had said.

She longed to raise her hand and show the Felonarch just what she could do now. This time, she would not try to distract him. This time he would die. In her hand, the invisible thread from the Gwylfan's tapestry loosened again, and slipped from first one finger, then the next, until it hung loosely in her failing grip, all but forgotten. The evil root curled enticingly around her other finger, a tiny tendril spreading to her wrist, wedding her to her choice.

"Free the prisoner of your heart," Thrissa's words insisted faintly.

This time, she would. . . . Aylith clutched the acorn with all her might and strode forward to finish her sentence.

"No! He's mine, Aylith! Stand back," panted Lorris, the vein at her temple pulsing with fury as she charged upon them. "He has hurt Jedhian, and he has taken my father, too. But he is my countryman, and *I* will finish this. It is my right!"

Nazir knelt in the snow, holding out his hand to them. His eyes were burning, his energy having returned at the prospect of gaining back his life. But there was no repentance in them. Only desperation and madness. He was an injured beast. A snake that would turn and strike the instant he was healed. Aylith shook her head.

"No, Lorris. He has been mine since the Maker spoke the words that created us all. I am the Mender. . . . "

Like a bell on the wind, the truth of her words chimed in her heart, and with that utterance, Aylith finally, truly, believed that she was the Mender. She said it again, more softly: "I am the Mender."

Lorris faltered in her step toward Nazir.

Aylith could now clearly see how the rage distorted Lorris's face, twisting her features out of place, giving her beauty away to a hard, fierce scowl.

"I must look just like that. Just like Raphos. Just like . . . Nazir," she whispered.

Thrissa's voice resounded in her ears: "Look for his true nature. . . . " True nature. Not what she now saw in this defeated man, not the ugliness, the pain, the feral rage. His true nature. Like the wall of fire, where she had passed without damage. Imagine him healed. Imagine him well.

"And I will be healed also. . . . " she breathed. The World Weavers' invisible thread snapped tight and again knotted itself fast upon her finger. The last tendril of the evil vine shuddered off and fell away.

Lorris stood rooted to the spot, seemingly unable to move, the power in Aylith's voice compelling her to hold her peace, to let this happen. Tears streamed down her face, and her hand trembled helplessly upon her sword. Aylith had spoken.

Aylith raised her hand, called forth the Clan Tree's power, the green fire flaring upon her fingertips. And placed it on Nazir's chest, over the mark of the curse.

"I release you," she cried, and plunged into the black depths of Nazir's pain, her only protection the life-giving power Logan had bequeathed her.

At her searing touch, Nazir's eyes flew open, the mark on his chest on fire like never before. He thought he was dying again and struggled with Aylith, trying to remove her hand, tear away the green energy that flowed into his body. He summoned strength from some unknown reserve, thrashing as her hand seemed to meld with his flesh. She felt as though she were losing herself completely, all self-awareness burning away with the effort of turning the curse and trying to hold the struggling man still to maintain her contact. Aylith felt as though she were losing the fight, but then a strong hand, its lightning scar white with effort, was helping her, a hand that had held a sword only moments before. She could not see Lorris, but Nazir buckled under the force of the warrior's restraint. Aylith seized the moment to regroup her power.

Then suddenly she Saw it, the vision leaping before her eyes. A huge, twisted bitteroot, growing tall and wide in Nazir's heart, crushed every bit of goodness in him, squeezed the life from his soul and body, leaving his spirit dry and cold, like the moors and mountains of his kingdom. She moved toward the great black vine, repulsed at its stench and ugliness. She reached out to slash down the bitteroot, but it loomed up at her all the larger.

"Do not look on it. See him as he is. Look for his true nature," came the gentle words of the prophetess.

Aylith closed her blinded eyes, and remembered a different Nazir. One that she had never known. A vigorous, healthy man, who walked about with no pain, who did not need Malvos's medicines. A kind man, a benevolent ruler. A man who loved. A man free from the Curse.

Through her touch, she told Nazir who he really was. Told his body, and it began to fill with vigor, new, healthy flesh emerging as the corruption of the mirke peeled away. Told his mind, and the madness there was filled with peace. Told his heart, and it was transformed.

Aylith relaxed into the Memory, knowing it was right. Then she put out her hand to sunder the horrid vine. But it was already dead. The dark pieces of the putrid plant lay at her feet, tangling in themselves, foul and smelling of decay. Nazir was free.

He gave a great gasp and Aylith lost her hold on him, falling backward into the snow, the precious acorn rolling from her pocket. Lorris fell back also, completely exhausted.

Nazir woke as though he saw the world for the first time. He felt his chest where the burning mark had tormented him all his life. The fire was gone. Only a thin, painless line remained, the silver cord of an old, healed scar. And by him lay the glittering acorn Aylith had taken from the Clan Tree's crown. Nazir picked it up reverently, transfixed by its glow, and clutched it tightly in his hands, its light filling the space exactly between his palms. Nazir knew he was different inside. He smiled, feeling his face take a new shape, the perpetual sneer replaced by the lines of a genuine smile. Nazir held up one hand, marveling at the power he knew he held in it. His fingers glowed with a new color, the mirke gone, the old blue of the cold anger changed to green.

Green!

Nazir shook his head in amazement. He looked out toward the west, and instead of seeing the barren wasteland he had always known, he saw a verdant pasture, full of so many shades of green that he could never count them and never tire of trying. Nazir had never seen such color, such life. He heard the music of the grasses in the warm breeze, the work of the insects in the flowers, and the songs of birds in the trees.

He knew the names of every living thing.

He knew the light spell.

"By Nohr! I have them. I have the Memories!" he shouted, jumping to his feet in exultation. "And the Clan Tree's seed! The Curse is lifted!"

He closed his eyes and opened them again. The ground lay barren as before. He called forth the power in his hands—and the land came alive in his mind.

Nazir laughed. Not the hideous, pain-ridden laugh of his past. A glorious, musical laugh, full of love. He sighed, tears streaming down his face. He knew things he had never known before. He knew he lived and took joy in it.

He knew the equinox was only an hour away.

He must work the light spell at Inys Haen's blessing stone. Malvos would have to be found . . .

Something stirred behind him.

Nazir slowly turned to look at Lorris, bending over Aylith. She lay in the thin snow, her sandy hair tumbling over her face, her hands tinged blue from the cold and smeared with the dust of the tree fungi. Lorris pulled herself up and looked at him, her face unreadable. Nazir bent and gathered Aylith in his arms and touched her face. She did not awaken. He tried her pulse, so faint that it could have been a trick of his mind.

How could he have never seen it? How lovely she was. An odd, new feeling stirred in Nazir's heart.

Suddenly, his long-nurtured revenge did not seem at all important. The world became very small, and the past did not exist. Nazir held Aylith's hands in his own, willing them to warmth, his fingers glowing green.

"Come back, Aylith."

Aylith's lashes fluttered briefly, and he could sense how hard she fought to return. But it was not working. There was something in the way; he could not reach inside her heart, could not connect.

"How is it you could heal me and I cannot do this for you?" he pleaded.

Moments passed, and he went over and over what he had felt when she touched him, every sensation, every emotion. The eastern horizon began to glow, the faintest hint of the equinox's arrival. There was no more time. Lorris saw it, too.

"Soldier, will you help me take her home?"

Lorris nodded. And then saluted.

Nazir smiled, his features almost those of a different man, thought Lorris. They gathered Aylith up, wrapped her as warmly as possible, each giving her one of their garments, and started at a run toward Inys Haen, trying to outrace the daylight.

CHAPTER
30

LORRIS AND NAZIR, CARRYING AYLITH, stumbled across the moor with greater speed than either of them had thought possible. Though the Far clanners and the Haenish had indeed joined battle with Nazir's troops, they managed to get up to the fording point of the Sobus, and were within a few yards of crossing the ice when a man rose up before them, sword drawn and ready. Nazir buckled at the sight of the white-eyed man glaring down at him, but Lorris pushed on, despite the words of the Albion leader, a man in a red cap, a man with only one hand.

"Stop, girl. I have no desire to kill you. It's him I want," said Morkin, his handless arm waving at her in warning.

Lorris did stop. Nazir took her hand and said, "You are Morkin. They told me you were dead."

"Not very. And the Albion nation would like you to know that there will be no light brought back to Cridhe. You can live if you'll just come quietly. I would

like to speak to you about compensation for my loss."
He waved his handless arm again.

"But Morkin—how can you want that? What about
everyone else? What about the rest of the world? And
if I did that to you, I swear, I will make things as right
as I can," said Nazir.

Morkin eyed him warily. "When have you ever cared
for another, Felonarch? What has befallen you out
here, eh?"

"Morkin, let us pass. No more blood. The Curse is
lifted. The equinox comes." Nazir pointed to the eastern horizon, where a thin ray of red light now pierced
the cloud cover.

Morkin slowly shook his head. His hand tightened
on his sword.

Nazir looked him straight in the eye and took a step
forward. Morkin raised his blade, his legs instantly bal-
ancing, despite the awkwardness of his missing hand.
Nazir had less than a second to wonder where the man
had learned his fighting skills and how he had slipped
his chains. The sword came down with a blinding flash
inches from Nazir's head, the Felonarch twisting aside
just in time.

Still carrying Aylith, Nazir corrected his stance and
ran past Morkin's undefended side, low and out of
range, and never looked back. At the same time, Lorris
edged by on Morkin's right, sweeping the man's heavily planted feet in Nazir's old sparring trick. Morkin
fell heavily, but Nazir had no time to appreciate
Lorris's skill. The thornwall was only yards ahead.

They rushed the open gate, the two soldiers man-
ning it preparing to defend until they saw who
approached. Lorris waved Nazir on as he bounded for
the Blessing stone, just as the ray of light hovered at
the gate and passed through the gap. Nazir stood
Aylith against the stone, removed the acorn from his

pocket, dropped it into the gap in the stone, and began the litany of light.

"Fourth prime: north. I bind and break the hand of winter . . ."

Aylith stirred at his side, and Nazir lost the words. He began again, picking up the phrase.

". . . the claw of frost, the strength of storm—"

"The blade of ice, the covenant of crystal." Aylith spoke the words with him. Nazir smiled; her voice, however small, carried in the wind like a bell. She seemed to gain strength as they continued.

"Third prime: west . . ."

"She's comin' down early, man, shift yourself!" raged Sims as the last of the sappers scurried to the surface, the tunnel falling in behind them.

It was too soon, too soon, and what had happened? Sims cursed and swore, his lungs filling with choking white dust, the remains of the foundations of the house of Nohr. The tower creaked horribly, like a ship going under, the big rocks grinding one on the next, the stone shuddering over Sims's head in its death throes.

I thought at least to have seen it from the outside, he wished, *but only tell me that Nazir is as trapped as I, and I'll pull away the last stone myself.* Sims braced himself for the end.

But a moment later, the building settled again and, still creaking, fell no further. And there was—could it be?—a strong light at the end of that tunnel. His eyes stung from its brilliance, the white one rhythmically pounding with pain. He turned and started the other way, down toward the comforting darkness. The sappers were calling out to him, to hurry, that they could see the sun. The sun? Sims thought they must rave, or he himself must be breathing dead air to hear such as

that. Then it occurred to him that he could possibly see
the tower fall from above after all. That maybe . . . it
wasn't over just yet.

His hope reborn, he carefully stepped over debris
and rubble, the way out clear now that the dust had
more or less settled. There was some kind of sound
ahead as well—a gurgling, wet noise. He began to inch
along the tortuous path, gaining confidence with every
step.

"Sims, wait, not that way—come toward my voice,"
Klaer called, and waited several moments for a reply.

"Sims?"

But Sims could no longer hear him. Sims could no
longer hear anything from inside the gullet of the frog.
The beast sat in its same place, amid the mire and filth
of its past feeding, contentedly digesting, completely
oblivious to the unimaginable weight of the tower bal-
ancing precariously above it.

"I don't hear nothin'," said Spens, a man of fifty-seven
winters, one of the original Mirkalbions.

Outside the leaning tower, the rest of the crew
crouched at the tunnel's entrance, reluctant to leave
their boss.

"Look out, men—she's crumblin'!" shouted young
Klaer, his eyes on the tower.

A huge, black bitteroot growing up the tower by his
foot snapped and dropped away, its tendrils unfurling in
long black ropes as it crashed to the ground. The sappers
ran for cover, just as the undermined heap collapsed, the
other bitteroots seeming to release their grip all at once.
Within seconds, all that was left of the Tower of Inys
Nohr was a pile of boulders and a thick cloud of dust.

"Well. What now?" said Klaer from under the wall.
"Sims . . . "

"I know, boy. He's in his grave," said Spens, looking beyond the ruined tower. "As will we all be soon. Look."

He pointed to the north face of the first mountain, where the strong light had, indeed, begun to wilt the precious colonies of ardré, turning their lovely blue plates a sickly brown.

Arn wanted to run for his life, but his feet refused to move under him. The sky seemed to open up in a limitless expanse, the ever present clouds rolling away in a great wave. The brightening beyond them was too much for him to look at, too much to comprehend all at once. Brilliant light streamed down upon his face and shoulders, bathing him in warmth. Rays of gold touched the gray land, and Arn saw the granite take color and glitter as the great rocks of the moors caught the sun. Shades of red and brown and purple and orange and a color Arn had no name for sprang up before his startled, sun-struck eyes. Cridhe had a new face, and it was beautiful beyond Arn's imagination.

The line of Far clanners behind him had fallen to the ground, trembling, their weapons scattered like toys around them. They shielded their eyes and muttered curses and prayers, some wept, and others laughed hysterically. The Haenish Speaker invoked the Maker. Odser and Baz danced around Wathel, who bellowed an off-key serenade. Whether in protest or accompaniment, a sheepkeeper barked close by.

Another sound came to Arn, and Arn alone, conquering every other voice. The Clan Tree's sweet melody came to his ears and swept over him, like a song he had never heard before but knew completely, thoroughly. And the clouds continued to roll back, from Inys Haen, from the Far territories, all the way to

Inys Nohr, they withdrew, leaving a clear blue sky
behind them and a warm breeze in their wake.

Arn broke through another line of bewildered rebels,
walking, then running swiftly toward the source of the
glorious song, over the glittering pools of melting ice,
despite the heavy mud clinging to his leather boots.
The dog he had heard earlier—he would later learn it
was Aylith's dog Nesa—joined him, nipping at his flapping shirttail. The rings of the Far Clans jingled as he
ran. He smiled, thinking that he had fulfilled his
promise "to bring home the entire Far Clan nation in
his pocket."

When he got to the Sobus, the ice was breaking up
and passage over it seemed impossible. But Arn was
not to be denied. What was the Sobus after the Slicks?
He hopped onto a large floating berg, then onto the
next, until he had skipped his way to the other side of
the river, his boots soaked, but his clothing still completely dry. When he was seventy, he would recall this
day, and think of the danger he could have come to in
the freezing water, and caution his grandchildren
about the spring thaws to come. But today, he thought
only of getting to the Clan Tree.

Aylith and Nazir stood in the gap of the broken
Blessing stone, bits of light from the spell still settling
over them and falling to the thawing ground like soft
rain. Arn stopped, completely shocked. They began to
glow, the new day shining fully upon them, the sunrise
taking them in a brilliant ray of blinding light, their
shadows falling as one, long and straight behind them.

The lines of Haen and Nohr had merged.

"In a point of light . . ." Arn breathed. "The
prophecy is fulfilled."

Aylith was standing on her own, her face glorious in
the new morning, speaking with Nazir. Well, it looked
a little like Nazir. The spell was finished, the sky was

clear of clouds, and then Arn and Nesa stood staring at the gap in the Blessing stone.

Where the new Clan Tree curled slowly upward from between the two halves of the stone.

He had expected a gigantic oak to grow, its branches hanging protectively over the clanhold, its leaves fully thrown and obscuring the sky, but when the Tree stopped its magical, instant growth, it was just a small twig bent in the warming wind, a sapling, only a few feet high, with several small branches and a few new leaves.

"This is the Clan Tree?" he asked, the crack returning to his voice. He did not care. Only the dog and the two Nohrish soldiers stood in back of him now, their mouths gaping as their Felonarch and Aylith disappeared in a shimmer of light.

But at the sound of his voice, cracking or not, the Tree had begun to shine. Arn felt a surge within his heart he could not resist. The Tree summoned him closer with an inaudible voice, a kind of sound that Arn felt rather than heard. The boy put out his hand upon the little Tree.

To feel wood!

Arn startled as the mysteries of the Tree opened up to his touch. It seemed as if he suddenly looked into the heart of Cridhe—and Saw three women weaving at a huge loom. One pointed to the wall where a tapestry hung, and it was the Clan Tree, grown and full of limb and leaf, and standing beside it was Aylith. A gold-green thread was worked into the Tree's roots and trunk. The women smiled and raised their hands when that thread pulled tight at the top of the tapestry, mending its tear. A white-haired elven woman looked up from her book and began to sing.

Then he Saw down the long years, and the Tree in front of him began to grow, its roots pushing down into the earth, grasping the rocks at the center of the world again, bringing everything back into alignment after its long separation. The stars found their places in the sky again. The seasons came and went as they had before the Parting. He Saw the Tree in a hundred more years, huge and towering; he Saw it in a thousand, standing strong. He Saw the clan united, and Inys Nohr had become a shining city, Inys Haen a great spread of grain fields and pasture, huge orchards and gardens.

He Saw the life stories of a new people, stretching forth into Cridhe's future in a long, uninterrupted line. His hands warmed to the power within the Tree. Arn knew he would never leave Inys Haen again.

He was the new Keeper.

Feryar flew overhead, circling for a moment, then dropping gracefully down to land behind the cow byre and change to his elven form. Zell, who had wisely given over his command to a more senior officer and was currently hiding behind the byre in a last attempt to never again see what he could not believe, simply shook his head and shrugged his shoulders, then offered the elf his cloak. Feryar smiled, accepted it, and made his way over to Arn.

"Feryar. You were never a fool, were you?" said Arn.

"Oh . . ." He looked down at his crooked little finger. "Yes, boy, I was." Tears welled in his golden eyes.

"Feryar, will you give me your hand?" said Arn.

Feryar tilted his head in question, but gave the boy his hand. With one hand on the Tree, Arn closed his eyes and imagined the crooked finger whole and well. Arn's fingertips began to glow, the green fire urging the elf's hand into wholeness.

When Feryar looked down again, his little finger had straightened.

"Thank you . . . thank you," he said in amazement. His golden eyes met Arn's blue ones. *Blue . . .* "I have to go now, Keeper," he said. "I have a new charge, it seems." And he was off in a flurry of pale wings, Zell's cloak falling at Arn's feet.

Morkin, his face in a growing puddle, sputtered awake only when the owl spoke to him.

"Morkin. I am Feryar. I believe I can help you . . . "

The Albion leader shook his head and pointed into the clear, bright sky with his missing hand.

"No, my friend. You cannot. No one can help the Albions now. The ardré is dead."

"Not so. You came far from the mines and the blue fields. Do you not carry ardré with you? I believe it travels best in spore form. Morkin, I know a place where there is enough darkness. It will grow again, and your people will live. There is a place where you and your people can be healed . . . Loch Prith, at the edge of the Western Sea."

Morkin felt for his scrip and patted the pouch of ardré. It was dry and intact. He looked at the owl in bewilderment, a smile beginning at the corners of his wide mouth.

At the first ray of light, Jedhian awoke with a start, his head aching miserably, and his erstwhile patient gone. Malvos was nowhere to be found. The blanket, the bedding, everything had been packed up and taken. Jedhian splashed water on his face and tried to stand. Then he realized—the water! It was water and not snow. . . . The spring had come. Aylith had brought the Spring. . . .

He charged out of the hut, into the sloppy common, and went sliding straight into Lorris, laughing, tangling in each other's arms and falling into the red mud.

"You are here, you live! I could not find you again after I left to follow Nazir. The gateman told me you must be dead, that Malvos had gone, and you not with him. I have searched this entire village," she said, catching her breath.

Jedhian tried to wipe the mud from her face, but succeeded only in putting more on it. He sighed.

"Yes. I live. And so do you. Lorris—look . . ." He pointed to the Blessing stone, where Arn and the new Tree stood.

Lorris squinted, disbelieving her eyes. "Arn? He looks so different . . . "

"I think he is different. I think everything is different." He looked around for a moment, puzzled.

"Lorris—over there," he marveled.

Lorris found his line of vision. In front of the village, in the midst of the befuddled armies, Aylith and Nazir, both of them well and whole, walked among the wounded, Nohrish to Haenish alike, taking the healing power of the Tree into the ranks. Wherever they passed, the hack disappeared, wounds closed, the pain, and maybe just a little of the hatred along with it, dissolved.

Jedhian looked long into Lorris's gray eyes, the sunlight adding silver sparkles to them.

"Let's go. No one needs me here. I have a promise to keep to your father."

She nodded solemnly. The wall at Inys Nohr. RoNal would have his record set straight.

Jedhian lifted Lorris's chin, found a clean place on her face, and kissed her.

EPILOGUE

SHAKING FROM A CHILL, MALVOS LAY uneasily in his tent under a morass of furs, silks, and woolen bhanas. He seemed unable to get warm, even though he could plainly see the clouds had rolled back, and this part of Cridhe, maybe all of it, had begun to thaw. So the Haenish girl had done it. Or maybe even Nazir. But Malvos doubted that; he still had Nazir's only supply of ardré-laced tonic. The Felonarch was probably dead by now, if not of the madness that cursed his house, then by the mirke and its sudden, rampant attack upon his body. But Malvos cared not that the spring had come again, nor even who had brought it. He did not have the strength to care. He had run this far and could go no farther. Unless Tempé came for him. Unless she would give him another chance.

Cool air over his rotten teeth gave him sharp pain as he drew his labored breath. Dozing now and then, he would snore horribly and wake himself. Dozens of times this night, he had ceased the trumpeting to lie completely still, breathless, hovering near death, his huge body crushing the air from his overburdened lungs. Then he would rouse, and gasp for breath, and continue to live.

Cridhe's small, blue moon crept into its highest seat, marking the first hour of the new day. Staring up at it through a hole in the tent, Malvos sighed.

He was surprised that Tempé had not already come. He figured she could not resist taunting him one last time and then leave him in manaless Cridhe to ignobly die the death of mana starvation.

Malvos had seen it before. Seen it happen to the man he had replaced, in fact. The wisdom of hindsight . . . His eyes would go first, then his remarkable hearing. Finally, his joints would freeze and he would stultify into an unmoving mass, his intelligence still intact, his mind screaming from stony lips unable to form the words that could give voice to his pain. That could last for months before his soul separated and went free. It would be a hideous death. And all it would take to avoid it would be a little mana—a very little sweet mana, just enough to touch the tip of his parched tongue.

Malvos dreamed the restless dreams of the damned, of the guilty, of the hoarders and wasters of the world.

He knew he was responsible for his own plight. If only he had taken what Tempé had offered instead of enough to really sate his hunger. When he had stolen mana, he had believed he could never want again, but all his theft had done was increase the need, increase his capacity. The hunger had grown, far beyond his control, and had clawed at him like a wild beast over the last five hundred years. It raged in his veins now, despite the easy appearance of his head upon the luxurious pillows. He weighed more than three hundred pounds, but Malvos was starving to death.

He dozed again, then wakened as he thought he heard the sound of a night bird overhead.

The silken tent flap stirred only a little as Tempé entered. She knew he was not quite asleep. He could never fool her very well.

"Malvos, my darling, it has been too long since we had a nice chat. And are you running from me? How absurd, my dearest. Why won't you tell me what I wish to know?" she purred.

Tempé's burnished copper hair fell in seductive waves across her chiseled face. She pouted her red lips at him as Malvos dropped the charade of his sleep, edged up awkwardly upon an elbow, and blinked tiredly at her. He knew her too well to be grateful for her visit just yet.

"I have been expecting you. Have you come for me? Or do you toy with me further? I sift your words, Tempé, and you truly mean for me to answer you. What is it you would know, and I will trade the information for my life."

She laughed, her voice humorless and dry. "My dear, your life is not worth discussing. Just tell me, and I'll decide whether your information is worth any kind of payment. Tell me where the mana is here, Malvos. I know you are hiding it from me. Cridhe has long had the reputation among Walkers for barrenness, but I feel something here after all. And you certainly would not have used my sword had there been no reason to believe it could help you leave. Even you are smarter than that. So, that means you are holding back. Where is the line, Malvos?"

Malvos sighed again. He had nothing to lose. "The Tree—there must be a new one—holds it, and some kind of warding shields the actual line from your senses. Only the Tree's Keeper can detect the line, and for some strange reason, I also can sense it, though I

cannot really tell you exactly where the line runs. That
is all there is. What more would you have of me?
Would you see proud Malvos beg? Then I shall. Please,
Tempé. Take me with you. You know I will die here. It
has been overlong for me. Have I not suffered enough?
Would you waste the best Finder in twenty planes for
your revenge?"

She laughed, her white teeth sharp against her lips,
and gestured gracefully in the air—his old sign for
marking a Find. "You think me an idiot after all these
years, my dear Malvos? I cannot believe you would.
Surely you know now, especially after you discovered
why I let you keep Soulslayer. Sort of a warning
device, you know? Should you have tried to use it, as
you did, and challenge my claim upon your hands, you
would have to choose between life and continued
imprisonment. Either way, I knew where you were. For
keeps. And it has been such fun knowing that one day,
you could no longer resist and would touch the sword
if there were mana around. . . . Of course, I cannot let
you have mana—you are starving for it. We both know
you could not restrain yourself. You would consume
everything I own if I let you take even one sip. You are
beyond my help, old friend. Give me the line here, and
at least ease your mind—die with your debt repaid."

Malvos bit his lip in frustration and despair and felt
the blood pour into his mouth. She was a cruel one,
always had been. Cold. Just like Cridhe before the
Mending. "Please, Tempé. There is no more to tell. I
would live." His eyes met hers beseechingly.

"No, Malvos. My rules. I have searched this place up
and down, including your silly tree."

He shook his head and dropped back upon the pillow.

Maybe he told the truth this time, she thought.
*Malvos had never been able to hold out this long
before. Especially in this condition.*

"Malvos . . ." she said softly.

He raised his head again, daring the tiniest of hopeful smiles.

"I *will* grant you one thing. You always wanted to know where Soulslayer had come from. I will tell you. I won it in a duel with the Thorn. He works the storm lines. I should have killed him, I suppose, but it wasn't worth it at the time. Consider that a Parting gift, eh?" She chuckled at her pun.

Malvos's eyes lingered upon her face. "You fear him. The Thorn. I sift it in your words. And I think maybe he works more than the storm lines now. Maybe he works the death pools, too."

Tempé's brow arched indignantly. "Is anyone more ungrateful than a Sangrazul? After all I've done for you . . ."

She shook her flame-colored hair, but could only glare at him, caught out in the truth he had heard in her voice.

How her age shows in the dim moonlight, thought Malvos. *How hard she looks.*

He collapsed upon the pillows, raising a small cloud of perfumed dusting powder. He fixed his eyes on the peak of the red-and-blue tent and waited for her to go. What more could she demand of him? The attention of a dying man was his to give or keep.

"Have it your way, you old fool. I have already replaced you, as I said. Do you think yourself to be so necessary to me that I would risk your ravenous hunger upon my hard-won lines? You people come cheap. And if you weren't so useful, I simply wouldn't bother. There is the constant problem of disposal," Tempé finished, her face the same color now as her hair. "Still, if you would only apologize . . ."

Malvos did not reply to her hurled insults. He did not even move. He would never apologize. He was a

Sangrazul. His attention seemed already far away, as though she had left the tent long ago.

Tempé smirked as she watched him stare at the moon through the sagging weave of the fabric over-hanging his bed. Then she followed his gaze. Her eyes went wide momentarily and she laughed aloud again, barely able to contain herself, delivering one last barb.

"Sleep well, Malvos."

She laughed wickedly again, the tent flap rising slightly at her passing.

Malvos drifted quickly into another troubled dream. He thought he heard elves singing and saw the won-ders of the fabled Loch Prith. He was young again and had the body of a strong warrior, a man among men, his height and strength legendary. Women adored him, and he had all the mana to eat that he could ever want. The hunger was satisfied; he felt released from its grip, from its tyranny, and he was free to leave Cridhe at last. Malvos smiled as he heard chimes and bells and the sweet sounds of glass pipes on the breeze.

And then he heard something else, low and feral, barely audible, in the lowest registers of his remarkable range. It snuffled and growled and made ready.

Too late, Malvos awoke from the dream, from the sleep song of the shroud, from the sound of another hunger. He clawed his way to consciousness, only to find himself trapped in another dream, and another and another, and another, until he gave up in a silent wail for help, unable to rise, or even move.

When he was beyond struggle, beyond conscious-ness, the red-and-blue tent flap rose, loosed itself from the double poles, and fell gently, hungrily upon him, still singing its fatal lullaby.

Teri McLaren, under the name Teri Williams, has coauthored two previous novels, *Before the Mask*, and *The Dark Queen*, and the short stories, "Mark of the Flame, Mark of the Word," published in *The Cataclysm*, and "The Final Touch," published in *The Dragons of Krynn*.

She teaches literature, medieval culture, and writing at the University of Louisville, in Louisville, Kentucky.

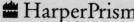